Also available from Roan Parrish
and Carina Press

The Garnet Run series

Better Than People

Also available from Roan Parrish

The Middle of Somewhere series

In the Middle of Somewhere
Out of Nowhere
Where We Left Off

The Small Change series

Small Change
Invitation to the Blues

The Riven series

Riven
Rend
Raze

Standalones

The Remaking of Corbin Wale
Natural Enemies
Heart of the Steal
Thrall

BEST LAID PLANS

ROAN PARRISH

carina
press

carina
press®

Recycling programs
for this product may
not exist in your area.

ISBN-13: 978-1-335-92480-3

Best Laid Plans

Copyright © 2021 by Roan Parrish

This edition published by arrangement with Harlequin Books S.A.

For questions and comments about the quality of this book, please contact us at
CustomerService@Harlequin.com.

Carina Press
22 Adelaide St. West, 40th Floor
Toronto, Ontario M5H 4E3, Canada
www.CarinaPress.com

Printed in U.S.A.

For Timmi.

BEST LAID PLANS

Chapter One

Rye

After sixteen hours of driving and a miracle that prevented his car from dying, Rye Janssen was exhausted and slap-happy, but hopeful.

Around hour three, his cat, Marmot, had realized she could squeeze between the headrest and Rye's neck and bat at his hair as he drove. By hour nine, Rye had consumed so much gas station coffee he was practically vibrating and Marmot had exhausted herself and curled up on the dashboard, snoozing in the sun.

As the road spooled out behind him and before him, Rye felt like he could breathe for the first time in years. He used to love Seattle. As a child, the city had felt like a world of possibility. When had it become claustrophobic?

His car stereo had broken ages ago, so Rye hummed to himself. Then he sang, loud, belting words he hadn't thought of in years, letting the wind rushing by his open windows snatch the sound away.

When Marmot crawled onto his lap and looked up at him with her alien eyes, he realized he was crying. Marmot licked at his chin and he smiled.

"Best decision I ever made, pulling you out of that oil can," he told her fondly.

And it was.

Rye only hoped the decision he was currently making turned out anywhere near as well.

When Rye had gotten the call three days before, informing him that he'd inherited a house from a grandfather he'd never met, Rye assumed it was some kind of scam. He hung up, irritated it hadn't been someone calling about one of the many job applications he had submitted. But after several more hours of phone tag and internet research, eventually Rye believed it.

He had inherited a house in some town he'd never heard of in Wyoming, a state he wasn't absolutely positive he could point to on a map.

In the end, the decision was surprisingly simple. Rye was broke. He'd been crashing with different groups of friends every week since he and his housemates had been evicted two months before. It had been his third eviction, and this time there were no more places to scrape together first, last, and security for.

Throw in the fact that he was pretty much out of cat-friendly couches when he wore out his welcome on this one, and suddenly a house of his own sounded pretty damn appealing. Maybe he didn't know anyone there; maybe he had to google map it; but at least he'd have a roof over his head.

So Rye had packed his few belongings into his untrustworthy Beretta, grabbed Marmot, and hit the road as the sun set over the bay.

When he arrived at the address the lawyer had given him in Garnet Run, Wyoming, Rye thought he'd been punked. Hoped he *had* been, because if this was what he'd just left Seattle for, Rye was utterly screwed.

The house stood in a wind-blasted field surrounded on two sides by woods, with nothing around but a horror movie scarecrow clinging to its post and a pack of chipmunks that

★ ★ ★

Rye unrolled his sleeping bag in the corner of the living room that looked in least imminent danger of collapse. Marmot curled inside the sleeping bag with him, her tiny weight a great comfort.

Then Rye did what anyone who'd spent their whole life figuring shit out for themselves would do: he went on You-Tube and looked up *how to build a house.*

The results were overwhelming, and mainly featured teams of very strong-looking men hoisting walls in groups of seven or eight, so Rye refined his search.

How to fix a house that's falling down alone.

Not good.

How to fix a house that's been abandoned alone.

Very not good.

How to fix a hell site that's clearly been blasted by an other-worldly curse. Alone.

Interesting ghost hunter videos that he bookmarked for later perusal, but not useful.

Rye sighed. He didn't want to waste his phone battery but panic was starting to creep in again, so he put on Riven's first album and let himself listen to his favorite three tracks to distract himself enough to go to sleep.

Theo Decker's voice sank into him, honey warm and sharp as a razor. The album was years old, but it soothed him every time. Now, it helped drown out the terrifying sounds that Rye assumed were nature.

They definitely *weren't* the creepy scarecrow becoming animate in the moonlight and hunting for prey. They certainly were *not* wolves or bears or whateverthefuck terrifying animals lived in Wyoming coming to eat him and Marmot. And they absolutely, one hundred percent, *weren't* a mob of torch-wielding villagers coming to spit the clueless city boy and roast him over their ravenous flames. Nope.

"Everything's fine. It's just nature," Rye told Marmot,

whose sleeping purrs indicated that she wasn't the one who required reassurance.

Theo Decker sang, and Rye fixed his whole attention on the music, squeezed his eyes closed tight against the darkness, pulled the sleeping bag over his ears, and tried to sleep in the crumbling house that was now his only home.

Chapter Two

Charlie

In the thin light of dawn, Charlie Matheson woke up gasping. The dream was an old, familiar haunt of meat and bones and loss, and he shook it loose like a spiderweb. It didn't do any good to linger on dreams, good or bad.

Instead, he ran. Out his kitchen door and through woods springing to life after winter's long spell. Up and up the rock-strewn path to the promontory, Lake Linea still half-frozen far below. Up here, the air was thin, and Charlie's temples pounded with exertion. Up here, he was a dot, blasted to nothingness by immensity.

Not responsible for anything or anyone.

But as the sun crested the trees, Charlie couldn't afford to be nothing anymore. He *was* responsible for things, so he made himself head for home.

Inside the kitchen door sat Jane, waiting impatiently for her breakfast. Her black and gray fur was ruffled like she'd just writhed herself awake, but the tufts at the tips of her ears stood straight up as always. She meowed at him, a sound like tearing metal, and he bent to offer her his hand. She twined herself around his ankles instead, rumbling a purr of welcome and demand.

"Hi, baby," he cooed to the huge cat, and scratched between her tufty ears.

A drop of sweat dripped off his nose and landed on her paw. She looked up at him as if he'd defiled her.

"Sorry, I'm sorry," he soothed, and Jane, placated, jumped onto the counter so she was at kissing height.

Charlie had never let anyone else see him do this. He couldn't be sure, but he'd always imagined that the sight of a very large man exchanging nose bumps and whisker kisses with a very large cat might be cause for amusement. And Charlie and Jane took the ritual seriously.

Even on the counter, Jane had to go up on her back legs and Charlie had to bend down. They locked eyes, Jane's glittering green to Charlie's placid hazel, and Jane ever so slowly bumped Charlie's nose with her own—a tiny, cool press, her luminous eyes so close to his own that Charlie imagined he might follow the rivers of color inside her. He slow-blinked once, and she slow-blinked back to him. Then she brushed her whiskers over his beard and he kissed the top of her furry head, right between her ears.

Ritual completed, Jane yipped—a sound very similar to her metal-tearing meow, but shorter and more demanding—and Charlie poured her food.

"I'm gonna take a shower and then get to the store," he told her.

She crunched her breakfast.

"I saw a hawk out at the promontory," he told her.

She crunched her breakfast.

"I'm gonna put you on a leash someday and take you out there with me," he told her.

She crunched her breakfast.

"Okay, maybe I'll just take you to the store and you can be a shop cat and get pet by strangers," he told her.

Her meow of protest rang through the house and Charlie smiled as he stepped into the shower.

Matheson's Hardware and Lumber opened at eight, and

Charlie arrived by 7:30 to make sure things were in order. There was always something: the register was out of receipt tape; 12d nails had found their way into the 16d nail bin; the key-cutting machine was out of blanks; someone had spilled coffee in aisle three.

Charlie walked the store, plucking this screw out of that bin, straightening coils of wire, and sometimes just running his fingers over the shelves he'd installed and the inventory he'd ordered. He knew every inch of this place, and there was a comfort to its predictability, even if it sometimes smothered him.

Marie arrived as he was turning on the lights, carrying her blue camping thermos of coffee. She high-fived him, tied on her apron, and shooed him out from behind the cash wrap. She never spoke until a customer entered, saving every iota of energy for the day's interactions.

He'd known Marie for ten years and she was the best manager he'd ever had. Also his best friend. Fine, his only friend. Marie didn't lie and she didn't sugarcoat—mainly because she didn't say much. But when she did, it was considered, concise, and final.

Charlie spent the first few hours of business squeezed into the desk in his tiny office at the back of the shop. It had been a closet when his father ran the store, and Charlie's broad shoulders barely cleared the walls. His father had done all his bookkeeping at home on the kitchen table—perhaps why, when Charlie took over the business, the books had been a hopeless mess.

He processed orders and filed receipts, answered a few emails and returned some calls. This part of the job wasn't something he enjoyed, but it had to be done and he was the only one to do it.

When Marie took her lunch break, Charlie went into the store to do what he liked more: helping customers find the right tools for their projects. He listened carefully to what they wanted to achieve, then walked with them, gathering the things they'd need and explaining different ways they might proceed. He loved problem-solving; the more arcane the project, the better he liked it.

He was just walking Bill Duff through replacing his garbage disposal when he heard a clanking and scraping sound from outside.

Through the glass front door, Charlie saw an ominously smoking car grind to a halt in the parking lot. It looked like it had originally been a late-eighties two-door Chevy Beretta but had since been Frankensteined of multiple vehicles' pieces, many of them different colors and some of them clinging desperately together, helped only by electrical tape and grime.

Charlie winced, fingers itching to put the car together properly—or, perhaps more practically, drive it to the junkyard and put it out of its misery.

Marie was bagging Bill Duff's purchases when the door burst open. In stepped a man Charlie'd never seen before.

He certainly would have remembered.

Long, dark hair fell messily over his shoulders. He was slim and angular, with a slinky walk that made him look like he was made of hips and shoulders. The cuffs and collar of his long-sleeved T-shirt were worn rough and the knees of his jeans blown out. He looked like ten miles of dirt road.

Charlie raised a hand at the newcomer.

"Welcome to Matheson's. I'm Charlie. Can I help you find anything?"

The man's light, kohl-lined eyes darted around, as if Charlie might be talking to someone else, then, looking confused, said, "Uh. No."

He hurried off down aisle one and Charlie let him alone. Some people didn't want help or attention while they shopped, and Charlie was just glad of a new customer—and a young one at that. Business was okay, but with each passing year overnight shipping and Amazon ate further into his profit margin, particularly with customers under forty.

The stranger walked up and down the aisles, muttering inaudibly, swearing audibly, and consulting his phone every minute or so, as if the answers he wouldn't accept from Charlie lay there.

After the better part of half an hour, he approached the register, arms full, though there were baskets and small carts available.

"Find everything okay?" Charlie asked as the man dumped his purchases on the counter.

"Uh, sure."

He sounded distracted and was glaring at the items he'd chosen.

"You need any help with…" Charlie gestured at the hardware equivalent to marshmallows, cheese, and spaghetti before him.

The man raised a dramatic dark eyebrow but didn't say anything. His eyes, Charlie could see now, were gray, and his skin was pale, as if he were a black-and-white image in a color world.

That pale glare lanced him, and he looked away, ringing and bagging things up.

The man swiped his credit card like he was ripping something in half and had to do it again when the machine didn't get a read. He glared at it.

When Charlie handed him his bags he couldn't help needling the man a little.

"Need any help getting things out to your car?" he asked, as he'd ask anyone.

The man glared down at the bags he was holding, then up at Charlie.

"No," he said, like the word was his favorite one and, in his mouth, capable of expressing every feeling and thought he had.

"Okay, then," Charlie said, purposefully cheery. "Have a good one."

The man narrowed his eyes like there was a barb hidden in the words he simply hadn't found yet.

"Uh-huh," he said, and wrinkled his nose suspiciously, backing out the door.

"Who was that?" Marie asked. Charlie turned to see her lurking in the doorway from the back room.

"I don't know," Charlie said.

But he was damn sure gonna find out.

The glarer was back the next day, bursting through the door in a palpable huff. Marie elbowed Charlie subtly—as subtly as a pointy bone to the ribs can be administered, anyway.

"Welcome back," Charlie said. "Help you find anything?"

The man shook his head, glaring, and walked to the back of the store. After that, Charlie didn't see him for long enough that he got concerned and went to make sure he hadn't impaled himself on an awl or stumbled into the band saw.

When he turned the corner on aisle six, though, Charlie didn't see any carnage. What he saw was the man's back, messy hair tumbling around his shoulders, and his phone screen as he watched a YouTube video that appeared to be about framing in a wall.

Charlie snuck back to the cash wrap without the man seeing him. He helped another customer, sent Marie to cut the wood for Ms. Mackenzie's decking order, and organized an endcap of gardening tools, seeds from the local seed company Kiss Me Kale, fertilizer, and seed starting soil. He was adding hose nozzles to the display when the man walked to the front of the store with a pack of common nails, a hammer, an axe, sandpaper, and two flashlights, even though he'd bought one the day before.

"Do you sell wood?" he asked. "Like, cut wood?"

Charlie nodded. "Yup, any dimensions, cut to any length you want. We don't have everything in stock, but I can get it for you. What do you need?"

"Um, I'm not sure yet."

"Okay. Well, just let me know, and we'll take care of you."

The man nodded, eyes narrowed, and piled his purchases on the counter.

Everything in Charlie wanted to make sure the man had used an axe before and knew how to do so safely. Every year vacationers chopped off bits of themselves thinking that chopping wood meant whaling on a stump they found in the woods. But given how this guy had responded to a simple friendly greeting, Charlie doubted he'd take well to being questioned.

This time when the man left the store, his shoulders were a little lower than before.

Two days later the man arrived just as Charlie opened the store. His hair was messier than ever, and his clothes even more rumpled. There were dark circles under his eyes, and instead of a glare, his face was fixed in a nostril-flared pinch.

"Morning," Charlie drawled.

"Hey, um, can I get that wood?"

"Sure. Tell me what you need and I'll see if we have it or if I need to order it."

The man took out a faded, spiral bound notepad from his back pocket. "I need, uh, 2x4s. About nine feet each."

There were unspoken question marks after each statement.

"And how many of them do you need?"

"Oh, uh." The man squinted, as if picturing the project. "Ten. No, twenty… Uh, yeah, twenty."

"Twenty 2x4s at nine feet each?" The man nodded. "No problem. I can cut those for you right now."

"Okay, cool."

Charlie cut the boards quickly, forcing himself not to ask

the questions he so badly wanted to. This guy obviously didn't know what he was doing, and Charlie yearned to get involved.

When he went back out front, Marie was ringing the man up. For the first time, Charlie took a moment to watch him. He was a bundle of energy, fidgeting and biting his lip as he waited. But the longer Marie went without speaking to him, the more he relaxed. His shoulders dropped and his chin lifted, and Charlie saw his nostrils flare as he took a deep breath.

Charlie also saw that he was beautiful. Utterly, heart-stoppingly beautiful. Without the glare, his light eyes framed by dark lashes were tempestuous and deep; his cheekbones and chin were delicately pointed; his nose was strong and straight. And his mouth—cruelly bitten red—was a luscious pout, painted more brightly than the rest of his coloring.

He was wearing jeans and a long-sleeved T-shirt, as he had been the last two times he'd come in, and the lines of tattoos snaked out of his cuffs and collar. Today he also wore a gray bandanna tied around his neck as if to pull over his mouth and nose, and Charlie wondered what DIY abomination the man was attempting that would require such a thing.

"Hey, Charlie," Marie called, jerking him out of his reverie. "Are we sold out of those blue plastic tarps?"

"Yeah. But we'll be getting more in next week."

At least they would be now.

The man shook his head.

"'S fine," he muttered.

"Depending on what you want it for," Charlie ventured, "I have one in the back. It has a small tear in the corner and some paint splatter, but you're welcome to borrow it."

"Oh, um. Okay," the man said. "Yeah, thanks."

Charlie got the tarp and loaded the cut wood onto a cart. He wheeled it to the parking lot, where it was immediately clear that it wouldn't fit in the death trap parked there.

The man came outside, purchases in hand, and Charlie said, "I'll follow you with this in my truck, all right?"

"Oh, it'll fit," the man said.

Charlie raised a doubtful eyebrow as the guy tried to shove one of the 2x4s diagonally through the passenger door and between the seats. It didn't fit.

"I can just drive with the door open," the man said, biting his lip. "No one's ever around here anyway."

He jammed another 2x4 in the same way. All twenty were obviously not going to fit. After he shoved in three more, he kicked at the ground, nostrils flaring, and crossed his arms.

"I can make another trip..."

"Three more trips," Charlie corrected. The man glared. "Why don't you just let me follow you in the truck?"

The guy was either incapable of gracefully accepting help or he was worried about Charlie knowing where he lived. As a big guy, Charlie knew quite well that sometimes people equated *large* with *menacing*.

"Or Marie can follow you?"

But the man just rolled his eyes, so Charlie didn't think it was fear. After kicking at the ground again, he sighed, "Fine." Then, as if it were physically painful for him to utter, "Thanks."

Charlie hadn't heard a more grudging *Thanks* since his younger brother, Jack, had broken his leg the year before and needed Charlie's help around the house.

"No problem," Charlie said easily, a spark of satisfaction flaring inside him that he got to intercede on behalf of this total disaster.

"Marie," he called in the door, "I'm gonna drive this wood to— What's your name?" he asked the man.

"Rye."

"—to Rye's house. I have my cell."

She raised an eyebrow that said *Can't wait to hear how that goes*, and saluted. Charlie loaded the wood into his truck, taking the 2x4s that Rye had put in his car out so the passenger door could close.

"I'll follow you," he said.

Rye's nostrils flared again but he just nodded. The car started after two attempts and Rye set off down the road, car clanking and coughing exhaust. Charlie let a bit of distance grow between them so he didn't have to breathe it in and enjoyed the clear, sunny day.

The window of Rye's car rolled down and Rye stuck his arm out, elbow resting on the door, fingers trailing through the air. The wind whipped strands of his hair out the window too, where it flapped like dark wings.

He turned left on Lennox, right on Oakcrest, and then swung onto Owl Creek Road. It was the route Charlie took to his brother's house. He decided he'd text Jack later and invite him and his boyfriend Simon over for dinner next week. Simon liked a lot of notice for social plans; it eased his anxiety if he had time to mentally prepare.

Rye slowed at the turnoff just before Jack's. Crow Lane was a long dirt path through the trees that terminated in a clearing and a house. A house that looked like the before shot in a home renovation show where a home was saved from demolition.

Had Rye bought the place to fix up? To flip? Certainly not, when he clearly had no experience with construction.

Rye got out of his car swearing at it, shoved his hands in his pockets, and glared at Charlie.

"My brother lives about a half mile south of you," Charlie told him, nodding in that direction.

Rye nodded. He started pulling the lumber out of the truck and carrying it to the dilapidated house. Charlie followed him, dropping his own armload beside Rye's, on the front stoop.

"Did you buy this place?" Charlie asked, when no explanation seemed forthcoming.

"Inherited it," Rye said.

Charlie's stomach clenched. Had Jack's neighbor been Rye's parent?

"Oh, I'm sorry for your loss," Charlie said haltingly.

Rye waved him away.

"I didn't even know him. My grandfather. I dunno why he left it to me. No one else to leave it to, I guess?"

And he walked past Charlie to get another load of wood from the truck.

"Are you going to live here once it's fixed up?" Charlie asked.

"That's the plan."

"Where are you staying until then?"

Rye raised an eyebrow. "You ask a lotta questions for a total stranger out in the middle of the woods."

Charlie raised his hands, palms out.

"Sorry. Didn't mean to pry. Just, we don't get that many new people moving to town. I was curious."

"Well, I'm not gonna murder your brother in his sleep or anything, if that's what you're worried about."

"I am *now*," Charlie muttered.

For the first time, Rye's mouth quirked into a smile, revealing sharp, slightly overlapping teeth and a dimple.

A mew came from behind Rye.

"I better…" He gestured to the house and the lumber.

"Sure."

"Thanks. For the tarp and the help."

Charlie knew he should just nod and leave but he couldn't help himself.

"This looks like quite the job. Do you have people helping you? Experience in demo and construction? Because if you want—"

"Either you've got a mad hero complex or you're bossy as hell, man," Rye said.

Charlie drew himself up to his full height, which wasn't insignificant.

"Who says it isn't both?" he said. "I'm Charlie, by the way. Charlie Matheson." Then he winked and walked back to the truck.

He only let his eyes flick toward Rye for an instant as he threw the truck into gear, but he thought the man was smiling.

Chapter Three

Rye

Charlie Matheson was huge, with broad shoulders, muscular arms, large, rough hands, and a jaw like a superhero, even if it was hidden under a reddish-brown beard. He had short reddish-blond hair with a bit of a wave to it, and his eyes were a hazel that reminded Rye of the woods around his new house.

He was kind and hot and bossy and irritatingly pleased with himself for being helpful. But he had saved Rye three trips.

Rye dragged the wood inside after Charlie left, pulling his sleeves down over his hands to avoid splinters. Marmot sniffed the wood, then jumped onto it, walking each board like a balance beam, leaving tiny damp paw prints.

The YouTube video had said to shore up the structure by placing 2x4s that ran from the floor to the ceiling.

"Okay, so we just stand these up and, like, nail them… to…shit, what do we nail them to?"

Marmot looked on as he stood up the first 2x4, little face cocked curiously.

It didn't fit. There was at least an inch between the top of the 2x4 and the ceiling.

"What the hell? I *measured* you!" Rye accused the room.

He tried another 2x4 with the same results. Then he

moved the 2x4 to a different spot along the wall. This time it was too long.

"Shit," Rye muttered. "You janky motherfucker."

After much trial, error, and swearing, Rye was able to fit three of the 2x4s into places that actually were nine feet tall. He couldn't nail them in place—the floor was too soft and he couldn't reach the ceiling—but probably just having them there was helping hold things up. Right?

With a full-body sigh and a lancing glare at the pile of misfit wood, Rye got back in his car.

"Can you, like, add an inch to a piece of wood?" Rye mumbled, internally cursing the second it was out of his mouth.

Charlie didn't laugh, though the twinkle in his eye betrayed his amusement. Rye glared.

Very slowly and very gently, Charlie said, "It would really help me answer your question if you would tell me what you're trying to do." Then he added, "I mean that in a totally professional, nonbossy, nonheroic way."

Rye snorted. He *hated* not knowing what he was doing. Even more, he hated not being able to fake that he knew what he was doing—after all, acting like you had your shit figured out was ninety percent of survival. But clearly this Charlie dude knew his shit, and Rye had to acknowledge that could be useful.

"Fine. I need to prop up the ceiling of the house and my boards are all the wrong length." At the first sign that Charlie was going to say that he had *not* cut the boards the wrong length, Rye specified, "I mean, the house is the wrong height. Different heights. All different fucking heights. It's, like, droopy."

Charlie's eyes narrowed.

"Are you not doing demo inside first?"

Demo. Demolition. Right.

"Uh. Well. I'm just seeing if I can… What would that look like, exactly?"

"With a structure like yours—and I've only seen the outside; it'd help to see inside—usually you'd want to demo the old interior to check that the foundation and load-bearing posts are sound, and see about the roof. If the floor is sagging, that might mean it just needs to be replaced, or it could mean the foundation is buckling, from age or from water or from termite damage. If there's any drywall in there you'd want to rip that out so you can reframe the walls square. Really, you'd want to take it down to the studs and give yourself a clean canvas. That would allow you to check the wiring, the plumbing, the heat."

Each word Charlie said gathered in a haze around him— thick and oily green-black, it cracked over his head like an egg and slid down his neck and into his eyes.

Rye shook his head, trying to dislodge the haze, to stuff it back down in the tiny place it lived in his gut. He fisted his hands so tight his knuckles cracked and looked around the hardware store like perhaps the magic tool that would enable him to succeed lay right out of reach.

What the hell had he done? He'd moved away from the only place and people he'd ever known. He had no job, no prospect of a job, and from Charlie's words it was clear that what little cash he had was nowhere near enough to fix up this damn house. If he was *lucky* he'd be able to sell it for the land. If he was lucky he could at least camp there through the summer. If he was lucky…

But Rye didn't believe in luck. Luck was just what happened when you were privileged and didn't know it. Inheriting this godforsaken house was the quote unquote luckiest thing that'd ever happened to him, and look how that was turning out.

"Fuck," Rye breathed. "Fuck, fuck, fuck."

He needed to get to a place where he could be alone and

think this through. And by think this through, he meant get to a place where an entire hardware store wouldn't see him lose his shit in public.

Chapter Four

Charlie had just been trying to get Rye to see that he needed help—help Charlie was happy to provide. But the look on the beautiful man's face when Charlie outlined even the basics of demoing the house…it betrayed an emotion Charlie recognized with his whole being: despair.

And if Charlie could intercede so that Rye didn't have to feel it, then he'd do anything he could.

"Marie, I'm gonna go…"

She just raised an eyebrow and nodded knowingly after Rye, her expression half sympathy and half amusement—both, he was fairly sure, for him. And, fine, the person who'd first told him he had a hero complex? It was her.

When Charlie got to Rye's house, his car wasn't there, so Charlie figured Rye'd gone back to his hotel to rage or panic or whatever his version of despair was.

He knew it was an invasion of Rye's privacy, but curiosity about the scope of the project drove him to approach the house and try the door. It opened easily. With a quick glance at the road to make sure Rye wasn't coming, Charlie went inside. Maybe if he saw what the project entailed, he could subtly point Rye in the right direction when it came to tools and materials.

Unsurprisingly, the house was cold and smelled of mold, damp, and disuse.

Charlie switched on the flashlight on his keychain to inspect the place before he ventured in. He was heavy and he didn't want to fall through a weak spot in the floor.

Sweeping the light over the interior revealed sagging walls and a water-damaged floor, which almost certainly meant a leaky roof. The walls and floor were all dark wood, making the source impossible to see. When it reached the corner, his flashlight lit on what looked like a mummy, and Charlie took a step backward. Then the form recontextualized in his mind and he realized it was something wrapped in... was that the tarp he'd lent Rye?

Charlie crept closer to it, testing each step before committing his weight. The floor was warped and sagging, but it didn't seem in immediate danger of splintering.

Yes, it was Charlie's blue plastic tarp, swaddling a sleeping bag. Next to it was a bag full of clothes, a pair of boots, and a dog-eared paperback copy of—

The attacker hit Charlie from behind with a hiss and the bite of razor-sharp claws in his neck. When Charlie tried to pull the thing off him it scratched at his hands. Charlie pictured something huge and rabid, its gnashing teeth and knifing claws tearing him to pieces. A bear? A wolverine? Some cryptid composed of both?

Charlie sucked in a breath through his nose, then pulled the beast away from his throat and held it at arm's length.

It was...a cat? A very, very small cat—with teeth and claws bared, yes, but still almost comically tiny.

"Jesus Christ, you almost killed me, you murder cat," Charlie said. "I'm not gonna hurt you."

He kept the cat at a distance. If it was a stray he didn't want to pick up any diseases he could pass on to Jane. But, though small, it didn't seem underfed, and when he ventured a finger to stroke its head, its eyes closed peacefully like it was used to being pet. He'd never seen a cat enjoy a petting with its teeth bared before.

"The fuck are you doing to my cat?"

Charlie spun to face the door. Rye.

"Of course this beast belongs to you. It tried to kill me."

"C'mere, Marmot," Rye said tightly, and the second Charlie loosened his grip, the cat jumped silently to the floor, sprang gracefully onto Rye's shoulder, and nuzzled the side of his head, purring loudly.

"This is breaking and entering, you know," Rye said blandly.

Charlie absolutely could not take him seriously with the cat perched on his shoulder like a parrot.

"Well, the door wasn't locked, so it's really just entering."

"Trespassing, then," Rye said with a sniff.

"I'm sorry. I know I shouldn't've come in. But you seemed really upset and I wanted to help."

"Fuckin' savior complex. Told you." But his voice was without heat. He just sounded tired.

"Is that the same or different than a hero complex, because I think that's what you said last time."

"You don't even know me, man. Why do you care if I'm upset?"

Charlie wasn't sure what to say to that. He always cared if people were upset. But there was something so vulnerable about Rye beneath all his glares and scowls. Something lost and needy. And, okay, Rye wasn't the first to point out that Charlie couldn't resist trying to help people sometimes… Fine, many people…compulsively.

So since Rye clearly didn't react well to him trying to help, Charlie put it a different way.

"I can't stand watching people do things badly," Charlie said. "I've worked construction, I've built houses, my own included, and you obviously have no idea what you're doing.

You're lucky I'm offering to help instead of trying to sell you a bunch of shit you don't need at the store."

There was an instant when Charlie thought he saw Rye take his words like a fist to the gut, but it was gone so quickly he might've imagined it, replaced by a jutting chin and look of grudging respect.

"I don't believe in luck," Rye said.

Charlie forced himself to leave. He forced himself to sweep past Rye and the tiny murder cat on his shoulder, looking like an Edgar Allan Poe caricature. Then he forced himself to get in his truck and drive away, only glancing back through his rearview mirror at the derelict house looming behind him. In the open doorway, Rye, now cradling the cat in his arms, looked small and lost.

Marie said nothing when he got back, but her raised eyebrow spoke volumes, the first of which began with *How'd that go?*

"The house is a wreck. It's at the end of Crow Lane, before you'd get to Jack and Simon's place. Do you know it?"

She narrowed her eyes and shook her head.

"He says he inherited it from a grandfather or something."

Her eyebrow said, *You're such a gossip.*

Charlie shoved his hands in his pockets, trying not to crack his knuckles. Lately his hands had begun aching at the end of a day working on the house or when it was cold. He wasn't supposed to feel this old at thirty-six.

Marie turned away to ring up Marla Martinson and Charlie inquired after Marla's sister.

"He doesn't know what he's doing at *all*," Charlie continued when she'd left. "He's just buying wood and nails and trying to prop the thing up like plastering more icing on a crumbling gingerbread house."

He got horrified all over again just saying it. Marie's smile said, *Mmm, gingerbread.*

"And I think…"

Charlie would never share these suspicions with just anyone—despite Marie's wry eyebrow, he wasn't a gossip—but
Marie was a paragon of discretion. Most people didn't know
a thing about her. Even Charlie, after ten years working beside her every day and eight or so of being friends, knew
less about some aspects of her life than he did about some
regular customers'.

"I assumed he was staying in a hotel or with family while
he worked on the house, but I think he's sleeping there."

Marie's eyebrows said, *Poor kid.*

"Right? He's liable to get himself killed, sleeping there—
the damn roof could collapse! So I need to help him work
on the place. I just have to figure out how to convince *him*
of that."

Marie's eyebrows went into overdrive: *You don't need to
help him; you want to. You're not responsible for him. And if he
doesn't want your help then it's not up to you to convince him.*

"Your eyebrows are certainly talkative today," Charlie
grumbled.

Marie smiled sweetly at him, "Yeah, they tend to seem
that way when the person looking at them already knows
exactly what I'm gonna say."

Chapter Five

Rye

"I've built houses," Rye mimicked broadly at Marmot. "You don't know what you're doing. I own a hardware store and I'm an asshole who goes around telling people they're bad at everything."

Marmot hissed. Rye agreed.

"Fuck that guy. Fuck him and his...his fucking shoulders and his hands and his power tools. *He's* a fucking tool. Asshole."

Rye started to punch the wall but stopped at the last second, worried the whole house might fall down as a result. That just made him madder because for once he was in the position to punch a wall he owned and he still couldn't.

"Fuck!" he yelled, and stomped furiously.

The wood gave way with an ominous *thrunk* and Rye's leg burst through. For a sickening moment Rye thought he'd broken his ankle, then he realized the sharp pain was just jagged ends of wood digging into his skin from the edges of the hole.

"Hulk smash," he said softly, and slumped down where he was, leg still stuck in the hole. Marmot sat down next to him as if to guard her stupid human with his leg in a hole. "Fuck, Marm."

Marmot commenced cleaning herself, unconcerned, and Rye felt something move against the skin of his ankle.

"Gah, fuck!" He jerked his leg out of the hole, imagining all the revolting things that could be creeping around down there. And he'd basically given them a portal to climb up and into the place where he slept. Wonderful.

Marmot sniffed at the hole, sneezed, and walked away.

Rye tugged up his pant leg warily. Scratches and smears of dirt mostly, but one long cut over his shin where the skin was the thinnest. Rye wiped at the blood, hoping it'd just reveal a scrape, but apparently the wood wasn't as soft as his ability to stomp through it had implied. Blood welled out of the cut and Rye swore.

He'd gotten a gallon of water at the gas station for drinking and brushing his teeth, and he soaked his bandana to clean the cut, swiping at the bits of wood and dirt in it. Finally he just poured a slug of water over his leg hoping it'd wash out anything bad and tied a clean bandanna around it before pulling his pant leg down.

The second he didn't have the cut to focus on anymore he realized he was trembling. Anger, frustration, fear; take your pick. He fisted his hands, trying to resist the urge to scream. Then he remembered there was fuck-all within hearing distance in this clearing in the middle of a state with like seven people in it and roared.

"You think you can fucking defeat me, you piece of shit?" he yelled at the house. "Your rotten wood and fucking falling down walls and stupid no electricity? *Fuck you!*"

He felt a tiny bit better.

He awoke to screams. He'd've thought he was still dreaming except that Marmot clearly heard them too, as she was scrambling up his chest to escape the sleeping bag. She darted away into the dark, her movements silent.

"Shit," Rye muttered. That damn cat was too brave for

her own good. He fumbled with the flashlight he kept next to the sleeping bag and stepped into his shoes. He forgot about the cut on his leg and hissed in pain when he bumped it with the flashlight.

It was freezing outside the polar warmth of the sleeping bag and he briefly considered climbing right back in, but although Marmot acted like a tiger, she was so small.

The screams came again, from above him, and Marmot hissed.

"Oh fuck, fuck, fuck."

Above him meant braving the stairs. Rye hadn't touched them. He just saw visions of getting up them only to have them fall away behind him, stranding him on the precarious second story of a house, like a cat caught up a tree.

But he couldn't let Marmot get hurt. And he certainly would never sleep again with that slasher movie soundtrack of screams.

Rye tested the first step. It seemed sturdy enough. He crept slowly up the second and third. They groaned dramatically, but so did the whole damn house. Rye couldn't decide whether to cling to the bannister or the wall, so he kind of braced himself against both—not that either would save him if the steps gave way.

Halfway up the staircase his foot hit something that gave way and he threw himself up instead of down, sprawling across the top half of the staircase.

He braced for disaster, but the stairs didn't move, so the only disaster there was him.

Having inadvertently tested their structural integrity with his whole body, Rye ascended the rest of the stairs quickly. The room at the top had probably been a bedroom—Rye's flashlight revealed a bathroom to the left—but instead of a bed frame or a dresser it contained only six chairs set in a circle.

"I do *not* have the capacity for this house to contain a satanic summoning circle," Rye said.

A thrashing sound in the corner drew his attention, and there was Marmot, tail flicking, pawing at...something.

Rye crept closer and swept the light tentatively over the corner, afraid of what horror it might reveal.

But it was just a squirrel—or, at least, something squirrel-like; Rye didn't know what the hell animals lived in Wyoming.

It seemed to be caught halfway into the room, its little arms scrabbling at the wood. Marmot crouched two feet away, ears back, hissing, but the little squirrel thing didn't seem like a threat. It seemed terrified.

"Okay, buddy," Rye said, in what he hoped would seem a calming voice to a squirrel thing. "Please just don't be rabid, all right, cuz I don't have insurance. Can you even *cure* rabies?" he wondered aloud. "Whatever, just don't have them."

He pulled the sleeves of his sweatshirt down over his hands and held the flashlight in his mouth. The squirrel thing was thrashing and screaming, Marmot was hissing, and Rye just thought as loudly as he could, *Don't bite me don't bite me don't bite me don't bite me.*

Unsure whether the critter would more easily slide in or out, but sure that he'd rather have it out of the house than in, Rye tried to squeeze it back through the hole it'd come in. First it fought him, then, as Rye changed its angle, something gave and the squirrel thing slid back through the wall.

Screaming was replaced with a chittering sound and then the sound of tiny claws scampering. Then nothing.

He collapsed on his butt on the floor, breathing heavily. The sound of the animal's panic had been harrowing, and Rye was utterly relieved for it to end.

"Jesus Christ," he muttered. Marmot jumped onto his thigh. "Good looking out, you fruitcake."

Flashlight in hand, Rye looked around the room for something he could put in the hole so this didn't happen again. There was a moldy looking blanket draped over the back of one of the chairs, so he stuffed the corner of it into the hole, wincing at the cold dampness of the cloth.

How had his grandfather lived in this falling-down place? Or had it decayed after he died and before the lawyer found Rye?

Now that the dual threats of rabies and a collapsing second story seemed to be past, Rye looked around. This room and the bathroom were the only things the stairs led to—there was no second floor over the kitchen. A mattress had been stood up against the wall in the far corner of the room and remnants of wood that had perhaps once belonged to a dresser or nightstand were stacked against the opposite wall.

On the floor in the center of the circle of chairs was a milk crate cluttered with burnt-out candles. Most were the kind you could buy at any dollar store—white pillars in clear glass, some with the Virgin Mary on them. A few others were dark green and dusty, and Rye didn't touch them but he bet they'd smell like pine. His mother had put out similar candles around Christmas when he was a child, often surrounded by fake pine boughs studded with plastic cranberries.

"Come on," Rye said to Marmot, exhausted now that the adrenaline had drained away.

Marmot pranced down the stairs in an instant and Rye followed slowly, reminding himself that if he'd gotten up without them giving way, he'd be able to get down.

He kicked off his shoes and slid back into the warmth of the sleeping bag. As he closed his eyes and pulled his hood up over his head, Rye's brain produced a phantom whiff of the fake pine smell those candles had produced, and a vision of those fake cranberries attended it. His mom would set the boughs out on the shelf over the television and the table next to the kitchen.

He wondered if she still did.

Chapter Six

Charlie

Rye was back.

Charlie saw him come in from the doorway to the office and stayed out of sight.

He looked tired, angry, and sheepish, and Charlie's heart beat a little faster. Rye looked like a wild animal that had crept cautiously close enough to feed.

He said something to Marie that Charlie couldn't hear and Marie pointed him toward the back.

"So," Rye said, standing in the doorway. "You, um, helping me. With the house…thing. What would that look like?"

He had his arms crossed over his chest, nearly hugging himself.

Charlie felt a rush of satisfaction and relief. He was going to be able to fix this. He wasn't going to have to watch Rye get crushed by a falling beam, or do everything wrong, or get taken advantage of by untrustworthy contractors.

"Well," he said, keeping his voice calm so he didn't scare Rye away with his enthusiasm. "I'd need to come into the house and see what we're dealing with. Then you and I would talk about what your goals are for the space. And we'd go from there."

"Fine."

"I'm assuming there's no electricity?"

"So?" Rye was instantly defensive.

"So, I'd like to come while it's light out so I can see."

"Oh. Right. Okay."

Rye glared at the floor, hands fisted by his sides.

"I could meet you there in about an hour if that works?"

"Okay." Rye almost seemed to squirm away from the word. "I don't know why you'd want to do all this work to help me, but okay."

"I'll meet you there in an hour," Charlie said.

Rye nodded and took a shuffling step.

"Thanks." He said it without turning around and left before Charlie said anything. He seemed be limping a little.

Rye was sitting outside on the sagging front step, hood up and arms wrapped around his knees, when Charlie pulled up. His long, dark hair tumbled out of the hood and around his shoulders, and when he looked up his gray eyes flashed. He looked young and sad.

When he stood, though, that glare was back; Charlie was starting to think it was just his default expression, so he decided to ignore it.

In fact, Charlie decided he'd just do what he'd do if he were alone, and not worry about Rye. He'd walked through a lot of houses and evaluated a lot of construction jobs. This wasn't any different.

His willpower on that front was instantly shattered when they walked inside and he saw a hole in the floor and Rye's wince as he put weight on his right leg. His heart started to beat faster at the thought of what might have happened.

"Did you fall through the floor?"

"Uh, kinda stomped through it."

Charlie got slowly to his knees and shined his keychain flashlight into the hole in the floor. The boards were water-damaged, certainly, but he couldn't see enough this way to determine if there was foundation damage too.

He didn't even like to contemplate all the things Rye could've been exposed to—six different types of mold, animal droppings, rabies—

He cut off his thought spiral and pictured windshield wipers clearing the troubling images from his mind.

In the first year after his parents' death, Charlie had been in survival mode. Take care of Jack, make sure they didn't lose the house or the business, learn how to be a grown-up.

It was the year after that, around his nineteenth birthday, when the images had begun—broken, bloody thoughts forced into his head against his will: turn on the garbage disposal—see a mangled hand. Stop at the gas station—see it going up in flames. Watch a coworker climb a ladder—see it falling and smashing them to the ground. That they didn't feel like his thoughts at all made them even more upsetting.

He'd gone to a therapist then, trembling as he told her about the horrifying pictures slipped unbidden into the slide projector of his mind. He had admitted his deepest fear: that they *were* his thoughts—dark, violent thoughts that meant something dark and violent about him.

She'd settled that fear by giving them a name—intrusive thoughts—and an antidote: the windshield wipers that scraped the images away as if they were a fallen leaf or a sluice of rain. He'd used the trick ever since. The intrusive thoughts had lessened over the years, but had never gone away. Now when they happened, they were mostly about Jack. The fall he'd taken in the autumn had exacerbated them for several months.

He'd begun to get them back under control recently. At least he'd thought so.

Still on his knees, he took a deep breath and put a hand on Rye's shoe.

"Can I see?"

Rye looked down at him, frowning, but then he bit his lip and gave one short nod.

Charlie lifted the leg of his jeans gently. Rye's ankle looked slightly swollen, but probably just tweaked, not sprained. He untied the gray bandana. The bottom half of Rye's shin was a mess of bruises and a long, fairly deep cut ran through the middle.

Rye was holding his breath. The cut looked painful but probably not so deep that it required stitches. Charlie could see just by looking at it that it hadn't been well cleaned, though.

Infection, disease, blood poisoning, gangrene, amputation—

Charlie pictured the windshield wipers, scraping every frightening thought clear.

"Come home with me," Charlie said, chest tight. He re-tied the bandanna and rolled down Rye's pant leg. Then he stood and made for the door.

"What? No."

"We need to clean that cut. Dress it properly."

"I thought you were gonna look at my house."

"That can wait."

"But you're here now," Rye said, looking genuinely confused.

Charlie sighed.

Wipe, wipe, wipe. It's not an emergency. Rye isn't going to die. It's okay to wait. Waiting won't make things worse.

"All right. I'll look at the house, then you'll come home with me. We can take care of your leg and talk about the house then. Okay?"

"Sure."

Charlie walked through the house, testing the floors, prying back boards to look at the joists, and tapping at the drywall, trying not to imagine infection blooming in Rye's blood and traveling through his whole body. Rye trailed behind him, asking questions and biting his lip when Charlie found something structurally unsound. Which was a lot of things.

When he was examining the fireplace, Rye pointed to some fragments of wood that lay unburnt among the ash.

"I think someone burned the dresser from the bedroom. Maybe the bed frame too."

Charlie looked closely at the wood.

"Could be."

"Maybe kids, hanging out? Or, uh, you know, satanists."

Charlie assumed he was kidding.

"Guess it depends on whether you found candy bar wrappers or a goat carcass in a pentagram," Charlie said dryly.

Rye grinned. A real, natural, can't-help-it grin, and it was like someone turned on the sun. He had two perfect dimples and his crooked teeth were utterly charming. The smile lit up his eyes and made his face inviting and warm.

Damn.

"I found cheap candles," Rye said.

"Hmm. Could go either way."

That got a laugh out of Rye, who looked surprised by it. Charlie was used to that. People told him all the time that he had no sense of humor.

Something niggled at the back of Charlie's mind and he looked up into the chimney to check the flue.

"In the fall, my brother told me he saw smoke coming from over here," Charlie remembered. "He kept saying the smoke was coming at a different time than usual. I thought it was just because he'd broken his leg and was going all *Rear Window*, making up a mystery to occupy him. But now I wonder if he saw people squatting here."

Rye's eyes cut to his sleeping bag and duffel bag in the corner at *squatting* and he walked away. Charlie followed him up the stairs. It was a small space relative to the rest of the house, as if Rye's grandfather was so sure that he'd always live alone that he didn't even leave space for that to change.

The idea made Charlie sad.

He'd spent the last two years turning his own house into

a place with the possibility for anything. Some days—many days—he'd wondered why he was doing it. Sure, Jane loved to roll around in the sawdust and plaster dust his renovations created, but beyond that...

Because the truth was that he could have turned the spare room into a woodworking studio. He didn't need a bigger kitchen because he cooked basic, practical meals for one. When he wanted to see the sky and the trees he simply walked outside.

But something had driven him to create something more. More flexible, more welcoming...just *more*.

Only very early in the morning and very late at night was Charlie able to admit to himself that maybe it wasn't *his* dream house he was building. That maybe he was building it for someone he hadn't met yet; for a life he didn't yet have.

"So?" Rye was looking up at him in a way that made Charlie realize he'd been standing at the top of the stairs, staring.

Mismatched chairs were set up in a circle around a milk crate with candles on top; the mattress pushed up against the wall.

"Probably kids," Charlie said. "If it was squatters, I'd think the mattress would be on the floor." Rye bit his lip, frowning. "Chances are they started burning the dresser and bedframe when it got seriously cold."

Rye nodded.

"Where are you from, anyway?" Charlie asked.

"Seattle."

"Hear it's nice there. Temperate."

Rye nodded. So much for conversation, then. Charlie got back to his inspection. When he began to tug a piece of fabric out of the wall, Rye stopped him.

"Oh, wait. Leave that. It's...there's a squirrel...situation. I don't want it to get stuck again. It screamed."

Rye shuddered and a tiny warmth bloomed in Charlie's gut, imagining scrappy, tattooed Rye rescuing a squirrel.

"Okay, let's go."

"You're done?" Rye asked.

"I've seen all I can see without tools. Let's take care of your leg."

"But—"

"There's nothing more we can do here today. So let's see to your leg and talk this over," Charlie said firmly.

Rye frowned. He took the stairs slowly, as if now that their business was done he could let himself acknowledge that he was in pain.

On the ground floor, Rye made a kissing sound and the hell beast that had attacked Charlie came prancing in.

"Can I bring Marmot?" Rye asked.

Charlie frowned. "Why?"

Rye's eyes flashed. "Because."

Well that explained that.

Charlie ran a hand through his hair.

"I have a cat. Not sure they'll get along." He eyed the tiny cat suspiciously, imagining it hurting Jane.

"Oh." Rye chewed his lip mercilessly. Marmot sprang into his arms and then his shoulder, purring audibly. Rye pressed his cheek into the cat's fur. "She could—" he started to offer, then shook his head. "Never mind. It's fine."

"Does she just stay with you? She doesn't run away?"

"She always comes back," Rye said. Marmot curled her tail around Rye's neck like a scarf, tip twitching against his throat.

Charlie reminded himself that although Rye was a little snarly, he *was* in a brand new place, clearly roughing it in a house he was now responsible for, with no idea how to take care of it. The cat seemed to relax Rye, so if that's what it took to keep him calm enough to care for his leg, Charlie could make it work. Jane would probably be curled up on his bed, happy to snooze through the whole incident anyway.

"She can come," Charlie said, mentally rolling his eyes at himself for being such a sucker for Rye that he was letting a hell beast come to his house.

"Yeah?" Rye's face lit up and he quickly looked down. "Okay, thanks. C'mon, Marmot."

"Why don't I drive. I'll drop you back after."

"Do you have a phone charger thingie?"

"I have a USB adapter."

Rye nodded and grabbed a cord from his car. "You mind?"

Charlie plugged the cord in and handed Rye the end. He put his phone to charge.

Marmot sat on Rye's lap as they drove, occasionally putting her front paws up on the dashboard to peer out the window. It was a little bit cute, Charlie decided.

"She's pretty fierce for a tiny little thing."

"Yeah, she can take care of herself."

"Why'd you name her Marmot?"

"Oh, uh. I found her stuck in an oil can outside where I used to work. And when I pulled her out she was all sticky and covered in oil. I thought she looked like one of those little seals—the kind that get stuck in oil spills. And I kept calling her a little marmot because I thought it was a kind of seal, cuz there's the outdoor company Marmot, right, and that's where I got my sleeping bag and it's called something like a seal sleeping bag. I don't know. I googled marmot later and realized it's not a seal—it's like a big squirrel, but whatever."

Charlie found that utterly adorable.

It was about a twenty-minute drive to his house. Rye fiddled with his hair, untangling the long, dark strands, and Charlie forced himself not to look at him. When he finally allowed himself to glance over at a stoplight, Rye was asleep, head resting against the back of the seat, Marmot curled up in his lap.

In sleep, Rye's face was lovely. The angles of his cheekbones and jaw, his expressive eyebrows, and delicately pointed chin. The curve of his lips and the long line of his throat. Inky barbs clawed their way out of his collar, but Charlie couldn't tell what the tattoos were of.

He must have been exhausted to fall asleep so quickly. Charlie drove carefully, avoiding any bumps that might wake him.

He turned off the truck in the driveway and had the strangest sensation of something momentous occurring.

Even after they stopped moving, Rye didn't wake. Charlie kept expecting him to, but one minute turned into five, and five turned into ten, and Charlie realized he was watching Rye sleep as if he had any right to such intimacy. Marmot yawned, blinked her eyes open, and stared at him from Rye's lap.

"We're here," Charlie forced himself to say, under the cat's scrutiny.

Rye blinked awake and as the second consciousness returned so did his furrowed brow.

"Did I fall asleep? Jeez, sorry."

"It's fine. Come on in."

Rye carried Marmot from the car, eyes everywhere.

"Whoa. Did you really build this?" he asked, taking in the not-quite-finished addition to the side of the house.

A rush of pride washed through Charlie.

"Not all of it. It was a small house originally. I gutted it and redid the interior about ten years ago. I've been adding to it over the last few years."

When he closed the door behind them, he heard the familiar thump that was Jane jumping off the bed to greet him.

A minute later, she appeared at the end of the hallway and slunk majestically toward them.

"That's Jane."

Rye snorted. "I guess that makes you Tarzan?"

Charlie shook his head. It was exactly what Simon, Jack's partner had said, when he'd begun feeling comfortable enough around Charlie to joke around.

Before Charlie could say anything, Marmot jumped from Rye's arms and shot down the hallway. Charlie rushed after her, ready to throw himself between this cat bullet and Jane, but his movements were slow motion in comparison.

He had visions of a vicious fight—tufts of fur flying and claws scratching at his sweet Jane, who might've been large but would never hurt anything. He vibrated with tension, ready to pluck the hell beast off Jane at any sign of aggression.

But Marmot didn't attack. She slid to a halt a foot from Jane and stuck out her nose. Half Jane's size and sleek where Jane was fluffy, Marmot circled Jane, sniffing at her. Jane stood still and let herself be sniffed.

Marmot yipped and Jane meowed her ripping metal meow. Then Jane plopped down in the middle of the hallway and Marmot began licking her all over as Jane purred.

Charlie couldn't believe his little lone wolf was instantly won over.

"Not what I thought was going to happen," Charlie said. No longer worried about Jane, he could focus on Rye. "Let's get you taken care of."

He led Rye to the master bathroom. He loved this bathroom. The floor was a deep indigo penny tile and the shower a herringbone of a sea glass blue so light you had to look twice to be sure of the color. It had taken two weeks to tile.

The shower was the most luxurious thing in the house. Once his back had begun to ache at the end of a long day and his knees twinge with too much kneeling, he stood under the shower and let the heat pour over his aching body and imagined that the warmth of it could follow him when he dried off. It was the one thing in the house he'd designed just for himself.

Charlie got the first aid kit from under the sink and turned to find Rye staring at the shower with naked longing. Probably sleeping on the floor of an unheated house with no water didn't provide many opportunities to take one.

"You wanna take a shower?" Charlie offered.

He could see the moment when Rye's kneejerk *no* was coming—the flared nostrils and narrowed eyes—but then Rye looked down.

"So bad," he said sheepishly, and raised his eyes to Charlie's.

Charlie forgot to speak for a moment. In the light of his bathroom, Rye's gray eyes were the same saturation as that sea glass tile—luminous and tumbled smooth by the violence of the oceans that surrounded them.

"Uh, yeah, be my guest," Charlie said.

He looked at Rye's clothes. Jeans streaked with dirt, a faded black long-sleeved T-shirt for some band he'd never heard of, a too-big jean jacket lined with fleece.

"If you put your clothes outside, I'll stick them in the wash and leave you some sweats," he offered.

Rye's pupils dilated.

"Thanks," he said softly. "Or...maybe you better let me do it. They're probably a little ripe."

Charlie waved his concern away.

"Take your time. I'll just...check on the cats."

Chapter Seven

Rye

Rye groaned as he stepped under the hot waterfall of Charlie's shower, but his groan turned to a whimper when water ran down over the cut on his leg.

He'd never liked blood and just thinking about the cut made him woozy.

He luxuriated under the water for a while, then washed his hair with Charlie's shampoo. It was jasmine, and made Rye think of dark, secret gardens strung with fairy lights a thousand miles away from Wyoming.

When he got out of the shower he found clothes on the other side of the bathroom door. He wrapped his dripping hair in the towel and pulled on navy blue sweatpants and a gray sweatshirt that said WYOMING in brown letters outlined in yellow and a man riding a horse underneath it in the same brown and yellow. It was hideous. The clothes clung to his damp skin. Both were so huge he felt like he was being swallowed.

He hung up the towel and crept out of the bathroom, the extra fabric of the sweatpants pooling at his ankles and his hair dampening the shoulders of the sweatshirt. Following a cattish sound, he found Charlie, Jane, and Marmot in a high-ceilinged living room with exposed wood beams and a wood floor covered with a deep gray rug. On the rug, Jane and Marmot were playing a kind of tug-of-war with Charlie, who was on his back with a sleeve in each of their mouths.

Jane had clearly played this game before, but Marmot was losing her shit, tugging at Charlie's sleeve, then getting her claws caught in the flannel and flipping over onto her back to free them. Charlie laughed and teased her with his fingers, and Marmot jumped onto his chest and began making biscuits on his sternum.

"You won her over," Rye said.

Marmot acted tough but she was a little softy at heart.

Charlie tipped his head and looked at Rye upside down. He smiled an upside-down smile, lines appearing around his eyes. Jane looked up at him just like her human.

"That's the biggest damn cat I've ever seen."

Rye padded into the room and sat cross-legged on the rug next to Jane. She was black with gray markings and had little tufts of fur on the tips of her ears. Her tail was practically the size of Marmot's whole body.

"She's a Maine coon," Charlie said, sitting up.

His movement displaced Marmot who protested by jumping onto his shoulder. Charlie's face lit up like a big kid's.

"Hi," he cooed to Marmot. Marmot flicked her tail in his face.

"Can I pet her?" Rye asked.

"Sure."

Jane lay on the rug, eyes half-closed, massive tail twitching lazily.

Rye sank his hand into her thick coat and scratched. Jane purred, a deep motorboat rumble. He scratched between her tufted ears and her eyes drifted shut. She was the softest thing he'd ever touched. He buried his face in her luscious fur and breathed in the scent of wood shavings and something lightly floral, like fabric softener. The combination reminded him of being outside in the Seattle spring when he walked through the woods and on the beach.

"You ready to take care of that leg?"

Rye muffled his groan in Jane's fur and dragged himself up.

Charlie stood also, plucking Marmot off his shoulder with one hand and depositing her on the rug. She stretched luxuriantly and then walked up on top of Jane to lie down on her back. Jane opened one eye, then closed it again in welcome.

The cats curled into a ball of gray and black and orange and white. It was impossibly cute.

Charlie pulled his phone out and snapped a picture.

Then he led Rye back into the bathroom and had him sit on the edge of the bathtub. The air was still humid from the shower and smelled of the jasmine shampoo.

"Guess you like it here, huh?" Rye said, suddenly wanting to delay this as long as possible. "Wyoming, I mean?" He pointed at the sweatshirt he was wearing.

"It's the cowboys," Charlie said.

Rye blinked. Okay, so Charlie Matheson was into cowboys. That was…really hot.

"The football team. The Cowboys. U of W."

"Oh." Well that was disappointing. "Did you go there?"

Charlie's face did something complicated and illegible.

"No."

"Oh."

Charlie sat on the floor at Rye's feet and tugged the sweatpants up to his knee.

"I should've told you not to let the fabric touch the cut," Charlie murmured.

Rye fixed his eyes on Charlie's red-gold hair, determined not to look at the exposed cut for one second.

"Okay, you have some slivers of wood in here. I need to clean them out."

"Mmfh," Rye said. He caught a glimpse of tweezers and squeezed his eyes shut tight. He smelled alcohol and then felt a flash of pain. He made himself freeze but the sensation of the cut being prodded was nauseating. He tried to breathe through his nose but that just made the alcohol smell stronger.

"Whoa, whoa, hold on," Charlie said, and Rye opened his eyes as he rocked backward off the lip of the tub.

Charlie caught him with a hand on his back at the same time as Rye caught himself.

"Come down here."

He eased onto the tile floor, vision swimming.

"Does it hurt a lot?" Charlie asked gently.

Rye shook his head, taking shallow breaths through his mouth.

"It's the alcohol. Don't like the smell."

The stink of it as his mother scrubbed every surface of the only apartment his father had been able to find at the last minute. He'd had a headache for days. Years later, on his hands and knees, he'd scrubbed with an identical bottle the mouse droppings and cockroach husks in another horrid apartment.

Charlie opened the bathroom door and flicked on the fan. Rye let his damp hair fall over his face, trying to smell jasmine instead.

"I'm gonna have to use it again to clean the cut. I'm sorry," Charlie said. "But I have to make sure it's not infected. Will you be okay?"

Rye wanted to say no. He wanted to bury his face in Charlie's shoulder and feel arms come around him and hold him. He wanted to hide. But hiding never did any good.

"Yeah, 's fine," he mumbled. "Gimme your shampoo?"

Charlie passed him the bottle of shampoo from the shower and Rye unscrewed the top and held it under his nose. He leaned back against the bathtub and closed his eyes again.

"Okay," Charlie murmured. "Just tell me if you need a break."

As Charlie poked and prodded his cut, Rye's mind drifted. He breathed in the scent of jasmine and imagined he was walking through Discovery Park in the late spring. He used to go all the time. There was a bend in the trail where the light broke through the mammoth trees and fell on passersby like glitter. There was a spot where the trees opened onto the outcropping that revealed the ocean. A place where you could trace the stratigraphy of thousands and thousands of years of rock, mud, rock, mud, sand, mud, rock.

Once, he'd seen a baby seal lying on the beach, fat and glorious and seeming to smile in the sunlight. He'd been with Maya then, and she'd packed a picnic of peanut butter and jelly sandwiches and Oreos. She said just because you couldn't cook didn't mean you couldn't have a picnic. They'd sat on the sand and tossed bits of the jelly side of the sandwiches on the ground to watch them be plucked up by gulls diving in reckless, graceful arcs.

That had been a good day.

"All right," Charlie said, voice soft and low. "Last alcohol smell and then I'll dress it."

Rye hadn't been to Discovery Park in years. It had been ages since he'd seen Maya.

"Okay."

Maybe once it got warmer here he could be outside again. Maybe he could walk through the woods around the house. Or find a cheap chair and sit outside. After all, he didn't live in the city anymore.

"Rye. Rye." A hand landed on his shoulder. "Hey."

Rye opened his eyes. Charlie was close and looked worried.

"Is it done?" He didn't look at his leg.

"Yeah."

He glanced down to see a white bandage taped around his shin.

"Is it okay?"

Charlie nodded. "I put antibiotic ointment on it. You need to keep it clean. I'll change the dressing in a day or two."

"Like salad," he heard himself say nonsensically.

Charlie squeezed his shoulder, then stood and offered him a hand. He got a whiff of alcohol and reached up to take it. Charlie lifted his weight like it was nothing and eased the shampoo bottle out of his hand.

For a moment, they stood close together. Charlie's eyelashes were a dark rust color. He had freckles on his forehead and on his cheeks above his beard. His eyes looked so fucking green. He had freckles on his eyelids.

Charlie gave him a small smile, his eyelashes fluttering.

Rye kissed him.

Charlie's full lips were soft and his beard tickled Rye's chin. Rye smelled wood shavings and clean sweat and a uniquely Charlie-smelling heat, but before Rye had a chance to taste him, Charlie pulled away and Rye lurched forward.

"What are you doing?"

Rye's head was swimming. "I thought... I... I don't know, shit. I'm sorry!"

His heart was pounding in his ears, threatening to take over his whole body. He backed toward the doorway.

"Rye, stop," Charlie called after him, but Rye was already out the door, heading for the living room.

He'd fucked it up. He'd completely fucked things up. Bad call, bad call, bad call.

Jane and Marmot weren't in the living room anymore. Rye called for Marmot but got no yip in response.

Charlie caught up to him.

"I'm so sorry," Rye said again.

He dared a glance at Charlie's face, not sure what type of anger or scorn he might find, but Charlie looked confused.

"It's okay," he said immediately.

"No. It's not."

Charlie called for Jane like he could deflect the focus onto the cat. It made Rye's stomach hurt.

Could he get a Lyft from here? His phone was still plugged into the USB cord in Charlie's truck. Where was Marmot?

"Let me get you some socks," Charlie said, and hurried away.

Rye's stomach was in knots. His clothes probably weren't dry yet and there was no way he could walk all that way in oversized sweats with a cat in his arms. And he needed his phone.

Charlie tossed him a pair of wool socks that bounced off his chest and onto the rug. Rye stared at them.

"Your laundry won't be done for another hour or so," Charlie said, all business again. "Do you want to wait, or should I take you home now and I can drop it off for you later?"

Rye blinked. Charlie wasn't quite meeting his eyes.

"Are we...? I...? Should we...?"

Charlie said nothing. The awkwardness was exquisite.

"Uh. Okay, then. Whichever's easier," Rye said.

Charlie shook his head. No help from that quarter.

Rye just wanted to get out of there. He couldn't stand looking at Charlie; being looked at.

"Now I guess," Rye got out. "I can get my clothes later."

"Okay."

But Charlie just stood there. He touched his chin, then his mouth.

"Do you know where the cats are?"

He walked out of the room and reappeared a few minutes later with Marmot in his arms. Rye reached for her, pulled her to his chest, and held her a little tighter than she liked. She smelled like wood shavings.

They drove back to Rye's in silence. He searched his brain for a single, solitary thing to say, but it was a vast, razed field, and every attempt stuck in his throat.

Rye was out of the car the second Charlie shifted into Park.

"Thanks," he said uselessly. "I'm sorry."

His stomach was a hollow pit.

"Come to the store tomorrow or the next day," Charlie instructed. He was all business. "I'll change the bandage. And I'll bring your clothes."

Rye nodded, then fled inside. The house smelled dank and moldy. The chill was biting. It would be dark soon. Rye scooped some food into Marmot's bowl and climbed into the sleeping bag. He was suddenly overwhelmed with exhaustion. Even with the padding of the bag, it wasn't nearly as soft as Charlie's rug had been.

Charlie's house had smelled good too. Clean and fresh and airy.

He stared at the ceiling until the sun set and he couldn't see anything anymore. Then Marmot came, pawing to be let into the sleeping bag and breathing cat food breath in his face. She settled in, her tiny body his only comfort.

"You made a friend, huh?"

Marmot purred.

"Sorry you'll probably never see her again," Rye said. "I fucked up. I'm sorry. I'm sorry," he said over and over.

He'd fucked things up before they'd even talked about the house. What the hell had he been thinking? He'd seen something in Charlie's eyes that he'd...badly misread, obviously.

He pulled his hood up, letting the jasmine smell of his clean hair surround him, and tried to escape into sleep.

Chapter Eight

Charlie

It had been three days and Rye hadn't come.

The day after he'd taken Rye home with him, Charlie carefully folded his laundered clothes into a bag and added first aid supplies. He took the bag to work and waited all day for Rye to come.

The next day, he got up early and went for a run, and then he did it again. For reasons he didn't care to examine, he washed Rye's clothes again, folded them again, placed them in the bag again. Rye still didn't come.

Rye, dead from blood poisoning, or lying on the ground unable to come in because of infection and pain.

He told Marie what had happened. The kiss. But when he told her Rye was probably just trying to say thank you, she frowned.

"Did it ever occur to you that someone might want to kiss you just because they like you?" she asked.

He dismissed it.

That night, Charlie made chicken in mushroom soup. He made it every Thursday. Monday, it was meatloaf; Tuesday, spaghetti and meatballs; Wednesday, pizza; Friday, beef burritos. On the weekends he ate the leftovers.

As he was eating, Jane on the chair next to him eating her

chicken pâté—he matched her meals to his; it was companionable—he thought about Rye.

What was Rye eating for dinner? Did he eat real meals at restaurants, or was he subsisting, as Charlie suspected, on gas station offerings? He put some leftovers for Rye into a container. Then he took them out again.

He wondered a lot of other things about Rye too. Like, did he feel the need to kiss anyone who did something marginally nice for him? And if Charlie hadn't pulled away, what else might he have done? Pressed his lithe body against Charlie's and let Charlie feel the lines of muscle and bone, the whisper of soft skin? Put his hot mouth on Charlie's neck and his hands all over Charlie? Charlie shivered with desire at what could have happened next, if Charlie had let him.

Rye was exasperating, defensive, stubborn, and snarly. But he was also determined and brave. He'd moved a thousand miles from home and taken on a huge project by himself. Charlie admired that, even if watching Rye take on that project completely wrong made Charlie want to scream.

On the third day that Rye didn't come into the shop, Charlie went to him.

Rye's car was there, but all was quiet when Charlie pulled up. He knocked, then called, "Rye?" when he didn't hear anything.

He heard swearing, then creaking wood, then Rye yelled, "What?"

"It's Charlie."

"Yeah, I know. What?"

Charlie rolled his eyes.

"You were supposed to come to the store so I could take care of your leg. Lemme in and I'll look at it."

"Um. That's okay."

"Rye."

Charlie heard his voice do that thing that Jack always called his dad voice and forced himself to change his tone.

"Do you want your leg to fill with pus and go septic and—"

The door cracked open before he could finish painting his grisly picture.

"Don't you have anything better to do than chase after people and tend to their wounds?" Rye grumbled.

Nope.

"Yeah, I do," Charlie said.

Rye eased the door open just enough to slide his slim form through. His hair was a mess and there was a crease in his cheek. He pushed his hair out of his face, crossed his arms over his chest, and stuck out his leg.

"You want me to do this standing outside."

Rye sat down on the step and stuck out his leg.

That's when Charlie noticed Rye was still wearing the sweats he'd given him the other day, only they had a layer of…was that dust? Dirt? It was in Rye's hair too. There was even a patina of it freckling his face. Charlie leaned in closer and swept a finger down Rye's nose.

"What the hell?" Rye said.

Charlie's heart sped as he recognized the grit.

"Did a wall fall down?"

Rye's eyes went wide, then narrowed.

"No," he snapped. Then added, "Not exactly."

Charlie pictured Rye sleeping in the house as it crumbled around him; Rye trapped under falling debris, screaming with no one to hear or help him.

Charlie's heart started pounding. He flung the door open and went inside, avoiding the hole in the floor. He could smell destruction. The half clean, half dirty scent of ozone and rotten wood.

The wall between the staircase and the living room gaped,

its rough-hewn beams a naked skeleton and splintered wood and plaster in a heap on the floor.

There was a band of tight heat around Charlie's chest, constricting his lungs. Terror. He swung around to Rye.

"Did this wall fall down and you stayed here anyway?"

Rye's gray eyes were narrowed, ready to fight.

"Not…exactly…"

Charlie narrowed his eyes. "Rye. Did you *tear* this fucking wall down?"

The flicker of Rye's gaze told Charlie he was right and he wheeled around and looked again. The load-bearing post was still in place, but he figured that was because Rye didn't have the tools to remove it, not because he knew what it was.

"The whole second story could have fallen on you!" Charlie yelled, breath coming shallow and heart slamming against his ribs. "What the hell possessed you to do such an idiotic thing?"

Rye glared beams of fire.

"*You're* the one who said we'd need to demo the inside before we could fix the house!"

Charlie gaped. "I— You— So—I—"

It was so *reckless*, so unthinking, so foolish! He could've been killed.

Rye scowled and hugged himself, Charlie's sweatshirt swallowing him up.

"You can't just *demo* a house! You need to know which walls are load bearing and you need a dumpster to haul the debris to. It could be full of lead or black mold or…or…anything. You need a mask and gloves and you can't do it by yourself. Jesus, the ceiling could've collapsed on you as you slept. You can't just *stay* here while you demo—"

He cut himself off, voice shaking so hard he was sure Rye could hear it.

Charlie felt a familiar tingling in his fingertips. The buzz-

ing in his ears came a few seconds later and he fled from the
house and into the clearing behind it.

He searched for the roof of Jack's cabin to steady himself.

He stared at the tiny distant triangle and forced himself
to breathe through his nose. He dug his thumbs into the
pressure points on his wrists and tried to calm down. It had
been months since he'd had to do this. Not since Jack's accident last year. But Jack was fine now. Better than fine. Jack
was thriving.

Charlie clenched his eyes shut, but all he saw with closed
eyes was his parents, dead two days before his eighteenth
birthday. Jack's face when Charlie told him they were gone.
Jack's chin wobbling like it had when he was a little boy. The
nights when Charlie would wake from nightmares into one.

"Hey. Are you okay?"

Rye stood to his left, Marmot in his arms.

Charlie nodded automatically.

Rye held out the cat like he was sharing a stuffed animal
with a friend on the playground. Charlie shook his hands out,
trying to dispel the tingling. When he took Marmot she put
her paws on his shoulder and plastered herself against his chest
over his heart. Her rumbling purr vibrated against his neck.

"I'm fine," Charlie said blankly.

"Yeah, you're clearly doing great," Rye muttered wryly.

Charlie kept his eyes on Jack's house. He wished he could
see Jack right now. Just to make sure he was all right. Maybe
he'd just send him a quick text—

"So what's the deal with your brother? You guys estranged
or something?"

"What? No. Why would you think that?"

Rye shrugged.

"You're looking at his roof like it's the closest you'll ever
get to him."

"No I'm not," Charlie grumbled. "We're not estranged,"
he felt compelled to add again.

They stood in silence for a while. It was a cool, sunny day, and the breeze felt good ruffling Charlie's hair and kissing his face.

When Rye spoke again there was a softness to his voice.

"I didn't just tear the wall down without thinking, you know. I googled it. I watched a bunch of videos."

Charlie sighed. It was mildly comforting that Rye hadn't simply started swinging a sledgehammer, but only very mildly.

"There's stuff you can't learn from a video. It's... I'm sorry I yelled. But it's so damn dangerous. Even if you've demoed a hundred houses, you can never completely predict what will happen. Sometimes there are places a house has settled or buckled or been eaten by termites and things just...happen."

"I get it," Rye said. "That's why I stopped."

Charlie nodded and his eyes scanned the horizon. Sometimes you could see elk around this time of year.

"Why didn't you come into the store?" he asked finally.

"I—" *Waited for you. Wanted to see you. Needed to make sure you were okay.*

Rye's eyes darted to Charlie's mouth.

"Because I was fucking embarrassed. Obviously."

His voice was acid but his eyes were pained and his cheeks flushed.

"About the kiss."

"Yeah, about the kiss. Of course about the kiss," he snapped.

Charlie didn't know what to say. He was embarrassed too, just for different reasons. Ones he had no intention of discussing with Rye at this time.

After a few moments, Rye sighed. "Okay, can we do this?" He gestured to his leg and Charlie nodded and followed him back to the porch.

"You have demo dirt all over you," Charlie muttered, rolling up the leg of his sweatpants.

"And you have a really irritating way of making every sentence sound like an insult. Did you know that?"

Charlie looked up into gray eyes narrowed with anger. Jack had told him that before. *Okay, Dad,* Jack would say in his late teens whenever he thought Charlie was being overbearing. A silly choice, since their own father hadn't been overbearing himself. Whenever Jack would say it, though, Charlie was hit with a complicated wave of anger and shame and satisfaction that usually made him walk out of the room and squeeze his eyes shut until the wave broke over him and he stopped shaking.

"Yeah. I guess I did," Charlie said. "Sorry."

He unpeeled the dressing and Rye hissed as the gauze stuck to the wound. That wouldn't have happened if Rye had just let him take care of it the day after like he'd said—but he stopped himself from verbalizing that, since it would sound very, very disapproving.

Charlie had thought they'd be doing this in the store, so he'd assumed they'd have running water. But he was pretty sure if he asked Rye to come back to his house he'd get a door slammed in his face.

"Hang on a sec," he said, and jogged to grab a bottle of water from the truck.

Despite Rye's neglect, the wound looked no worse for wear. It wasn't inflamed or weeping, and Charlie's heart stopped pounding. He applied more antibacterial ointment and put on fresh gauze. He carefully rolled the sweats down over Rye's leg and stood, offering him a hand up.

"Thanks," Rye said softly, gesturing to his leg and to the bag of his clean clothes Charlie'd brought.

Clearly, this was the way it was with Rye. He would never seek help out; he would only accept help that came to him.

"Okay, here's the deal," Charlie said. "I'll help you."

Rye blinked at him.

"Help me."

"With the house. *Obviously*, with the house," he teased.

Rye quirked a small smile.

"I'll help you demo. I can get some friends to help. We'll tear it down and get a sense of what would need to be done to rebuild. Then we'll make a plan. But this is not a joke or a game. If we do this, you have to listen to me when I tell you shit's not safe."

"Why?" Rye asked.

"Because that shit will get you killed! I already told—"

"Why are you *helping me*? After what I did," Rye clarified.

Rye's lips, soft on his for just one moment.

Charlie windshield-wipered the thought away.

"Why wouldn't I?"

"Is that supposed to be an answer?"

Charlie couldn't tell Rye the real reasons. *I couldn't stand to see anything bad happen to you. I don't really wanna let you out of my sight in case something bad* does *happen. You make me happy for some reason I haven't quite figured out yet. You're the most interesting thing to happen to me in years. I don't want you to go back to Seattle because you can't make this work.*

"I like demo," Charlie said simply. "I like projects. You've got a project. Besides, you're clearly helpless without me," he added just to watch Rye's nostrils flare wide enough to swallow his nose. "It'll be fun."

"Yeah, fun, great," Rye murmured. "I can't pay you. I have, like, a thousand bucks to my name. I don't suppose that would cover building a house?"

Obviously Rye knew it wouldn't, but Charlie was pretty sure he had no clue the magnitude—in time, work, or money—of a project like building a house.

"No," Charlie said. "But there are loans and ways to get cheap materials. We'll talk to the bank and see what your options are. As for demo, though, I can get Jack and Simon to help, and a few buddies who'll help us do the work if we buy pizza and let them listen to terrible honky-tonk while they work."

"Why?" Rye asked again.

"I guess they just really like a banjo."

"No, I mean—"

"I know what you meant. Because sometimes people like to help and it has nothing to do with who they're helping. Because there's not that much to do around here on the weekends. Because these folks grew up building things themselves and this is what they do. Because they like me and want to help me out. Take your pick."

"I don't know if I can get a loan," Rye said. "I've probably got pretty bad credit."

"We'll figure it out."

"And you trust me enough to do that? You don't even know me."

"It's a house. What are you gonna do—steal it?"

Rye was staring at the ground and when he glanced up his eyes shone. Charlie tactfully pretended not to notice.

"Okay," Rye said. "I think you're bananas, but okay."

Charlie winked. "Potassium's good for you."

Rye snorted.

"There's just one thing," Charlie went on, ignoring Rye's look of suspicion. He aimed for casual, but his muscles were tight with worry that Rye would say no.

"You can't stay here." Rye opened his mouth but Charlie waved him off. "No. We'll be ripping up the whole floor, Rye. The walls will come down. You might as well sleep on the ground outside."

"Maybe—"

"Please don't tell me you're such a city boy that you don't know why it's a bad idea to sleep in the middle of the woods with a cat."

"Don't worry, they have murderers in Seattle."

"Do they have bears in Seattle?"

"Sure, if you go to the right bar on the right night." Rye waggled his eyebrows. "I can't afford a hotel, man. I'll get a tent or something. I'll be fine."

"God, you're infuriating!" Charlie roared. Rye was like a cat with its claws caught in fabric that tried to bite you if you attempted to free it. "I have a guest room."

Rye snorted and clutched at his head, dragging fingers through his hair.

"You don't even know me!" he said again. "I could murder you in your sleep. Or, or steal your stereo, or..."

Charlie was beginning to think Rye was reminding *himself* of the fact that they didn't know each other.

"I know you don't know me, but there are locks on the bedrooms and I'm gone at the store all day. I promise, you're safe with me."

"Yeah, I bet Bluebeard gave the same speech."

Charlie laughed. "Well my locks are on the *inside* of the doors. But feel free to check the basement for murdered wives before you commit to anything."

Rye looked at his blighted house, then back at Charlie.

"Marmot can come?"

"Marmot can come."

Charlie could *see* the struggle inside Rye.

"I can just crash on the couch—"

"Why would I want you taking up my couch when I have a spare room?"

Charlie couldn't read the expression on Rye's face so he decided to interpret it as cautiously optimistic.

"You're, like, not a real person," Rye said. "You don't just invite strangers to live with you. You don't just offer to help strangers rebuild creepy houses they inherited from grandfathers they've never met."

"Is that a yes, then?" Charlie asked.

When Rye gave a slow, puzzled nod, Charlie felt like he had won a prize.

Chapter Nine

Rye dropped his duffel on the chair, and perched on the edge of the bed as Marmot sniffed the corners of Charlie's guest room.

For a few weeks, he'd been on his own, and now here he was again, crashing in someone else's house, preparing to accustom himself to yet another person's habits so they didn't kick him out.

"At least this time there's a bed," he muttered to Marmot.

Charlie had told him to make himself at home, but Rye had only felt at home once in his life. They'd called the house Skeletor for serpentine reasons of the moment that Rye no longer remembered. It was a five-bedroom house in Beacon Hill and there were six of them, so thrilled to have found it that they'd signed the lease even though the move-in was immediate and some of their leases weren't up.

They shared food, cooked together, rotated chores, calculated each person's rent based on their income and other expenses. They took care of each other.

It had lasted two and a half years.

Rye would move nearly every year for the next six years, until the eviction that found him couch hopping before he came to Garnet Run.

Through all those apartments, with all those roommates,

Rye had gotten a great deal of experience in living with a huge variety of people with different backgrounds, levels of cleanliness, attitudes, worldviews, and personalities.

Before, when he lived with his parents, even though he'd had his own room, it hadn't felt like home either. He'd still contorted himself—only those had been psychic contortions. The kind that made you smaller and smaller until you threatened to disappear if you didn't get out. So he had.

Now he had another room of his own in another person's home. But this one was nothing like any of the cramped apartments or sublets he'd stayed in. This was a grown-up's house, with a laundry room and hand towels and no detritus of previous housemates or furniture accumulated from the cast-offs of passers-through.

There was something ruthlessly practical about most of the choices Charlie had made about the space, as if they'd had to pass a test of neutrality so as not to offend anyone. Even so, Rye could extract patterns of color, shape, and angle. He could tell Charlie liked cool colors and natural materials, and that he enjoyed soft things to touch.

He could tell that Charlie didn't travel. There wasn't a single object in the house that seemed to come from anywhere else, nor was there anything that seemed to come from some*body* else. No inside jokes or decorative souvenirs; no gift books or magnets from Arizona. No shot glasses from a Florida airport or repurposed cookie tins with Christmas bears on them. No stash of pilfered hotel shampoo bottles in the guest bathroom. Nothing.

The only framed art was a series of color illustrations of animals: a moose, a bear, a lynx.

He should be happy. He had a shower again! A toilet and running water and an outlet to plug his phone into. A bed, and a washing machine. A kitchen. And he was happy... Kind of.

He also couldn't help feeling like he was right back where

he'd been when he was crashing on Kyle's couch in Seattle—
though at least he now had a bed and a door.

Was this how his life was always going to be: beholden to
others for the crumbs of generosity they offered him? Trying to live in empty corners of someone else's life?

"Fuck," he muttered, and Marmot sprang silently onto
the bed beside him. She seemed to have no problem making herself at home anywhere. She curled into a small spiral
in the direct center of the blanket and yawned, like a nice
big house with a comfortable bed in it was merely her due.
Rye wished he could feel more like her.

Rye woke with a start. He hadn't even realized he'd fallen
asleep, and for a moment he was totally disoriented. The
surface he was lying on was confusingly soft and he was
strangely warm. The only familiar thing, in fact, was the
purring form against his stomach.

"Rye? Dinner."

A knock at the door and that was Charlie. Right, he was
in Charlie's guest room. And Charlie had…cooked dinner?

Still sleep-sodden, Rye pushed the hair out of his face and
made a sound that must've sounded enough like communi-
cation that Charlie said, "Okay."

Marmot yawned and stretched, her tiny paws splaying
in the air. Rye darted in and pressed his cheek to her belly.
Claws caught in his hair and he drew back before they tangled there.

"Dinner," he echoed, to see if it sounded as strange when
he said it. Yup.

He followed the aroma of food into the kitchen and found
Charlie dishing up something that looked like a casserole.

"You didn't have to do that," Rye said, voice rough with
sleep.

"Do what, cook dinner? I do it every night. Gotta eat."

"I just meant you didn't have to do it for me."

"I didn't do it for you."

Rye felt squirmy. *Intruder. Freeloader.* The first word was his own, the second was his father's. He squeezed his hands into fists to stop the word that usually came next and focused on all angles of what was. He was in a warm, safe place. He and Marmot were together. There was food, and Charlie was offering to share it with him. It felt hard to accept what Charlie was offering, but it seemed freely given. He was okay.

"No, I know, I only meant— Never mind. Thanks."

Charlie nodded and turned out a tin of wet cat food on a small plate and set it on the dining table—it looked like a cat food commercial. Jane slunk into the room, meowed her strange ripping metal meow, and jumped onto the chair in front of her food. She sniffed delicately at the plate and then began to eat.

Rye hovered, waiting to see where Charlie would go. When Charlie sat down next to Jane with his food, Rye did the same.

"Thanks," he said again. "For dinner and for letting me stay here."

Charlie was watching him with an assessing look.

"You're very welcome," he said simply. Then he went back to his dinner. And it was as easy as that.

The chicken with mushrooms casserole was what might generously be called *hearty* and ungenerously be called *bland*. But it was the first hot meal Rye'd had in two weeks and he scarfed it down gratefully, forcing himself not to add the cost of its ingredients to the ever-growing tally in his head of what he owed the man sitting across from him. He never got on the right side of those tallies, so he'd stopped keeping them.

They ate in a silence that might have been awkward except that every time their eyes met, Charlie smiled at him, as if maybe he was genuinely glad Rye was here.

★ ★ ★

Rye drove to the Crow Lane house the next morning, with instructions from Charlie that his brother, Jack, would meet him over there, and he should wait until Jack got there to do anything. Rye grumbled at this as a matter of course, but was secretly relieved. He didn't want a repeat of demoing the wall. He'd been terrified that every swing of the hammer would be the one that brought the house tumbling down.

Jack was there when Rye arrived. He was clearly a Matheson—a smaller, younger, slightly more refined-looking version of Charlie.

Jack raised a hand in a half wave, half salute.

Rye wished he could have brought Marmot.

"I'm Jack. I live right there." He pointed to the roof just visible over the rise.

"Hey. Rye."

"Simon will be by later to help," Jack said. "He had to do a work thing."

"Who's Simon?"

Jack smiled a smile of pure sweetness.

"My boyfriend."

Something unclenched in Rye's stomach that he hadn't known was tensed. He wasn't the only queer person in Garnet Run, thank fuck! And if Jack and his boyfriend were happy here, then maybe he could be too. Maybe.

Jack winked.

"Let's make a pile to the side of the house so when they drop off the dumpster everything will be in one place and out of our way," he suggested.

Rye wanted to argue out of habit, because it was *his* house and he didn't need a bunch of Charlies and Jacks coming in here and telling him what to do. But it wasn't like he had any idea what he was doing.

"You used a sledge before?" Jack asked.

Rye shook his head.

"Don't drop it."

Yeah, thanks, he was pretty sure he could've figured that much out. Then again, he *had* stomped a hole in his own floor.

Jack showed him where to hit, handed him a mask, and then left him blessedly alone. Unlike his brother, who seemed to watch Rye's every move. Was Charlie just waiting for Rye to mess something up in his house? Steal something?

They worked in companionable silence—well, companionable din—for a while, and Rye could acknowledge that doing this with someone who knew what they were doing—and with a sledgehammer—was preferable to doing it without.

When Jack's phone chimed, he stepped out for a minute. There was a furrow between his brows when he returned.

"Simon will be here in a few to help us," he said.

Rye nodded, but Jack didn't pull his mask back up. He took two steps closer to Rye, expression forbidding.

"Listen. Simon has bad social anxiety and right now he'll just want to hit shit with a hammer and not talk to anyone. So don't give him any shit."

This last was clearly a warning that if Rye *did* give him any shit he'd have to expect some in return from Jack. It was an unnecessary threat—Rye only ever gave people shit if they gave it to him first—but Jack's protectiveness of his boyfriend sent a frisson of heat up Rye's spine.

"Got it."

"I'm serious. Don't tease him and don't look at him funny, no matter what."

"Of course not," Rye said, raising his palms in peace.

Jack's eyes narrowed but he just nodded.

At the sound of tires coming up the drive, Jack put down his hammer and went outside. Through the dirty window, Rye could just make out a tall, thin man with wavy dark hair who must be Simon. Jack opened his arms and the man pressed tight inside them. Even though they were almost the same height, Simon made himself small enough to be folded up in Jack's arms.

They clung to each other for minutes. Rye smashed the wall with the hammer, but his gaze was drawn to the window again.

Jack rocked them slowly, running a hand through Simon's hair and Simon buried his face in Jack's neck.

Rye smashed the wall again. He looked out the window again and this time Jack was cupping Simon's face in his hands and Simon was saying something with his eyes closed.

Rye wanted to smash everything. He wanted to bust it all wide open. He wanted to hit someone. He wanted to tear the world apart.

He wanted someone to hold him as tight and as unendingly as Jack Matheson was holding his boyfriend.

Fuck.

Rye dropped the sledgehammer. It, predictably, busted a floorboard.

"Fuck, fuck, fuck."

He tried to pull the board back flat. Naturally, at just that moment, Jack walked through the door. But though he opened his mouth, he shut it again in favor of ushering Simon in.

Rye told Simon, "Thanks for helping out," without looking at him.

Simon made an inarticulate sound of assent. He grabbed the sledgehammer Jack had been using. Then, silently, single-mindedly, he beat holy hell out of the kitchen wall. When it lay in rubble at his feet he glanced up at Jack, and gave a single nod.

Rye could feel blisters coming out on his palms from swinging the sledgehammer and his back was complaining, but goddamn it felt good to hit something. To see the concrete proof of his actions. He let those newly earned pains swell until they eclipsed the pain in his shin, the pain of leaving Seattle, the pain of starting over, and the pain of yet again needing help.

By the time Charlie showed up midafternoon with two more helpers named Rachel and Vanessa, they'd reduced most of the interior walls to wreckage, and Rye's entire body ached. He felt wrung out and light as air, cares smashed out of him.

Charlie stood with his hands on his hips and surveyed the scene, looking utterly at home in the midst of controlled demolition.

"You got a lot more done than I expected," he said, and Rye rolled his eyes.

"Thanks for the superlow expectations, bro," Jack said, and Rye liked him three percent more. "Hey, Van. Rach."

"You know that's not what I meant," Charlie said.

"*I* know," Jack said, shooting a look at Rye.

Charlie turned to Rye. "That wasn't what I meant. I think with Rachel and Van's help we can finish today. I'll get the ladder for the second floor."

"Okay," Rye said, as if any of this was actually being run past him.

He tried to redo his ponytail to eliminate the hair that had escaped to cling to his neck in sweaty strands and hissed as his abused hands stung.

At the sound, Charlie crossed to him, took his hands, and turned them palm up. He frowned at the red, pinched skin and the blisters beginning to emerge on his fingers.

"You should've worn gloves," he scolded.

But whereas before Rye had felt reprimanded, now he saw clearly that Charlie's reproach was on his behalf. Charlie ran his fingertips over Rye's reddened palms and cringed.

"Jack, why didn't you make him wear gloves?"

"Cuz I'm not his dad," Jack said. "I offered."

That was true.

"I'm fine," Rye said.

"You won't be tomorrow," Charlie forecast darkly. "I've got some salve at home."

He squeezed Rye's shoulder and began carrying armfuls of debris outside to the pile they'd begun.

At home.

Vanessa and Rachel had clearly done this before—they worked as an efficient unit, finding time to tease Jack about something that Rye couldn't quite track.

"Are you afraid of heights?" Charlie asked, and when Rye shook his head, showed him how to pull shingles off the roof.

From the ladder, he could see more of Jack and Simon's house—could see, as well, the swath of trees surrounding them in every direction, tops so soft and green that Rye felt like if he fell backward onto them, he'd be cradled like a baby.

The sky was crayon blue and the clouds were perfectly fat and white, like the drawings in a storybook, and why the hell couldn't he stop thinking about Charlie?

And watching him. The breadth of his shoulders and the gentleness of his corrections. The way he squinted slightly when he was thinking and how the muscles of his back moved under the soft fabric of his green and black flannel shirt.

After they'd removed the shoddy shingles, Charlie declared the roof beams salvageable. When Rye climbed down the ladder, he nearly collided with Charlie. For a moment their eyes locked, then Charlie kept walking.

Three hours, two minor injuries, and one snake later, the house was down to its gnarled bones.

Charlie ordered pizza for everyone and they ate leaning against his truck with the pizza boxes in the bed.

"Remember the time Charlie hired Jack and me to demo that lake house?" Vanessa was saying. Rye, of course, did not remember that time, and his attention drifted. He ate a piece of pizza without tasting it.

Everyone was laughing and Charlie was smiling and shaking his head while Jack and Vanessa looked sheepish. Rye shot a glance at Simon, who was standing next to Jack. He was leaning in, body language signaling that he was paying attention, but his eyes were fixed on his feet.

Jack had a casual arm around his waist. Vanessa and Rachel were leaning against each other. Were they a couple, too? Vanessa caught him looking and shot him a wink, then squeezed Rachel closer. Rye grinned at them. Apparently he'd fallen into the queer web without even trying.

Jack and Simon soon took off, citing a need to walk the dogs, and Vanessa and Rachel followed a few minutes later. Rye carried out a few more loads of debris, but as the sun set, it became harder and harder to see. When he tripped over a hunk of drywall and Charlie caught him by the arm, Charlie declared the workday over.

"You can leave your car," Charlie offered, since they'd be coming back together the next day. It sounded pretty great not to have to lift his arms to operate a steering wheel, so Rye climbed into the passenger seat without complaint, groaning as he settled back against the cushions.

Charlie started talking about the dumpster and something about the roof but Rye couldn't pay attention. Lassitude crept through every limb. He said "Mmm-hmm" every now and tried to nod but wasn't quite certain his head actually moved. Charlie said something as they pulled into the driveway and Rye *Mmm-hmmd* him, and Charlie snorted.

When Rye tried to get out of the car, his muscles locked in place, and he groaned as he jolted to the pavement.

"Whoa," Charlie said.

"Mfine," Rye said. "Just need a shower."

The hot water did help, and Rye slouched toward the kitchen, where Charlie was pulling a pizza out of the oven and beer out of the fridge. Though he'd had a slice earlier, Rye's stomach growled. He could never get sick of pizza.

Instead of putting the food on the dining room table, Charlie took it to the living room. They ate pizza and drank beer on the couch. The cats emerged at the smell, Jane from one hallway and Marmot from the other.

It was so comfortable here; so goddamned nice. Charlie? Was so nice. Bossy, yeah, but nice. And the bossiness was... kind of hot? Wait. Surely Rye must've just been addled from so much physical labor.

"So, um, how'd you learn all that shit?" Rye asked.

Charlie snorted.

"By *that shit* do you mean carpentry?"

"Yeah."

"My dad taught me some. Then when I was sixteen or so I started working construction in the summers. A friend's dad ran the crew so he got a couple of us jobs. I liked it. I've always liked building things. Then after my parents died and I took over the store, I learned a lot really fast so I could help customers. And I started doing construction on the weekends for extra cash."

"When did your parents die?"

"When I was seventeen. Almost eighteen."

Rye sat up.

"Jesus, that's awful. Both of them?"

Charlie nodded.

"Car accident."

"Shit, I'm sorry."

Charlie accepted the apology with an offhand nod that said he'd done so many, many times before, but Rye saw the tension in his jaw.

"Is Jack younger than you?"

Charlie nodded.

"He was thirteen when they died. So for a while it was just the two of us. It was..."

He shook his head like there was simply too much to say. "You raised him."

Rye knew it was true before Charlie nodded, and several pieces clicked into place.

For the first time Rye saw Charlie in a very different light. The man who had interceded in his disaster and given him a home. The man who cooked dinner every night and did laundry and ran his business in an orderly and practiced way. The man who knew about mortgages and loans and cosigning. Who worried about safety standards and about his brother, and always, always, always other people, but not about himself. He wasn't bossy and overbearing—well, okay, he wasn't *simply* bossy and overbearing. He had been a caretaker out of necessity and was a caretaker still.

"That sounds really, really hard."

Charlie looked at him for a few moments and Rye wondered if he was going to lie. Then his eyes got a faraway look.

"It was. I think I spent about five years straight completely terrified. Terrified Matheson's Hardware would fail, terrified we'd lose the house, terrified something would happen to Jack. Just terrified of everything. It was exhausting."

"Were you close with them?"

"Yeah. My dad… I always wanted to be like him."

He looked sheepish as he stroked his beard.

"At the time I didn't say it because it wasn't cool, right? You were supposed to think your parents were a pain. But my dad was great. He got the store from his parents. It was more of a farm store then, but he went in the hardware direction. Made it what it is today."

In fact, the other day, Marie had mentioned that Charlie completely overhauled the store in the last ten years, adding the entire lumber department and partnering with as many local and sustainable businesses as possible. But it was just like Charlie not to mention that.

Charlie fumbled with the remote and flicked the TV on,

signaling he was done talking about his parents. Rye got them each another beer and settled back on the couch, fatigue creeping through him.

"Tired," he mumbled.

"Mmm," Charlie agreed, his eyelids fluttering. He had put on an episode of *Secaucus Psychic*.

Rye raised an eyebrow.

"Shut up—'s good," Charlie said, and bumped Rye's shoulder with his. But because Charlie was huge, he kind of shoved Rye over on the couch. "Oops."

Rye had never actually watched the show, though one of his old roommates had been obsessed with it, saying she wanted to make a pilgrimage to the East Coast to meet Jackie and have her contact her long-dead grandmother.

To Rye's surprise, it turned out to be better than he expected.

"Isn't she a medium, if she can talk to the dead?" Rye asked.

"Yeah," said Charlie.

"But the title says she's a psychic."

"Are mediums psychics? Or are psychics mediums?" Charlie mused distractedly.

"I guess then it wouldn't be...whattayacallit? Two *s* sounds. Catchy in a title."

"Alliteration," Charlie murmured.

On screen, Jackie told the man his deceased sister agreed that he should take a new job and move if it would make him happy. The man cried.

"Do you believe in this stuff?" Rye asked.

"Psychic stuff?"

"Yeah."

"Nah," Charlie said, but his eyes were glued to the TV.

A few hours ago, Rye would've said that figured, given how practical Charlie was. How grounded. But now that he knew about Charlie's parents dying when he was young, he wondered if rather than dismissing it out of hand he'd had plenty of time to consider his stance.

"Not even a little?"

Charlie tipped his head to look at Rye. His eyes were the kind of hazel you forgot was a combination of green and brown except when they were fixed on you, paying attention to you, and then you didn't know how you ever forgot.

"On the show, she calls some people blocks. People who aren't sensitive to vibes or energy or currents of feeling. Jack says I'm a block."

He shrugged and Rye took a moment to enjoy the notion that both Matheson brothers apparently watched this show.

"Do you feel like a block?"

"I think that's the thing about blocks—they don't feel things."

He said it casually, like an offhand truth he didn't need to consider.

"But…that's just about psychic, ghosty stuff, right? Not about, er, earthly emotion?"

Charlie mumbled something Rye didn't catch.

"What?"

But Charlie didn't repeat it.

Up until now, Rye had thought Charlie was rather terse about personal matters. Now he wondered if Charlie simply wasn't used to having someone to listen. So instead of dropping the subject, he pushed a little harder.

"Would you find it comforting to think that your parents are still around, in another form?"

Charlie's eyes were fixed on the screen, but his jaw tightened.

"I dunno, sometimes. In that first year, I used to talk to them constantly. I had so many questions. No idea what I was doing. I'd ask them things and hope for an answer. Once I even—"

He cut himself off with a shake of his head.

"What?"

Charlie rolled his eyes.

"Once, I tried to ask them. Jack had this Ouija board that he'd gotten from a friend at Halloween the year before for some sleepover they had where they tried to scare the bejesus out of each other, and he hadn't given it back. And I… you know."

Rye imagined eighteen-year-old Charlie, really just a kid himself, trying desperately to ask his parents how to be an adult, and it broke his heart.

"What happened?" Rye asked gently.

"Nothing whatsoever except that I felt really foolish and hoped Jack wouldn't notice I stepped on that little thingie that you use to move around the board."

Charlie gave a ghost of a smile, then raised an eyebrow at Rye. "Do you? Believe in this stuff?"

"When I was a little boy—probably six or seven, given which apartment we were in—I saw a ghost. At least, I thought I did."

He had Charlie's full attention now.

"I woke up to the sound of someone crying and there was a small form in the corner of my room. Hazy, kind of, but there. It was a child, and they were sobbing."

Rye had whispered, "Are you okay?", not wanting the sound to wake his father, who would never accept *weeping ghost* as an explanation when he told Rye to stop making a racket.

The child had kept crying, the kind of snuffling, wet cries that can only last so long before they drain your energy out with them. Rye put a pillow over his head and went back to sleep, hoping it would be gone in the morning. When he woke, there was no evidence and when he asked if his parents had heard anything, his father just ranted about teenagers out until all hours of the night wreaking havoc.

He hadn't seen anything like it since, but it had left him with a powerful sense of possibility.

"It seems as likely to me as anything else, anyway," he said, shrugging. I guess the idea that the energy of life can leave a mark on the world after we're gone kind of appeals to me."

Rye's chaotic life had so far left nothing behind. If he died tomorrow there would be no tangible record of his existence on earth except a few government forms and his name carved very small at the base of a scarred tree in Discovery Park.

So when Charlie said, "I'm sure you'll leave plenty of marks before you die," with utter sincerity, it made Rye's heart pound a little faster.

"Thanks," he said, not sure that was quite the sentiment but wanting to say something.

When the episode ended, Charlie turned off the TV and lumbered to his feet. He held out a hand to Rye to help him up.

When Charlie's warm hand closed around his own, Rye hissed at the sting, having forgotten the damage he'd done that day from demo.

Charlie eased his grip instantly, but kept Rye's hand in his, and turned it over. He traced the blooming blisters with his fingertips and caressed the pinched skin.

"Shoulda worn gloves," he murmured, like he couldn't help himself. "Lemme get the salve."

He left Rye standing in the middle of the living room, hand out like he was dancing with a ghost.

"C'mere," Charlie said, and drew Rye back down on the couch.

He uncapped what looked like a shoe polish tin and scooped a fingerful of the stuff out. It smelled like mothballs and cloves.

"Maybe you just pretend to be a block but you're actually anointing me with a potion right now," Rye said.

Sleepy, tipsy Rye said silly things.

"I am anointing you with a potion," Charlie said. "It's a keep-your-hands-from-hurting-so-much-you-can't-use-them-tomorrow potion, and it's potent as hell."

Rye closed his eyes and willed himself to be silent as Charlie worked the salve into his abused skin. Charlie's strong thumbs dug into the tight tendons and muscles of his palm and fingers, like he could rub out the pain all the way down to his bones.

"Just relax," Charlie murmured, and Rye pressed his shoulders to the back of the couch.

As Charlie switched hands, Rye's attention wandered, and he imagined Charlie really was a witch. Charlie was giving him a potion that made him feel no pain, that made him good at demolition and construction, that gave him great credit and a high school diploma.

And hey, while it was magic, why not throw in the power to have a deep and lasting connection with another person?

Charlie rubbed the salve into his wrists too, and even though they weren't blistered it felt heavenly.

"What are these of?" Charlie asked, tracing the tips of his tattoos.

"Oh." Rye tugged up his sleeves, revealing the woodcut-style tattoos that ran up and down both arms. "Roots."

To his great relief, Charlie just looked at them appreciatively instead of asking about them. He'd rather not talk about the way he'd gotten them a decade ago in the hopes of feeling like he was a part of something, since he had no contact with his parents, no siblings, and moved so often he never let his belongings swell to more than the two duffel bags and a backpack he kept in the closet.

He'd also rather not talk about how it hadn't worked, so he'd gotten more, and those hadn't worked either.

Instead, he let himself drift away on the river of peace that Charlie's warm hands provided.

"Why didn't you want to kiss me?" Rye heard himself ask, as if from a long ways off.

Charlie's hands on his froze and Rye swallowed hard. But he didn't want to let Charlie off the hook. He wanted the truth, even if it hurt. Even if it humiliated him.

"I... I did," Charlie said.

Rye opened his eyes to see Charlie holding both his hands and staring at him awkwardly.

"You don't have to say that," Rye said. "You pushed me away from you like I was on fire. Which is fine. I just wondered why."

Charlie noticed that he was still holding Rye's hands and dropped them. Rye instantly missed the feeling of them being held.

"That wasn't what I meant when I—I didn't want— It seemed like you were thanking me or something, and I... I didn't want that."

Rye had questions, but he was too tired and too tipsy for this conversation.

"Okay, no problem. Night," Rye said, and stood to go to bed.

At the doorway, though, he turned back. There was no reason not to be honest. He'd learned a long time ago that not being clear led to vastly more problems.

"Charlie. It wasn't because I was thanking you. I thought... I thought you wanted me to. And I wanted to. So I did. I know I should've asked, but... Anyway, I'm sorry I didn't ask, but I'm not sorry I kissed you."

Charlie's eyes, dark and serious, went wide and his lips parted, but he didn't say anything. He just nodded.

"G'night," Rye said again, and hurried off to bed.

Chapter Ten

Charlie

Charlie Matheson was in hell. Well, heaven. A hell of a heaven. Whatever. And he'd done it to himself. He was thirty-six years old and he'd finally circled back to where he'd been at seventeen: wondering, yearning, afraid.

Trevor Oasco. A running back on the team Charlie's junior year. He'd been an army brat who showed up at the start of second semester. Outgoing, funny, and tough, he'd been the kind of person who made friends quickly and easily, and Charlie'd been no exception.

When he noticed the way Trevor's muscles bunched as he exploded from a crouch across the field, or how his dark skin slid gloriously over the tendons in his forearms, Charlie initially thought he was just attending to a teammate's form. His skill. When he found his eyes magnetized to the droplets of water that crept down the side of Trevor's neck after he showered in the locker room and how graceful his fingers were when he held a pencil in physics class...well, Charlie hadn't let himself think about it, really.

He hadn't thought about much at all back then. He'd had no need to.

He'd studied as hard as he needed to to make the grades that would get him into school, practiced football until he puked, worked construction on the weekends to save up for truck parts, and helped his dad out in the store when it got busy. All that didn't leave much time for thinking, and that was fine with Charlie.

All that not thinking meant that when Trevor sat down next to him one day, after the rest of the team had dispersed, looked into his eyes, then leaned in and kissed him, he was shocked. But curiosity and desire had chased the shock away almost instantly and he'd leaned into the kiss, letting his palms and fingertips learn the muscle and skin he'd stared at; letting his mouth learn the smile that had lit warmth in his belly he hadn't even noticed until it was replicated and exploded.

They didn't talk about it. There was no need. They both knew Trevor would be leaving soon. They both knew it wasn't the kind of thing you mentioned casually to the other guys on the team.

Then one day after practice Trevor had shot him a look and he'd stayed and when they'd come together there was something *more* in it. More than mouths and hands and jerking each other off because it felt so, so good.

Something like a friendship of the flesh.

Before they'd parted, Charlie had kissed Trevor's lips for no reason other than that he wanted to, and Trevor had squeezed his hand. They'd smiled shyly at each other and they'd both looked back when they were walking away.

That had made Charlie think. He hadn't been able to stop thinking about Trevor after that. About how Trevor made him feel things he'd never felt before. And want to feel things he'd never wanted to feel before.

Trevor's mother had gotten transferred, as was inevitable, and his family had moved a week before Charlie's eighteenth birthday. At the time, Charlie had been disappointed because it would've been nice to have Trevor there for his birthday. He imagined Trevor's kisses given to him like gifts—more notable for being proffered on a special occasion.

But his disappointment—and any chance he might've had to miss Trevor—had been obliterated by his parents' deaths three days later.

Charlie never had the option to not think about things again.

Now, Rye's kiss—hell, Rye's very presence—was making him think about desires and questions that had lain dormant for twenty years. Things he hadn't thought about because he'd been so damn busy thinking about everything—and everyone—else.

Rye's kiss had stirred his memories and his desire. But it was what Rye *said* that stoked it. Rye wasn't sorry he'd kissed Charlie. He'd wanted to do it. And so he had.

What might it be like to simply desire something, and then let himself have it?

"Let's go over what it will take to get your house built," Charlie said. He'd just showered after a run and found Rye in the kitchen.

Rye took a seat next to him at the table and Charlie pulled a notepad toward him.

"Now, this is just going to be an estimate, but it is based on work I've done for other people and the cost of the work I've done to my own house."

Wary as a stray cat, Rye nodded.

Charlie made the list. Lumber, drywall, roofing, insulation, flooring, cabinetry. He wrote numbers next to each, approximating them without labor, except for plumbing and electric, which Charlie knew enough to fix but not to install.

"This is bare bones," he said, explaining down the list. "It doesn't include stuff like paint or bathroom tile or carpet. This is just to get a solid roof over your head and walls underneath them."

"Yeah good plan, ceiling on top of the walls, I like it," Rye muttered, eyes flickering over the numbers.

Charlie wrote the total estimate at the bottom of the list and circled it. It was best to show people things in black-and-white whenever possible.

"Seventy...um...seventy thousand." Rye's voice was a dry scrape. "Dollars. That's...that's in dollars?"

"It's an estimate," Charlie reiterated. "But yeah. I'd say that's about what you're looking at for materials, permits, inspections, and someone to do plumbing and electric."

"I'm... I don't..." Rye looked ill. "I had no idea it was anywhere near... How?"

"Well," Charlie began. This was why you wrote things out for people. "I can get the lumber at something of a discount because of the store, but—"

Rye shook his head and pushed the notepad away, like he could banish the numbers themselves.

"How can I *do* this?" he choked out. "When you said we'd figure it out, I thought you meant like *ten* grand, Charlie. I don't have a job. I don't...*fuck*!"

Rye pushed back from the table and started pacing.

"God, I thought I had a chance here, man. I thought maybe I could finally have a place that I wouldn't share with a hundred housemates. That I wouldn't get fucking evicted from or priced out of, but of *course* it was too good to be true that some fairy godfather would just materialize and give me a house. God, I'm so stupid!"

Charlie realized he'd made a fundamental miscalculation. He'd known that Rye didn't know what it took to build a house; but it hadn't occurred to him *how* far off Rye was in his estimations. For Rye to have left Seattle and come all the way to Garnet Run, where he didn't know a soul, he'd've had to believe there was a house waiting for him that was, well, habitable. If he'd lived in rental apartments, why *would* he know how much it cost to buy lumber or repair plumbing?

"You could get a loan for the cost of the renovation," Charlie began.

Rye winced.

"I don't think so. My credit is… Well, I don't have much. And what I do have is bad."

Charlie frowned. "I wonder if you could get a mortgage against the property itself."

He did some quick calculations in his head. If Rye could get the mortgage and then refinance…

"I don't know what that means, but if it happens through a bank then probably the same issues apply."

"I don't suppose you happen to have very rich parents?"

Rye glared at him.

"Friends?"

"Yeah I was crashing on a couch in a tiny apartment with five other people, a dog, and a baby cuz my friends are rolling in it."

Charlie took a moment to imagine prickly Rye living with a baby.

"Well, I don't think you have many other choices, then," Charlie said. "Let's go talk to someone at the bank. You won't know if you don't ask."

"Dude, I told you."

Charlie took in the defeated slump of Rye's shoulders, the slouch of his head. He looked utterly hopeless and Charlie wanted to take it all away. He wanted nothing more than to have the perfect solution, gift wrap it, and place it in Rye's wringing hands.

"We'll go to the GRCFCU. Talk it all through." At Rye's blank look, he added, "The credit union."

The blank look didn't go away. "Charlie. No one in their right mind will give me a loan. Or a mortgage. Or a whatever. I've got no…*anything*."

"Let's just go get all the information. Then we can make a plan."

This had been one of Charlie's first and deepest lessons all those years ago, after his parents died: gather all the information first. You might think you know, but you don't know, and there's no sense having a reaction until you do.

Rye shook his head and slouched back onto his chair. He opened his mouth and before he could doom-monger anymore, Charlie put a hand on his arm.

"A community credit union doesn't have the same requirements as other banks. There might be more wiggle room than you think. Worst case scenario, they'll say no, and you're in the same position you're in now. Right?"

Rye sighed and it seemed to come from his very depths.

"Okay," he said.

"Let's go."

Charlie rose.

"Oh, now? Okay."

Rye shoved his phone and wallet in his pocket and looked at Charlie expectantly.

"Do you want to change?" Charlie suggested.

Rye was wearing tight black jeans blown out at the knees and a black long-sleeved T-shirt with some kind of undersea monster holding a wrecked ship in its tentacles and the name of a band Charlie had never heard of arced across the chest in letters dripping blood into the ocean of blood that held the ship and the sea monster. His hair was loose and the smeared remains of yesterday's kohl darkened his eyes.

"Oh, no, I'm okay," Rye said, pulling on a boot.

"Er, I meant that you should probably change. Bank, you know? Helps to look professional. Make a good first impression."

Rye blinked at him. "Changing my clothes doesn't change my credit, Charlie."

He stomped into his other boot.

"No, it's just…how things are done."

Rye cocked his head and Charlie wondered if he was being contrary or if he sincerely believed that things like first impressions and professionalism didn't matter.

"I don't have any of the kind of clothes you're talking about," Rye said. "Nothing with buttons or a pocket protector."

"Do you have a shirt that isn't a horror movie poster?"

Rye looked scandalized.

"It's a Carapace shirt."

Charlie gave him a look.

"Fine, look for yourself."

Rye stomped into his room and dumped the contents of his duffel bag onto the bed for Charlie's perusal.

It was all black band shirts except for a few worn white undershirts and a peach T-shirt with a cartoon vagina on it that said *GET OUT OF MY CUNT, CUNTS*. Charlie laid it aside with the rest.

There was no way that his own clothes would fit Rye so he returned to the black shirts. One of them just had a large red triangle on the back and was blank on the front. He held it out to Rye.

"What's funny is that Horseshoe Crab Mafia has the filthiest lyrics out of any of these bands," Rye said.

"May be, but since they aren't printed *on* the shirt I think it's your best bet. Do any of your jeans not have holes?"

Rye pointed to the only pair of pants that were in the bag. They were...leather?

"These are your only other pants."

Rye nodded, a glint in his eye.

Charlie sighed.

"Okay, well, at least change the shirt."

He turned to leave the room and give Rye privacy while he changed and heard a little snort of laughter.

When Rye came back out of the bedroom Charlie considered him.

"Maybe tie your hair back?"

Rye flipped his head over and gathered his hair up in a messy knot on top of his head.

"Um, no. What about, like…a braid?"

A smirk hovered at the corner of Rye's mouth as he took his hair down. Looking directly at Charlie, he braided it, securing the braid with an elastic band he took from around his wrist.

Charlie swallowed a lump in his throat. There was something intimate about watching Rye braid his hair. He could imagine Rye's hands were his own, twining the soft, riotous strands together.

"Better?" he asked.

It didn't have the professional effect Charlie'd hoped at all—instead, it made him look younger—but at least with his hair out of his face Rye couldn't fiddle with it or hide behind it, two things he tended to do when it was down.

"Maybe you think a French braid would look more financially solvent?" Rye said, smirking fully now.

"Ha-ha."

"No, really," Rye continued as he pulled his coat on. "I could do Heidi braids. Or Princess Leia buns. You know, if you think that the associations might hoodwink a loan officer into giving me more money?"

"Get your financially insolvent ass in the truck," Charlie grumbled, but that didn't stop him from picturing Rye with two braids and with buns in his pretty hair.

They walked into the Garnet Run Community Federal Credit Union, and Charlie waved to Mike Brant and Felicity Martens. He introduced Rye to them both and Mike led them to his desk.

"What can we do for you, Rye?" Mike said. "Or is it Ryan?"

"Nope, just Rye. Um." He looked at Charlie. "I need a loan. Or…a mortgage?"

Mike looked at Charlie too.

"Well, it would help to know which…" Mike said.

Rye leaned forward, elbows on Mike's desk like he was about to tell a story.

"Okay, so, here's the deal," Rye said, and Charlie braced himself.

Chapter Eleven

Rye

"My grandfather died and left me his house for some reason—no idea why. Only, it's falling down. So I need to rebuild it. But I don't have any money. And Charlie said maybe you guys could give me a loan to buy all the materials for the house. Or, no, buy the property and then pay me for the... Uh."

Rye looked at Charlie, begging him to jump in because the particulars of what he'd said—foggy even as he was saying them—had now fled his mind completely.

Charlie bit his lip and Rye got the sense that he'd said things all wrong.

"He owns the home and the property free and clear, Mike. So I mentioned a loan for the cost of rebuilding. Or perhaps a mortgage against the property that would provide for the rebuilding costs. But I knew you'd be able to tell us what the best option was."

Rye thought Charlie was laying it on a bit thick, but he clearly knew what he was talking about because this Mike person nodded and stroked the bridge of his nose thoughtfully.

"Let's take a look at what we're working with," he said.

Thus began a process of looking up Rye's credit that he knew was likely to end in disaster. When a screen loaded on

Mike's computer, he visibly flinched, shot a glance at Rye, and grimaced.

"Not much here," he said.

"Yeah." Rye squirmed. "But with a house isn't it... I mean, it's not like I can walk away with it, ya know?"

Mike gave a contrived chuckle and said, "Ha, good one." But Rye hadn't been joking.

Mike asked question after question about his credit, his employment history, his rental history, and any hope that Charlie had managed to foment died a crushing death.

"He has a job now," Charlie said. "He's working at the store, starting this week."

Charlie nudged Rye's foot with his own, as if Rye didn't have a lifetime of experience lying about his financial status to find ways to live.

Mike nodded like that helped and tapped away on his computer.

"Wait, we're talking about Granger Janssen's property?" Mike said.

"Yeah, he was my grandfather."

Mike nodded, thoughtfully chewing on a pen that was branded with the bank's name.

"Granger Janssen was a longtime member of the credit union," he mused. "It would be nice to continue that into the next generation."

Rye might not have known anything about loans or mortgages, but he knew when to shut up and let people talk themselves into things.

Mike rambled on about value versus equity, refinancing, appraisal, and length of mortgage repayment. Rye tried to commit what he was saying to memory to look up later, but it all turned to mush in his head and his mind started to wander to questions he *was* familiar with—like how in the fuck any of this could possibly work.

He snapped back to attention when Charlie turned to

look at him and he realized Mike was looked at him expectantly too.

"Sorry, what?"

"I said that we can do the loan, but because of your credit, you'd need someone to cosign."

"What does that mean?"

"It means that someone else with better credit would need to enter into the agreement with you and vouch for your repayment."

"And I said I can do it."

Charlie.

"Wait, what?"

"I can cosign with you."

"No. No way," Rye said immediately. "I can't ask you to do that. You've already done so much. Too much."

He studied Charlie, large frame overwhelming the bank chair. Charlie, with his warm hazel eyes and his lumberjack beard and his strangely excellent posture and the way he knew how to do things. He wanted Charlie to like him, to respect him, and this sure as hell wasn't helping on either count.

"You didn't ask," Charlie said.

No, he hadn't asked—his very being was the request; the need.

Freeloader, loser, moocher, sponge.

Anger fizzed up his spine. The same powerless anger that he'd felt when he was ten and he'd come home to find his mother packing his things into garbage bags and his father stuffing a hole he'd punched in the wall with balled-up toilet paper and glue.

"Where are we going?" Rye'd asked.

"We're moving," his mother had said.

"But I don't want to move."

Rye had a favorite corner of his bedroom where he'd set up his dinosaurs and his books and a blanket to sit on to read them. He had a spot under the bed where he hid his box of treasures—special things he found outside that he rescued and brought home.

"Well it's happening," had been his mother's reply, one that echoed through their life for the next six years and three apartments, until Rye left home at sixteen.

The same helpless anger he'd felt when his best friend Ruth's sleeve had snagged on a branch at lunch in tenth grade and revealed her wrist braceleted in bruises. And when he'd gotten the final eviction notice that had sent him to a friend's couch.

An outward-facing anger that had nowhere to go so it stayed inside, racing through the veins like acid, eating away at everything it touched.

"I need to use the bathroom," Rye said, standing abruptly.

Mike pointed behind him and Rye made his escape.

He stared in the mirror. Plain black shirt. Hair tamed into a braid. The most respectable version of himself that Charlie had been able to cultivate given what little he had to work with. Rye glared at his reflection and pulled the hair tie from his braid.

He shook his head until his hair rioted around his face in messy waves.

The door opened and Charlie's face appeared in the crack.

"You okay in here?"

Rye glared at him.

"Yes. Jesus. What, is it unprofessional to have to use the bathroom now? Do they deny your loan if you're a human being who needs to take a shit?"

Rye could hear the defensiveness in his own voice and he knew well that Charlie wasn't the appropriate target, but he couldn't help his snarl.

Charlie came in and closed the door behind him.

"What's up?"

He said it calmly but Rye could sense his impatience. His

desire to get back out there, sign the paperwork, do the deal. Fix the problem. And, of course, the problem was Rye.

Rye swallowed in an attempt to keep the anger inside him where it belonged.

"This is bullshit, Charlie," he hissed. "I'm not letting you get yourself on the hook for this. You barely fucking know me."

If he hadn't been watching in the mirror he might have missed Charlie's faint wince. But he just cleared his throat and moved on.

"I would just be an insurance policy for them. Just another mechanism for Mike to point to and say everything is going to go fine. It's just a formality."

"When banks and signatures are involved it's a whole hell of a lot more than a formality! And I can't believe you would do this when you actually have something to lose. What if I'm a...a...a total con and I disappear and leave you owing the bank a bunch of money? And you have to sell the store or your house or...do whatever? It's stupid!"

Rye heard the word echo in the small bathroom. It was a word he tried not to use anyway, and directed at Charlie who was anything but...

"Shit, sorry," Rye said. "You're not stupid. It's reckless, I meant. You've gotta take care of yourself."

Charlie's brows drew together and he stroked his beard. He was so damn beautiful.

"I think this is your only shot," he said seriously. "If you don't want to sell the property, there isn't another option." He faltered and added, "Unless you *do* want to sell it. Go back to Seattle."

Charlie's voice tumbled over the words like water over rocks, a slight disturbance that clued Rye in that maybe Charlie didn't want him to leave.

"I don't want that," Rye said.

And it wasn't until he said it that he realized how completely true it was. He didn't want to go back to Seattle where there was nothing waiting for him but friends who'd forgotten about him, a string of interchangeable and temporary retail jobs, urban landmarks of who he'd failed and how, and always—*always*—the ineluctable push of new money, crowding him farther and farther out of the city.

"Well, then."

Rye sighed and shoved his hands into his hair.

"Shit! I don't know! It's so much. I just... I really don't want to fuck you over."

"Then don't."

He said it so clearly, so matter-of-factly, as if all it took was simply not to do something, that Rye almost laughed.

"Well obviously I wouldn't do it on purpose," he said, exasperated. "But it's not like I ever got evicted on purpose either. Shit happens and I don't want you getting caught up in it."

"I wasn't just saying that about the job at the store. If you want it," Charlie said.

"Yeah? I mean, yes, of course I do." Rye wasn't sure this was the best moment for discussing employment plans, but okay.

"Well then you'll be able to afford the monthly payments and it won't be a problem."

"Sorry, what?"

Rye felt like he'd missed a step.

"What what?"

"Huh?"

Charlie smiled. "Who's on first?"

"First of what?"

"Rye!" Charlie said.

"I have no idea what you're talking about!"

"Okay, okay. Can we just go back out there and Mike will lay out all the numbers. You'll see."

"Fine," Rye grumbled.

Charlie raised a hand like he was going to smooth Rye's riotous hair back into some kind of order, but stopped just before he touched him. They looked at each other for a moment and Rye wanted to say *Thank you*, he wanted to say *You can touch me*. He wanted to wrap his arms around Charlie's middle and melt into his embrace.

He wanted a hell of a lot of things. And for the first time, it looked like he might get some of them.

They went out to lunch to celebrate the loan, Rye still reeling at all that had taken place, clutching a folder of paperwork like his future depended on it. Because it kind of did.

"I can't believe you did this," Rye said numbly. It was the only thought in his head.

"You've said that thirteen times already," Charlie pointed out, unbothered.

"Yeah well, I'll probably say it at least thirteen more," Rye grumbled. "Cuz I just can *not* believe—"

"Okay, I get it," Charlie said, smiling as he parked the truck.

Peach's Diner was where Rye had gone his first morning in Garnet Run, needing a cup of coffee and a minute to get his head together. Its decor was a combination of floral prints and antlers that Rye was quickly becoming accustomed to in Garnet Run.

"Sit anywhere you like, Charlie and Rye," the waiter said, winking.

"How does she know my name?" Rye said out of the corner of his mouth.

Charlie waggled his eyebrows and smiled.

Rye glared at him and slid into the booth in the corner.

"How's the store?" the waiter asked Charlie as she handed them menus. Her name tag said Melba and Rye smiled.

"That's a joke cuz Peach's, right?" he said, pointing to her name tag.

Melba's brow wrinkled and she cocked her head, looking to Charlie for an explanation. Charlie cleared his throat.

"Nope, no joke, *Rye*."

"Oh. I just thought…because…you know. Peach Melba?" Both Charlie and Melba just looked at him.

"Peach Melba," Rye repeated. "The dessert. Named after the opera singer? Okay, never mind, sorry," he grumbled.

"I'll bring coffee and come check in with you in a minute," Melba said, leaving them with the menus.

Charlie shot Rye a look.

"I wasn't making fun of her name, I thought she was going by Melba because this place is called—"

"So you said."

"I mean, okay, who is named Melba these days, though?" Rye whispered.

"Reckon you just saw who."

"Yeah, yeah, yeah, okay."

After they ordered, Charlie started going through the things Mike had said he needed to process the loan and Rye wished he'd brought in the folder. He'd snagged a pen emblazoned with the bank's logo on his way out of the bank, so he scribbled some notes about what Charlie was saying on the paper placemat that cheerily announced *Peach's!*.

Their food came: pancakes and bacon for Rye and a Western omelet with biscuits and sausage gravy for Charlie. Sausage had always disgusted Rye, but he had to admit the smells coming off Charlie's plate were making his stomach growl.

"You want some?" Charlie asked.

He took a bite of Charlie's biscuits and gravy, and then another bite. It was spicy and salty and creamy and Rye grudgingly admitted that it was delicious.

As he was revising his stance on sausage, a shadow fell over their booth. It was a tall white man, skin leathered from the sun, with a full head of steel gray hair, dark brown eyebrows, and heavily wrinkled brown eyes. Rye guessed his age at around seventy-five, but with the sun damage it was hard to tell.

"Mr. Wayne," Charlie said in the voice that sounded like he was tipping a hat though he wasn't wearing one. "Been quite a while."

"Mr. Matheson," the man said. His voice was lighter than his appearance suggested. "And…" He turned to Rye. "Mr. Janssen, perhaps?"

Rye forced down the automatic Batman quip since his most recent comment on someone's name had gone over like a lead balloon.

"Yeah, Rye. Hey."

The man looked at him intently—studied him, really. His face softened and for a horrifying moment, it looked like he might cry. When he spoke again, his voice was husky.

"You look a lot like your granddaddy."

Such a banal phrase, but it struck Rye like a wrecking ball. He didn't look like either of his parents. They both had lighter hair; his mother had softer bone structure than Rye and his father had blunter features. He'd never been told he looked like anyone in his family and he'd never met any of them. His mom muttered about a sister she didn't get along with occasionally, but that was the only information Rye'd ever gotten.

"I…do?"

He nodded. "May I?"

Rye scooted in so he could sit down.

"You knew my grandfather? That lawyer guy said he didn't think he was close to anyone in town."

"I knew him all right. We had breakfast together the first Tuesday of the month for twenty-six years. Early, before most folks were even up. Here."

He placed a gnarled finger on the table.

"At Peach's?" Rye asked.

"At this booth. When Melba called me and said you'd

picked Granger's booth I about galloped over. Had to see for myself. And here you are. And I'll be goddamned if those aren't Granger's eyes stuck right in your head."

Ghoulish phrasing aside, Rye was strangely touched to have something in common with this man he'd never met. The man who was giving him the chance to start over—a chance he'd never thought he would have.

Rye's mind was everywhere at once. Had they been friends? Lovers? Well, if they were lovers, Rye hoped they saw each other more than once a month! But maybe they saw each other all the time and it was just that they had breakfast *here* once a month—

Rye darted a look at Charlie, who raised his eyebrows and nodded at him. Rye interpreted that as *Say something; don't just sit there speculating about your grandfather's decades-long love affair with an aging cowboy Batman!*

"Um. I'm very sorry," Rye said. "That he died. For you, I mean. I didn't know him."

Rye glared at himself, but then he heard creaky laughter from the man next to him.

"Sorry, what's your name?" Rye asked. "I feel weird calling everyone mister."

"Clive."

"Thanks. Anyway, I just meant—"

"I know what you meant, son. Your granddaddy didn't have the manners god gave a rock either. I liked that about him. Meant I was usually pretty sure what I was getting was the truth."

Rye shot Charlie a look: *See, I'm not rude, I'm honest.*

"So you were…friends?"

"That's right. I was his only friend around these parts. But that was the way he liked it. People found him odd. Off-putting. Probably because he didn't care for company much. Didn't ask after folks' families the way you ought to." He shrugged. "I never cared about that. But he was a good talker. Had big ideas and big wonder. I liked that. Over the years, we became friends. Eventually, I heard he had a son he was estranged from living out in Seattle with a family of his own."

Rye was trying to dredge up any bit of information his parents might've said about his grandfather and couldn't remember a single one. Had his father really never mentioned his own father? But, no, Rye didn't think he had. It struck him, suddenly, how little his parents had ever talked, period. At least about anything that mattered.

"When that lawyer called me and told me he'd left me a house I hung up on him. Thought I was being punked. I didn't know anything about him. Still don't, I guess."

Clive nodded. "He died in October. It took the lawyer a while to track you down."

That didn't surprise Rye. Given how often he'd moved and his pay-as-you-go phone, he was surprised the lawyer'd found him at all.

"He was a very principled man. A kind man. I respected him." Clive's voice went raspy with feeling and he cleared his throat. "How're you making out over there? I didn't know the place was falling down around him until after he'd died. Woulda done something if I'd known. Course, Granger woulda never asked for my help."

"It's a job all right," Charlie said.

"But I don't understand," Rye said. "That lawyer made him sound like a recluse. Like he had nobody. But if he had you, why'd he leave the house to me? He never even met me. Why didn't he leave it to you?"

Clive considered him soberly.

"He knew about you," Clive said. "When you were young, he reached out to your daddy, tried to mend the rift. It worked for a little while. He had three pictures of you. One when you were first born, one when you were a year old, and one when you were a few years older. Your daddy sent them. But they never brought you out here to visit. Never invited Granger to Seattle."

Clive traced the lines of gold in the Formica tabletop with his fingertip like he was tracing a map of the past.

"He was a proud man. Stubborn as hell too."

Charlie let out a muffled snort that seemed to draw an obvious comparison.

"What was their problem?"

"I don't think it was just one thing," Clive said. "Way he talked about your daddy, though. Phew. Made him sound like a—" Clive cut himself off with a cough. "Well now, what do I know."

Rye imagined that if his grandfather hadn't gotten along with his father, that only spoke well of Granger.

"My dad and I don't get along," Rye offered. "If that helps."

"Made him sound like a man with little patience for lives lived a different way than his own," Clive concluded diplomatically.

If he wasn't careful, his father's poisonous words leaked into his mind from time to time. His intolerance. His righteous belief that he was right and everything about Rye was wrong. The things he'd said echoed sometimes, when Rye was down or tired or scared. As did the things his mother *hadn't* said. Like anything to the contrary.

"Yeah, he's a fucking asshole," Rye agreed.

Clive nodded.

"Sorry to hear that. You don't seem like you caught the disease."

Rye smiled. "I'm probably an asshole in my own way."

Charlie muffled a snort, and then schooled his face diplomatically.

Clive smiled. "It's a wise man who knows he's an asshole."

Rye lifted his coffee and toasted the sentiment.

"I'll leave you to your lunch, gentlemen."

Clive unfolded his tall form from the booth, knees creaking. He dropped a hand on Rye's shoulder. "I'm glad to meet you, son. I hope I'll see you around town."

Rye's heart started to pound.

"Wait. Maybe—" he said, reaching out a hand. "Would you want to meet up again sometime? It's just, I'd love to hear more about my grandfather."

Clive's eyes softened and he gave a single nod.

"I'd like that."

Before Rye could fumble out his phone or hand him a pen, Clive slipped a hand in his pocket and placed a card on the table in front of Rye.

He nodded at Charlie, then turned and strode purposefully away, leaving Rye blinking after him.

Chapter Twelve

Rye

"Listen, I need you to be polite."

"Excuse me?"

"Yeah, like that."

Rye rolled his eyes. They were pulling into the parking lot at Matheson's Hardware for his first shift.

"I meant—"

"Rye. This is my business. I'm not kidding. I know you're not the small talk type and you've got that whole ruthless honesty thing going on, but this is a small, tight-knit town. People know each other and they know my place. They expect politeness. They expect to be greeted. They expect help if they want it."

Rye tamped down his automatic bristle.

"Of course."

"Today you can just observe, help out. Marie and I will show you things as we go along. I'll probably mostly have you at the register, since Marie knows all about our inventory."

"Okay."

Rye liked the way Marie went about her business and let him go about his. She was completely professional with customers, but seemed to lack any sense of obligation to make others feel comfortable at any cost.

"Don't try to get her to talk if she doesn't want to, okay?"

"Obviously."

God, what kind of asshole did Charlie think he was?

"Even getting to know you questions. She won't like it."

"Yeah that's pretty clear."

"Okay, good." But apparently Charlie couldn't help himself. "Just, even if you think you're being polite—"

"Charlie. I would never force someone to talk when they obviously don't want to. I've lived with a million different kinds of people, so I'm pretty good at picking up on their personalities. And although you seem to think I need a *Politeness For Dummies* book, I have worked in customer service since I was sixteen. I swear I won't embarrass you."

Charlie regarded him intently, then nodded.

"Okay."

Matheson's hardware. Oasis to the handy. to Rye, a hell of one thousand kinds of nails and noncomputerized cash registers.

Marie showed him the combination of buttons to push for the fifth time after the register spat out an itemized scroll of his failures.

Her raised eyebrow clearly said, *I thought you told me you'd used a cash register before?*

"The ones I've used were all manufactured after the invention of the World Wide Web," Rye grumbled.

After that, Marie set him to sorting out screws that had gotten mixed up with screws of a different size. It was tedious but blessedly free of cash registers.

"You're that Janssen boy," a man said behind him.

Rye was pretty sure that this was one of those moments Charlie had mentioned where friendliness and politeness were expected so he made his face neutral before turning around.

"Guilty," he said.

"What are you going to do with Granger's place?"

"I'm gonna fix it up," Rye said. "Did you know my grand-father?"

"I knew Granger."

Rye waited, but no further information seemed to be forthcoming.

"Okay. Uh, can I help you find anything?"

Politeness, thy name is Rye!

The man chuckled. "No, son. I know where everything is."

He patted Rye on the shoulder.

An hour later, the screws were sorted and Rye had developed a cramp in his neck from whipping his head around every time someone walked past him.

"Do they all know who I am?" he muttered.

Marie raised an innocent eyebrow, but he was pretty sure she was amused.

"Glad to provide the entertainment," he grumbled.

She grinned.

After his lunch break, during which Rye dropped off the loan paperwork to Mike at the bank, there were even more people.

"Damn, is it always this busy?" Rye asked Charlie. He didn't remember much of a crowd when he'd been in himself.

"Nope."

"You having a sale?"

"Nope."

"What's the deal then? A hammer convention in town or something?"

"They're curious. About you. Word will've gotten out."

Rye blinked.

"Word will have gotten out? Word of what? That a human being not from the state of Wyoming is working in a hard-ware store? Is that news?"

Charlie raised an eyebrow, but unlike when Marie did it, Rye didn't have the slightest idea what it meant.

"Charlie. Charlie?"

But Charlie had gone out back to cut wood for a customer.

Rye sighed and went to sort bolts.

Two white girls, one tall and one short, who looked about college age, turned down the aisle, engaged in an intense discussion.

"Help you find anything?" Rye asked them.

"Yeah, a roommate who doesn't suck, please," the taller of the two muttered.

"Cohabitation grief? I'm familiar," Rye said. He decided that if he couldn't help with hardware, maybe he could at least help with this. "What's the problem?"

"You're not from here, huh?" the other girl said.

"Nope. Seattle."

They both nodded as if that explained things.

"We have a new housemate. And she's cool, mostly. But she has all these weird habits. Like, she talks to herself constantly to hype herself up. And she only drinks out of teacups. Like, even her water, out of teacups. Orange juice? Freaking teacups!"

"Oh," the other girl added. "She also sings opera while she does yoga. Like, aren't you supposed to *breathe* during yoga? And she keeps food in her bedroom like she thinks we're gonna steal it or something."

She rolled her eyes.

Rye smiled. They had it easy.

"I once had a roommate who slept with a Tupperware of meatballs next to his bed and rolls on his face," Rye said. "He was worried he'd get hungry during the night and if he did he'd just make a meatball sandwich."

"Um. What?" the taller girl said.

"Yup. I could tell you roommate stories all day, but there's only one thing to do."

"What?"

"As long as they're not hurting you or doing something really shady, you just have to accept that people are all different and that whatever shit your roommate does that you think is weird, you probably do things that are totally normal to you that they think are just as weird."

The girls looked at each other doubtfully, all shiny hair and nondescript outfits, as if they couldn't imagine a single thing about themselves that might strike someone else as weird.

"It's true," he went on. "I promise. I've lived with probably a hundred people over the years. It's a waste of energy to be annoyed by that stuff and trying to get people to change stuff that's about them is pointless. All you can do is have clear boundaries about stuff that's actually a problem for you. Like that she can't eat food if you mark it with your name or something. Or asking her not to sing before eight a.m. That kind of thing. Other than that, she's just being herself."

Rye shrugged.

"You've had a *hundred* roommates," the shorter girl said with an awed expression.

"Maybe more, I never counted. So learn from my many, many roommate situations. Annoyance: waste of energy. Trying to change shit that has nothing to do with you: waste of time. You: just as annoying as everyone else."

The girls looked at the floor.

"You're not here to buy materials to wall her into her room or anything, are you?" Rye joked.

"Can you do that?" the shorter girl said. "No. No, right?"

"Uh, yeah, probably not the best idea," Rye confirmed. "But you could try a whiteboard where you write roommate agreements?"

Rye realized he didn't know if they sold whiteboards, but before it could matter the girls wandered off, their conversation muted.

Congratulating himself on both being polite and passing

wisdom to the next generation, Rye turned around and almost ran into a man and woman standing in the aisle, holding a pitchfork like a real-life *American Gothic*. Rye reminded himself that since they were in a place that sold pitchforks it wasn't as eerie as it would otherwise have been.

"Help you find anything? Else?" he said, taking a step away from the pitchfork.

"Busy in here today," the woman said.

"Yeah, I think that might be my fault," Rye said. "In a come-gawk-at-the-new-guy way."

The two exchanged a look and Rye said, "I get it. Small town. New person."

"And then there's the fact that you moved into Granger Janssen's old place," the man added.

"Did you know my grandfather?"

"No, no one really knew him," the woman said. "He kept himself to himself."

"We didn't even know he had a grandson."

Rye shrugged. "Well, I exist."

They both nodded and continued staring at him.

"Er, can I…ring up your pitchfork? Or did you need anything else?"

The man nodded happily and they followed Rye to the register. He searched for a tag and didn't find one.

"Why doesn't he put tags on anything?" Rye muttered to himself.

"Charlie?"

"Hmm?"

"Are you referring to Charlie?"

"Uh. Yes. I was just… Hang on. Hey, Marie!" Rye yelled.

Charlie came in from the back room.

"Hey, Marvin. Hey, Stacy," Charlie said. "How's the farm? The Bringhams raise alpacas," Charlie told Rye.

"The fuzzy llama things?"

"They're camelids, in fact," Stacy corrected.

"Oh, right, okay. Cool."

No one said anything else.

"Um, I couldn't find a price on this," Rye said.

Charlie tapped a few buttons on the register and Rye went back to the safety of sorting bolts.

Friday morning, they drove to work separately because Charlie planned to stay late to do inventory. When Rye left at 5:30, instead of going back to Charlie's place, he drove to the Crow Lane house.

Windows down, Rye breathed in the smell of pine. The air was crisp but not cold and it whipped his hair into his face as he swung around the final curve and the house came into view. Except it wasn't so much a house now as it was the hollow outside of a house with a dumpster of debris next to it.

All of which made it very easy to see the three people standing in the center of it.

Their heads jerked up as his car rattled into view. They looked at him, then at each other, and it was clear they were going to rabbit.

"Hey, wait!" Rye yelled, putting his hands up in what he hoped was a recognizable gesture for *I'm not gonna call the cops on you.*

Whether it was his gesture or the fact that the people could've run in any direction at any time and instantly evaded him, Rye wasn't sure. Maybe it was curiosity—the same curiosity that had resulted in unbearably repetitive and intrusive questions at work. Or maybe it was the simple fact that they outnumbered him three to one. Whichever, after a consulting look at one another, they came out to stand in front of the house.

When Rye drew closer, he could see that they were young. Fifteen or sixteen, maybe. And he'd bet dollars to doughnuts that they were the ones who'd set up the circle of chairs in the old bedroom of the house. Also, what did *dollars to doughnuts* mean?

"Hey," Rye said.

"Who are you?" The first one to speak was a tall girl wearing a beanie and an oversized padded flannel jacket. She had a pointy elfin face, and curly blond hair.

"I'm Rye. I…" He'd been about to say that he owned this house, but it was so absurd, so utterly not in line with any sense of himself, that he couldn't get the words out. "My grandfather used to live here. Apparently."

"Apparently?" This was said by a kid in beat-up tennis shoes, skinny jeans, and a baby blue bandana covering brown hair.

"Uh. Yeah. I never knew him, but he left me this place. Apparently. I dunno, it's weird."

The teenagers nodded. Weirdness they understood.

"You been hanging out here?" he asked.

They exchanged looks and nodded suspiciously.

"I was crashing for a while when I first got here. Thought maybe you were satanists when I found your circle of chairs and candles."

He said it lightly, just trying to ease the tension.

"Maybe we are," said the third kid flatly. He had dishwater blond hair that looked unwashed and angry acne over his cheeks and chin.

Rye smirked. "Yeah, well, just don't let me come back to step in any sacrificial goat blood. Or alpaca blood," he added, remembering the Bringhams.

They gave him a very strange look.

"Well I don't know what the hell kind of animals satanists sacrifice in Wyoming," Rye snapped.

Bandana Kid chuckled. "Imagine trying to sacrifice an alpaca. You've got your—I don't know, sickle blade or whatever?—and you go to kill it but you're like 'No, I can't do it, you're too soft, I'll just have to make a sweater instead, hail Satan!'"

Rye laughed along with them.

"I don't care, you know," he said. "That you were hanging out here."

"But you're gonna fix it up? Live here?" Greasy Hair Kid asked.

Live here, live here, live here. It echoed through Rye's head and settled in his stomach in a deep well of uncertainty.

"Uh. I dunno. I mean, fix it up, yeah. My...a friend is helping me. After that...yeah, I don't know."

Rye looked around at the vista of field and forest and huge sky; birdcalls and chittering and the susurrus of the pines the only sounds around.

He imagined waking up every morning and driving to Matheson's Hardware. Helping customers find the right size bolt or the correct grain of sandpaper. Coming home after work to this isolated little house. Slowly working off the debt he'd accrued to Charlie from all the materials and hours needed to fix this place up. Falling asleep alone, listening to sounds of bats and squirrels or whateverthefuck critters he hadn't been able to identify in the dark.

"Fuck."

He didn't realize he'd said it aloud until Flannel Jacket Kid nodded and said, "Yeah, get out while you can. Where're you from, anyway?"

"Seattle."

"Cool," all three of them chorused.

They stood in awkward silence for a minute, then Bandana Kid asked, "Are you about to do construction now?"

"Huh? Oh, nah. I just..." Rye searched for a reason why he should be here with no tools, then shrugged. "I didn't want to go back to the place I'm staying."

The three nodded in perfect understanding.

"You staying with your friend?"

"Uh, yeah. I dunno. We don't know each other that well so it's a little awkward."

That sounded better than *I'm really attracted to him but he's a freakishly responsible martyr who insists on doing things like co-signing loans for me rather than jumping my bones.*

They nodded again.

"Awkward home shit is the worst," said Greasy Hair Kid.

They all nodded together and Rye was reminded so much of himself at their age: desperate for someplace to be where no one would judge him, make him feel bad for just being who he was, assume the worst of him. If he'd had such a place, he would've guarded it with everything in him. And clearly they had too, if they'd been spending time here since Granger died in October.

"You can hang here with us if you want," Bandana Kid said.

Rye was genuinely tempted. For the first time since he arrived in Garnet Run he didn't feel on guard. Didn't feel like at any moment someone was going to take him by the scruff of his neck and escort him to the state line.

Well, except...there had been those few times with Charlie. Those companionable silences while they drank their coffee in the morning before work. Or the way they'd looked up at each other and grinned at the same moment over the cats' shenanigans.

"Um, thanks, but I guess I should get back," Rye said. "Make dinner or...something."

They nodded sympathetically.

"You gonna stick around for a bit?"

They nodded.

"If it's okay?"

"Yeah. Just be careful. Don't die in there," Rye said, and sketched a wave behind his back as he walked to his car. He shivered at the chill in the air as the sun set and turned back around. "And don't burn down my house!" he added.

He got three thumbs-ups in response and left feeling confident the house would still be there when he returned.

Chapter Thirteen

Charlie

When Charlie got home after doing inventory, he smelled something delicious and heard something loud. Ordinarily he'd stand under a hot shower before he did anything else, to try and forestall the ache in his back, but he was drawn into the kitchen where he found Rye dancing and singing along to the blaring music he was playing, while maneuvering two pans on the stovetop.

"Hey!" he yelled. "I'm home."

Rye jumped like a startled cat and clutched his heart as he sagged against the counter.

"Jesus fucking Christ, don't scare me like that!"

"Jesus Christ himself could sneak up on you with your music that loud and you wouldn't even notice."

Rye made a face Charlie was learning meant he was both amused and irritated at his own amusement because he didn't like what had been said. Charlie chose to focus on the amused part.

"What is that, anyway?"

"Riven."

Charlie shrugged and Rye smirked.

"Why am I completely unsurprised that you've never heard of one of the most famous rock bands of the last ten years."

Charlie shrugged again. Rye was right. Probably Jack

knew the band, but Charlie'd never been very good at keeping up with popular culture, even when he was younger. It had simply never mattered much to him.

"What're you making? Smells good."

"Sesame peanut noodles and a mango avocado salad. I hope you like stuff spicy."

Charlie wasn't sure about that. The only spicy thing he could remember eating was a mistakenly selected flavor of beef jerky on a construction site years before.

"I'm sure it'll be great," he said. "Do I have time to take a shower?"

"Yeah I still have to fry the tofu."

"Tofu."

Rye rolled his eyes. "Go shower."

Charlie emerged from a shower as hot as he could stand it feeling refreshed and starving. His stomach growled at the bowl of glistening noodles, veggies, and what he assumed was tofu, on the table.

"What *is* tofu?" he asked as Rye set a bowl of fragrant mango salad on the table and sat down next to him.

"Oh my god, seriously? It's bean curd."

"Oh. Thank you. For making this. It smells amazing." Rye's smile was a little shy and he busied himself serving the food. "For the record I know about tofu. I just didn't know what it was made of."

"Yeah, you're clearly an aficionado."

"Where'd you get it, though? And mango. Did they have all that stuff at Smith's?"

"No, I drove to the Safeway."

"Wow. Thanks," Charlie said as Rye heaped noodles and salad on his plate.

Flavors exploded on his tongue—spicy and salty and sweet; hot and cold; the familiar taste of peanuts and the unfamiliar taste that must've been sesame. The contrast of the warm, soft noodles and the cold crunch of raw carrot and cucumber...the creamy sauce and the slap of spice. It was like nothing Charlie had ever eaten.

"Holy cow," he said. His mouth tingled. He tried the mango and avocado salad, bright and limey and cool. "Where did you learn to cook like this?"

"I moved out when I was sixteen. Could never afford to eat out, so I had to learn to cook. I've lived with so many different people since then that I've learned dishes from a lot of them."

Charlie took another bite. He must have been even more exhausted than he'd realized because the taste almost brought tears to his eyes.

It was complex and bright and *alive*.

He'd cooked five meals a week since he was eighteen and never experimented. Food had always been about fuel; about surviving. This food was about thriving.

"Why'd you move out at sixteen?"

Rye glared. Charlie was becoming familiar with the spectrum of his glares and was pretty sure this was a glare at whatever he was about to say rather than a glare at Charlie.

"My parents kind of...sucked?" he said—the Rye version of diplomacy. Charlie was pretty sure they'd have to do more than just suck to make Rye leave home.

"Yeah?"

Rye chewed his lip.

"My dad was—is—really not a nice person. He's homophobic. Racist. Just a closed-minded bigot all around, actually. When I was fifteen, my dad saw me kiss my friend Jarrod. He flipped his lid."

Rye didn't elaborate, but his flinch told Charlie enough to hate Rye Janssen's father.

"I wasn't as... I didn't tell him the truth. I told him I did it on a dare."

Charlie realized Rye's cringe had been partly for himself and his anger intensified.

"You were a kid and you were scared of your father."

"I know. Still don't like that I lied. Anyway, my mom never said shit about it to him, or to me. I'm not sure if she agreed with him or was scared of him or just didn't care. My mom was…" Rye got a faraway look like he was picturing her. "She had some problems, I guess. A germophobe. But like, couldn't use a plate without wiping it down with alcohol first. My dad would say something awful and she would start cleaning, like she could banish his shitiness with antibacterial soap or something."

Rye was moving food around on his plate.

"When I was sixteen it just fell apart. I was so sick of hearing these awful things come out of my dad's mouth. Awful things about me and my friends and about other people. I had this… I don't know, I was worried if I stayed too long I might start to think like him or something. And then that year at Christmas, my mom kinda deteriorated.

"She started decorating our apartment in September and she would freak out if you touched any of the decorations, but they were everywhere and the place was really small. I tried to tell her that maybe she should talk to someone but she wouldn't hear it. So I went to my dad. He, uh. Didn't receive that well. Turned it on me. Basically said he would never let any wife of his see a therapist because only weak, crazy people see therapists, et cetera. And he told me to get out."

Rye shrugged.

"I could have waited him out, probably. Stayed with a friend for a few weeks then gone home once his temper cooled. But it felt so bad there all the time. So one night after school I packed my shit and I left. I tried to get my mom to leave with me, but she just waved me off. I stayed with a friend for a little while, and then I just…"

He shrugged again, a gesture to say *The rest is history.*

Then, self-consciously, he said, *"Anyway.* That's how I learned to cook."

It was clear that Rye didn't want to talk about it anymore, so Charlie just nodded and said, "I invited my brother and Simon over for dinner next weekend. Any chance I could convince you to cook?"

Rye nodded, looking relieved. "Sure."

The turning of the lathe always gave Charlie time to think and tonight was no different. Usually it brought with it meditations on store problems he needed to solve, improvements he wished to undertake on his house, or worries about Jack. Now, though, he thought of Trevor.

What if Trevor hadn't left? What if Trevor—and *Trevor,* understand, could be Trevor or another Trevor, or another— had been his? What if he'd had someone when the call came about Mom and Dad? What if, after he'd told Jack—so young, so scared, trying to act so tough—he'd been able to call someone and say, *I'm scared? I'm too young and too scared and I have to act tough for Jack because now I'm all he has?*

What if all these years he hadn't been alone?

He tried to stop thinking, then, because *ouch, fuck,* but then, Rye prowled into his mind like a sleek cat. What did Rye think of this and what did Rye think of that and what would Rye look like spread out naked in Charlie's bed, pointed chin tipped up to bare his throat as he screamed and screamed, body shaking with pleasure, and let Charlie see it? And where, *where* did that thought come from?

Charlie almost never thought about sex. He certainly didn't think about having sex with people. But now Rye.

As if summoned by the thought, Rye padded into the woodshop, Jane and Marmot following. Jane rolled in the curls of wood on the floor as she usually did and Marmot darted around the room, sniffing this corner and pawing at that tool.

Rye hovered. Charlie tried very hard to ignore him.

It was hard to ignore someone who rearranged the very molecules of your being like a magnet did filings.

Like a third curious cat, Rye peered at the lathe.

"You make chair legs and shit?"

Charlie smiled at the image of his whole woodshop filled with thousands of chair legs.

"I make bowls mostly, but yes, this is the tool you'd turn chair legs on."

He held up one of the bowls that was waiting for a coat of mineral oil.

"Wow."

Rye touched the satiny wood with reverent fingertips.

"Can I try?"

Charlie imagined his fingers caught in the lathe, broken bones, spurts of blood. He blew out a breath, conjuring windshield wipers to clear those images from his mind.

"Sure," he forced himself to say.

He clamped a chunk of scrap wood into the lathe and marked the center.

"It's about the angle of approach. You're the blade and you encounter the wood at different angles to change its shape into what you want."

He handed Rye the roughing gauge and a pair of safety glasses, and set the handrest so the rotating wood cleared it.

"So if we're gonna make a bowl, we start here."

He reached around Rye, chest to Rye's back, and held Rye's hand at the correct angle.

"Anchor your hand here, hold the gauge steady, and when I start the lathe, just move in a little bit. We'll just be taking the edge off."

Rye nodded. His hair smelled like Charlie's shampoo, but it smelled different on Rye. Darker, sensual, a garden at night.

He hit the power switch and the lathe began to spin. Rye's

hair fluttered and Charlie anchored him with his arms, holding him steady.

"Slowly," he cautioned, hand light on Rye's. "And hold tight."

Rye held so tight the gauge juddered when it hit the wood and Charlie clamped down on Rye's hand to keep it from hurting him.

"It's fine. Just go real slow."

He guided Rye's hand slowly and surely until the very tip of the gauge kissed the block, *snicking* off the barest whisper of wood. They pulled back, angled the gauge again, and slid forward, taking off another layer.

Slowly, gently, with his hand on Rye's, they shaped the curved edge of the bottom of a bowl. After a few minutes they were one body, breathing, pressing forward, pulling back, and changing angle together.

Charlie breathed in the scent of Rye's night blossom hair mingled with the fresh flick of wood shavings. It smelled like home.

When he stopped the lathe, Rye looked up at him, eyes wide, pupils nearly swallowing the gray of his irises. He blinked and slid his safety glasses off.

It seemed like he looked at Charlie forever. Charlie's heart pounded so hard he was sure it was audible in the sudden silence. A faint flush pinked Rye's cheeks and he licked his lips. Then he slid his hand around Charlie's neck and swallowed hard.

"I wanna kiss you," he said, voice rough. "And it's not a thank you or a payment. It's cuz that was hot as fuck and you're hot as fuck and...and..."

Charlie couldn't find any words. His entire being throbbed for Rye and all he could do was incline his head.

Rye's extraordinary eyes fluttered closed in the moment before his lips met Charlie's.

The last time Rye kissed him it had felt impersonal, and Charlie had ended it immediately.

This kiss just showed Charlie by comparison *how* impersonal that kiss had been. This was the *real* Rye kiss, he realized. This kiss was hot and lingering, and Rye's mouth was sweet, his tongue luscious, his teeth sharp. Rye's other hand cupped Charlie's jaw, like he was afraid Charlie might pull away. So Charlie leaned closer and gathered Rye to him.

Rye gave a small mew of pleasure and it shot down Charlie's spine like a caress. He wanted Rye to make that sound over and over again. With a hand pressed to the small of Rye's back he could feel the silken fall of his hair with the other. He twined his fingers into the glorious mess of waves until he felt the curve of Rye's skull. Every inch of him was perfect.

Charlie felt perfectly in control until they were falling.

He saved them from careening to the ground through sheer muscle and instead ended up with Rye crushed to his chest, one arm bracing them against the lathe.

Charlie didn't spare more than a fleeting thought to commend himself on his choice of a lathe that would take the hit of their combined body weight.

"You okay?"

Rye's response was a squeak muffled against his collarbone. Charlie stood them up and bent to look into Rye's face. Rye was all sharp chin and blinking eyes and swollen lips.

Charlie groaned, reached out a finger, touched them.

Rye's eyes fluttered shut and his mouth yearned toward Charlie's.

Then they were kissing and kissing until they were drunk, mouths made for kissing and hands for holding faces and hair and necks and each other's hands while kissing.

They ended up against the nearest wall, Charlie's back pressed to the drywall and Rye sagging against him, breathing heavily. Charlie searched for his mouth blindly, lips wanting to know only Rye's lips.

Rye started pulling at Charlie's clothing, hands wild, mouth wet, cheek a burning brand against Charlie's palm.

"Hang on," Charlie mumbled against Rye's mouth. Rye made a moue of discontent and pressed closer. Charlie lost himself in hot, heady kisses once more. He wrapped Rye's hair in his hands, tugging a little, and Rye gasped into his mouth.

"You okay?"

Rye nodded instantly. He was squirming.

"You sure?"

Charlie peered at him.

"Just, um." Rye glanced down. "Yup." He swallowed hard. "Just yeah."

"Rye?"

Rye huffed out a little irritated sound. "I like it when you pull my hair, okay? It gets to me."

A rush of heat pooled in Charlie's belly. He wanted to find out every single solitary thing that got to Rye. Just... not all at once.

Charlie slid his hand back into Rye's hair and tugged. Rye's eyes fluttered shut and he plastered himself back to Charlie's chest.

"How hard do you like it pulled?"

Rye's moan was wordless but heartfelt, and Charlie pulled a little harder. Rye dropped his forehead to Charlie's chest and groaned. Charlie stroked Rye's throat with his other hand, fingers gentle on his soft skin, and fisted his hair with the other, tugging more sharply.

Rye's gasp was the most beautiful sound he'd ever heard. He did it again and again until Rye was writhing against him.

"Stop, stop," Rye said. "Fuck, stop."

He was pressing even closer to Charlie, arms tight around him, but moving his lower body away.

Charlie untangled his hand from Rye's hair and just stroked it softly.

"You okay?" he asked again.

Rye wouldn't look at him.

"Rye?"

"God, yes, just you have to stop or I'll come all over you," he groaned.

Charlie froze. He'd been turned on before, buzzing with heat, but at those words a bolt of lust tore through him that made him physically jolt.

"But you don't...you don't want to now...right?" Rye was asking.

"Huh?"

Charlie felt like he was fighting to hear through an unfamiliar fog.

Warm hands slid up his chest.

"You don't wanna fuck. Or do you?"

The word cleared Charlie's head. *Fuck.*

"I don't...know."

"Then you don't," Rye said.

"But I want..."

Charlie didn't know how to say what he wanted. He didn't know if Rye would want it too. He didn't know if it was an okay thing to want.

Then Rye was kissing him again, hot and magic in his arms, saying, "Anything," against his lips like he really meant it.

"I want you to..."

"To come? You wanna see me get off for you?" Rye asked, voice breathy and low, and how could he *say* things like that?

"Yes," Charlie moaned. "And..."

"You want to pull my hair while I come for you."

Charlie's breath caught because *Yes, yes,* that.

"But you don't wanna come?"

"Not...not yet," Charlie managed.

Later, later when I'm alone in bed and there's no chance you'll see me do it wrong.

Rye kissed him, then, deep and yearning.

"Touch me, Charlie."

This desire was like nothing Charlie had ever felt. He fisted Rye's hair and pulled until Rye's face was upturned like a flower. Rye's breathing was already ragged.

"Can you really… Would you really have…" Charlie swallowed hard.

Rye bit his lip and nodded.

"Okay," Charlie said.

"Okay," Rye mouthed.

Charlie tugged on his hair and caught his open mouth in a brutal kiss, swallowing Rye's moans.

He pulled harder and felt Rye tremble. Rye pressed against him, all attempts to hide his response obliterated now. When Rye's hips pressed forward, Charlie could feel his erection, hard against his hip. Rye gasped and shuddered, and Charlie felt lightheaded.

"Charlie, Charlie, Charlie," Rye chanted.

He writhed in Charlie's arms like a live wire, pulling against his hand, pressing into his chest and hip and thigh. Desperate.

Charlie felt like a god.

His blood throbbed in his veins and his dick throbbed and his heart throbbed. Every bit of him throbbed for the man who was falling apart in his arms.

Charlie clamped an arm around Rye's waist, holding him so they touched everywhere, and pulled his hair with a sharp yank. Rye's head lolled and his mouth fell open. Charlie did it again, then massaged Rye's scalp with his fingertips to soothe the sting.

Rye's eyes were shut tight and his pale skin was flushed blotchy from his cheeks to his throat. Charlie couldn't comprehend how he could be touching someone so beautiful. So free.

In all his adult life, Charlie had never been that free.

Rye gasped as Charlie kissed him, trying to feel even a bit of what Rye felt. Rye slung his leg around Charlie's hip and pressed even closer to him, and Charlie could feel his hard cock through both layers of their clothes. He felt the moment Rye tipped over, pleasure peaking.

Rye came with a strangled groan, then his mouth opened on silence. He fisted Charlie's shirt and buried his face in Charlie's shoulder as tremors ran through him.

Charlie was suspended in a wave of arousal that held him like a cloud. Beautiful and unbelievable and new.

Rye whimpered and his fists eased. He dropped back to his flat feet and Charlie let go of his hair. Charlie listened to him breathe for a while before Rye looked up at him. His lips were swollen and his eyes liquid.

Charlie cupped his face, wanting to see what it was that made someone be able to *do* that. To want something and to take it.

Under his scrutiny, Rye scowled like a sleeping cat who noticed it was observed.

"No, no." Charlie smoothed his brow with the press of his thumb. "Sorry."

He kissed Rye's hair.

"Um." Rye's eyes darted everywhere but Charlie's.

Charlie kissed Rye's eyelids, forcing him to close them.

"You're so beautiful," Charlie let himself say with Rye's eyes closed.

Rye nuzzled into him, his breathing back to normal.

"I can't believe we just did that."

"Why?" Charlie had rather gotten the sense that this was the kind of thing Rye was used to.

"Because." Rye glanced up at him. "You... I... I thought you weren't... Fuck, I don't know."

Charlie unclamped their half-made bowl from the lathe and wiped sawdust from the arms of the machine. The wood shavings he left for Jane to roll in later. She and Marmot had disappeared back into the house at some point and he hadn't even noticed.

Sometimes Jane liked to come roll in the shavings while Charlie slept. On those nights, he would wake to the scent of fresh pine on her fur when she snuggled into bed beside him and curled up under his chin.

"Charlie."

Rye's hand touched his shoulder tentatively.

"I lied to you the other night," Charlie said. "When we were watching *Secaucus Psychic*. I do believe in ghosts."

Really, there was no belief involved. Charlie lived with them every day. When he swapped the contents of aisles five and two, putting the screws and nails in front of the cash register to discourage people from slipping one or two into their pockets as Charlie knew they often did, he'd heard his father's voice in his ear.

When he'd baked Jack a birthday cake the year after they'd died and thought baking powder and baking soda were the same thing, he'd heard his mother's voice.

If carrying them with him for the last twenty years didn't prove that ghosts were real, Charlie wasn't sure what would.

But now, in the aftermath of Rye's pleasure and his own desire, more than anything, he wished for them to go away. To dissipate and leave him in peace. His own man.

"I lied too," Rye said.

His voice sounded different and when Charlie turned, Rye was staring right at him.

"When I said I didn't know just now. It's… I was pretty sure you weren't into me like that."

Rye looked him up and down, gaze appreciative and lingering. "But you are, huh?"

Charlie swallowed hard, the fear of what it meant to admit his desire tightening his muscles. Then he nodded.

"I like you," Rye said. "I really do."

The knot in Charlie's stomach eased a bit.

"I like you too," he said, voice just above a whisper.

"I don't know why," Rye grumbled. "Cuz you're a bossy, perfectionistic—"

"Okay, okay," Charlie interrupted.

Rye grinned, his eyes soft enough to let Charlie know he was just teasing.

Chapter Fourteen

Rye

Rye's arms and back ached under the hot water of a long shower, and he was pretty sure that he didn't have a future in construction.

Early that morning they'd begun the first day of work on the demoed Crow Lane house and within an hour it was clear that while Charlie was good at demolition, he *loved* construction.

He was like some kind of annoying superhero, with muscles that never tired, an inhuman sense of depth perception, and the ability to tell when something was a fraction of an inch out of plumb—his words—by eye.

Rye was pretty sure sometimes he just *said* shit wasn't straight because, hello, crumbling cabin. But lo and behold when Charlie would apply the level, he always turned out to be right.

It had been three days since he'd come in his pants while Charlie feasted on his mouth and pulled his hair and Rye couldn't stop thinking about it.

When Charlie passed him a cup of coffee, when Charlie appeared behind him at the cash register, when Charlie sat across from him at the dinner table. They hadn't explicitly talked about it, but it was there, a current thrumming beneath every interaction; the promise of sparks if they reached out and touched.

But they hadn't.

Rye wanted Charlie to be the one to reach for him. He needed to know that Charlie wasn't simply going along with this because he lived to help people. He had to be sure that Charlie wasn't just doing it for him.

He threw on some clothes and gathered his damp hair into a hasty bun so it didn't drip down his back while he was cooking dinner for Jack and Simon.

In the kitchen he pulled things out of the refrigerator and tossed them on the counter.

"So what'd you decide on?"

Charlie leaned against the doorjamb looking unfairly hot with his reddish-blond hair darkened by his shower.

Rye wanted to throw himself against that broad chest and feel those arms hold him tight. He wanted Charlie to come up behind him as he was cooking and rest hands on his shoulders. He wanted to go up on his tiptoes and press a casual kiss to Charlie's cheek.

"Vegetable lasagna," he said, since none of the other things were going to happen.

"That sounds good," Charlie said. "Can I help?"

When he came closer, Rye could smell him. That damn jasmine shampoo and the woodsy scent of his soap that reminded Rye of how he'd smelled in the woodshop, fragrant shavings all around them.

"Sure."

"You can put on your music, if you want," Charlie said.

Rye shrugged.

"Come on, it seemed like you were having so much fun cooking the other day. I wouldn't've asked you to cook tonight if I thought it was a chore for you."

What a strange thing to say.

"I'm happy to do chores, Charlie. If I'm living here I want to pull my weight."

"Not necessary. I was used to cooking before and I can cook now."

"I do like to cook. I told you that. But that's not the point. What, you can work all the time and do chores you don't like and help everyone else but you think I'm only supposed to do things if I like them?"

Charlie shrugged. "Wouldn't everyone like to only do things they enjoy if they could?"

"Um, no. Only children, the ultrarich, and total narcissists think doing only what you want is any kind of life. The rest of us have, like, ambitions and empathy and obligations to other living things. You don't really think that, do you?"

Charlie shook his head, then shrugged.

"Do you?" Rye asked again.

"No, I...no. I guess not."

But it fit more pieces into place for Rye. It wasn't just that Charlie was used to *having* to take care of things and people. Charlie was willing to do things he didn't enjoy in order to protect the people he cared about from having to do them.

He wondered if anyone did things for Charlie.

"What would you do if you only did things you enjoyed, then?" Rye asked.

Charlie's chuckle was bleak.

"Jeez, I have no idea."

"Well, maybe you should think about it."

"Maybe I should," Charlie allowed.

Rye put on Theo Decker's second solo album on his phone and put the phone in a cup to amplify the sound.

"You need a speaker for in here," Rye said.

After that, Rye zoned out, listening to the music and losing himself in the familiar motions of crushing garlic, slicing onion, and sautéing vegetables.

He and Charlie worked easily together. When it was time to layer the lasagna, Charlie said, "You didn't boil the noodles."

"You don't have to. The sauce will cook them while it bakes. Plus it's a pain in the ass."

"Whoa," Charlie said. "I never knew that. I made lasagna once but it was such a pain I stuck to spaghetti and meatballs after that."

"Lots more tips where that one came from. Tune in to Rye's Recipes every Friday night."

Charlie smiled and nodded. Charlie's nods were serious agreements, not offhand gestures.

Rye liked that a lot.

At first, Jack hadn't seemed much like Charlie in anything but looks. But now Rye could see other similarities. They both had a certain acceptance of things as they were. An unflappability that seemed like peace. They both exuded a kind of steady calm, though Jack's was a more casual, easygoing state, while Charlie's seemed inviolable.

And though he wouldn't have thought it, they shared an unexpectedly dry sense of humor that seemed in character for Jack, who was a little grouchy, but always surprised Rye in Charlie, who seemed so stoic.

Then there was Simon. He knew from Jack's fierce injunction at the Crow Lane house—and Charlie's last-minute reminder before their arrival—that Simon's intense anxiety flared around strangers.

He'd noticed Simon was nice-looking, but since he'd mostly looked at the ground when they were working together, Rye was surprised to see that he was *beautiful*, with eyes the startling blue of a flame. He was also, once he'd warmed up a bit, much snarkier than Rye had previously seen, and Rye decided he liked him.

Jack and Simon talked about their animals and Jack told a story about how their St. Bernard (named Bernard—a joke?

Rye wasn't sure) and Box, the puppy they got a few months ago, had joined forces on walks to befriend a pack of chipmunks.

"To try and eat them?" Rye asked.

"No, no," Jack assured him. "Bernard is a gentle giant. He just wants to lie on the ground and have a bunch of chipmunks curl up on top of him."

"I follow an Instagram account like that," Simon said wistfully.

"My friend Kyle had a dog he used to bring everywhere," Rye said. "He'd wear his backpack in the front like a baby carrier and put her in facing out so she could see the world. And she just wanted to make friends with everyone she met."

As he said it, Rye realized that he'd been here for a month and Kyle hadn't texted him once, nor had he texted Kyle. Amazing how someone could be a part of your daily life and then simply have no bearing on anything at all.

To distract himself from that thought, he said, "I bet Marmot would like to go on walks. That's my cat."

At her name, the cat in question wandered into the dining room, sniffing at the air, and Rye patted his lap for her. She curled up on his thighs and tucked her head under her paw.

"Aww," Simon said. "She can come if you want."

"Maybe. Thanks."

Rye stroked Marmot's ears and she purred.

"The food's really good, Rye," Charlie said. His eyes were soft.

"It is," Jack agreed, as Simon said, "Really good."

"Just very relieved it's not meatloaf. Been a lot of that over the years," Jack said, winking at Charlie.

Charlie flipped him off good-naturedly, but said nothing.

Rye waited but Simon just nodded in anti-meatloaf sympathy. Fury and disbelief fizzed under Rye's skin as he stared at Jack.

"Uh, I'm sorry," he said. "Let me get this straight. Your eighteen-year-old brother put food on the table for you and you're *teasing* him because you didn't happen to like one of the foods he learned to cook in order to take care of you? What the fuck?"

Three pairs of very wide eyes blinked at him from around the table. Rye had more to say but he clenched his teeth and forced himself to relax by petting Marmot, who'd woken in his lap at the tension in his limbs.

Jack looked stunned. He opened his mouth several times before finding any words.

"I'm sorry, bro. I never meant... I didn't... You know I appreciate you, right? And everything you did for me?"

Charlie nodded.

"Sure. I know. Don't worry about it."

"I—It was just a joke. I didn't mean to be a dick about it."

"You weren't a dick," Charlie said.

He smiled and the tension between him and Jack was diffused. But Rye was not appeased.

"You were," Rye said matter-of-factly. "I believe you didn't mean to be," he added. "But you were."

Simon was examining the table intently, his hands clenched in his lap.

"I... I'm sorry," Jack said. "But he barely even likes meatloaf himself. It's...it's *meatloaf.*"

He said it like no one could possibly like meatloaf. Sure, Rye also happened not to be a fan, but that wasn't the point.

"You think every week for nearly twenty years, he's made something he doesn't like?" Rye asked.

Marmot stood up on his knee, arched her back in a languorous stretch, and ran off, done with any nonsense of humans that didn't result in her getting pet or fed.

"Well. But. Wait, Charlie?"

Jack looked at Charlie, who folded his napkin in his lap with concentrated precision.

"I like it," he said simply, shrugging.

Jack gaped.

"Shit, man, I'm sorry. I thought… Damn, I dunno what I thought."

"It's really okay," Charlie said.

"Sorry," Jack murmured again.

Charlie shot Rye an assessing look. He didn't seem angry, but it certainly wouldn't be the first time Rye got an earful after the fact. People were rather expectedly resistant to the truth when it made them uncomfortable.

Predictably, the night ended soon after that.

Jack followed Charlie into the kitchen, leaving Rye and Simon standing in awkward silence.

"Hey, Simon, um… Not to be a total weirdo but, uh, any chance you wanna be friends?"

Simon's eyes flashed wide beneath his dark brows and then he toed the ground.

Rye was asking someone who felt anxious around people to do the thing that made him anxious immediately after calling his boyfriend a dick, so he wasn't that hopeful.

He added, "We could just be, like, text friends, if you want? We don't have to hang out or anything."

Simon crossed his arms but didn't say anything.

"Never mind, man. I'm sorry. Didn't mean to put you on the spot."

Simon made a frustrated noise and gestured at Rye.

"Sorry, I don't— Oh, sure." He took his phone out of his pocket and made a new contact, then handed it to Simon.

When Simon handed his phone back, Rye texted him so he'd have his number.

Hi.

Simon's fingers flew.

Now we can talk about the weirdness that is the Matheson Brothers without them knowing we're sharing information.

"Sounds good," Rye said. "I really didn't mean to put you on the spot, though. Just because I'm staying with Charlie for a minute…"

Simon texted, Shut up, you didn't pressure me. I'm not good at talking—doesn't mean I can't make my own choices.

"Got it," Rye said. Then, searching for a topic that wasn't So about me calling your boyfriend a dick, "Is your new puppy really that cute?"

She's the cutest goddamn thing but she somehow corrals the other animals into mischief they'd never gotten into before we got her. She's basically a cult leader.

Then Simon sent two pictures, one of a very adorable puppy snoozing by the fire with her big paws sticking straight out, and the second of that same puppy in a room with lots of books and art supplies, a vee of cats and dogs behind her. Destruction was a promise.

It's hard when adorable things are evil, Simon wrote, and sighed.

The brothers came out of the kitchen and neither appeared to be damaged so Rye assumed things were okay. Simon's attention was immediately on Jack. When Jack smiled, Simon shot Rye a quick look that managed to communicate that his last text had referred to Jack as much as to the puppy.

Rye nodded at him just as Charlie appeared beside him and he heard Simon's little breath of laughter.

"Okay, uh, bye, bro," Jack said stiffly. "Rye, thanks for dinner. It was really good. Night."

Simon waved and they left with their arms around each other. Rye thought of the way Jack had held Simon at the

Crow Lane house when he'd been upset. Held him so tight it'd looked as if Simon could have lost all his edges, flowed free, and Jack would still have managed to contain him.

Rye swallowed his envy and turned to Charlie.

"I stand by what I said," he told Charlie before Charlie could say anything.

Charlie didn't look angry. He looked confused.

"You really think my brother is an ungrateful dick?"

"I don't think he *is* an ungrateful dick. I think he said a mean, ungrateful thing. And he said it without imagining that it might be hurtful, so I assume he's said similar things often enough to know you wouldn't tell him off."

Charlie shook his head. "It's fine. He doesn't like meatloaf."

Rye rolled his eyes.

"It's not about the meatloaf, specifically. But come on! At eighteen you learned how to cook and cooked him dinner every night and what he has to say about it is to make jokes about how you're a bad cook? You have to get that that's ungrateful?"

Charlie's brow furrowed even more.

"He was just a kid," Charlie said softly.

"So were you. And he's not a kid anymore."

"He… Jack's a sweetheart," Charlie said.

"I'm not insulting your parenting skills," Rye said gently. "It sounds like you stepped in and raised Jack so selflessly that he never had to think about it."

Charlie shook his head again as if he could erase the things Rye was saying like an Etch A Sketch.

"He…he was so young, and…"

Rye put his hands on Charlie's upper arms and squeezed. "I know."

Rye could feel how tense Charlie's muscles were and see the faint lines around his eyes.

"I gotta sit down," Charlie said.

Chapter Fifteen

Charlie

Charlie's thoughts were skittering all over the place. He was walking into his living room with Rye after dinner and he was walking into the living room of his parents' house with his grandmother. She'd flown up from Florida for the funeral and offered to take Jack with her for the remainder of high school.

Charlie, two weeks past the legal ability to claim guardianship, had claimed it, and sent her away empty-handed, the prospect of losing his brother as well as his parents unthinkable. He'd known it would be hard but he had been blessedly ignorant of *how* hard, because if he'd known then he might have taken her up on her offer.

Instead she sent what money she could, when she could, and came to visit for one week every summer, claiming that it was a relief to escape the July Tampa heat.

Every time she came she told Charlie that he was doing a good job. That his parents would be proud of him.

"You okay?"

Rye's voice was soft and he dropped onto the couch next to Charlie. Charlie focused on Rye's eyes, quicksilver limned in kohl. He'd never met anyone with truly gray eyes before. He'd known people with blue-gray eyes and brown-gray eyes and eyes that really light blue—like Simon's—that they looked almost gray in some lights. But never someone with eyes the color of Rye's.

"Charlie?"

They almost glowed. Like a church window with sun streaming through it, only this light seemed to come from inside Rye himself, blazing out—

"Charlie. Where'd you go?"

"What? Nowhere."

Rye's eyes were closer to him now, and they looked concerned.

"'M fine," Charlie said.

He was fine. He'd bought this couch so it would be big enough for him to lie down on. He'd painted the walls of the living room a warm cream color so it wouldn't look too stark against the pine flooring. He'd hung a painting from Jack's first book, *There's a Moose Loose in Central Park*, over the mantle because it reminded him of what an amazing artist Jack was. How proud he was of Jack's success at turning his passion into a career.

"I'm gonna do the dishes," he said.

Rye followed him into the kitchen and hovered in the doorway.

Charlie concentrated on the familiar task. Rinse, scrub, rinse, dry. A few dishes in, Rye came over and started drying. He was humming to himself, a song that Charlie thought he recognized from the album Rye'd been playing while they were cooking dinner.

"You have a really nice voice."

"Huh? Oh, thanks."

Rye dried the final dish and Charlie put the lasagna pan to soak in the sink.

"You wanna watch *Secaucus Psychic*?" Rye asked.

Charlie nodded, glad not to have to make a choice, and followed him back into the living room, the scent of dish soap clinging to his hands.

Rye hopped over the back of the couch and collapsed gracefully onto the cushions. He stretched to grab the remote off the coffee table and handed it to Charlie. He said it was annoyingly complicated to use.

He was so beautiful.

He must've stared a beat too long because Rye's eyelashes fluttered and he flushed.

"Charlie. Were you okay with what happened the other day? Because you seemed okay at the time, but you haven't mentioned it. So I just wanted to check."

"You haven't mentioned it either," Charlie said.

"I know. But I've thought about it a lot."

Charlie's breath caught. He had thought about their encounter at least ten times a day since it had happened, trying to commit it to memory in case he never got the chance to touch Rye again.

Those quicksilver eyes heavy-lidded with desire, his body shaking with need; the tiny gasps of pleasure when Charlie slid fingers into his long hair; the final shudder and jerk of orgasm while Rye was pinioned between Charlie's body and the fist in his hair.

He swallowed hard. "I didn't mean for you to think I didn't enjoy what happened between us. Because I did. I *really* did."

Charlie sat on the couch next to him and Rye drew his knees up, curling into the cushions.

"Then why hasn't it happened again?" Rye asked.

"You're the one who made it happen," Charlie said without thinking. "I never would have."

"Oh. Never?"

Was that hurtful to admit? Charlie wasn't sure. He never would have initiated anything because he never did—never had. He wouldn't have had the first idea how.

"Probably not."

"Why?" Rye didn't sound hurt, just curious.

Things to do with sex… Charlie had never talked about them with anyone.

Well, there had been Dickens, whom he'd met online and talked with for a while. Dickens had been an easy confessor, being completely anonymous and possibly on the other side of the world. Charlie—or JanesDad as he'd called himself on the site (he'd chosen the moniker while Jane lay on his stomach, making biscuits on his chest, so hush)—had spilled truths as he'd never imagined doing in real life.

He'd never needed to before. Now…

"Are you dying?" Rye whispered.

Charlie snorted. Rye's mental leaps were something.

"Ah, not that I'm aware of?"

Rye looked slightly relieved.

"Then what?"

"Did you really think the most likely reason I hadn't put the moves on you was that I was *dying*?"

Rye scowled. "No! I… Just making sure." He rolled his eyes. "Fine, I watched a show the other day where this guy knew he was dying so he pulled away…never mind, anyway."

He curled up even more and called for Marmot. Naturally, Marmot being a cat, nothing happened. Rye scowled again.

"I knew you could work the remote if you wanted to," Charlie said absently.

Rye ignored that.

"Charlie, what's up? I can't stop thinking about it. If you're not into me, that's fine. If you're not into guys, that's fine. If you're not into sex, that's fine. It's all fine, just please fucking tell me."

Charlie's heart started to race and his fingertips began to buzz and tingle. He had never said this out loud before.

"I don't… I don't know," he croaked.

"It really is. It's all fine, I promise."

The shame welled up from his guts to his throat, choking him.

"No, I... I don't know because I've never... I haven't... I haven't been with anyone. Well, one teenage fumbling. But other than that."

Charlie broke off and squeezed his eyes shut. He wanted to disappear. He wanted to go back to the moment before he had confessed that. To a moment when Rye still thought he was normal.

After moments of silence, he darted a glance at Rye's face, braced for laughter or shock, but Rye just looked like Rye. When he spoke, he sounded just like he usually did.

"Do you mean you've never had sex with anyone, or you've never dated anyone?"

"I...both."

Charlie swallowed acid. He scratched the edge of the couch cushion and heard the soft *thlump* of Jane's paws hitting the ground. Ten seconds later she was in his lap, her black and gray fur damp from a recent cleaning. He sank his fingers into her fur and felt the vibration of her purr.

"Why?"

Rye's question was simple and neutral, and though Charlie searched for the judgment in it, he didn't find any.

It was a question that had once plagued Charlie, then faded, slowly, into simple fact.

"Mom and Dad died two days before my eighteenth birthday. I was a high school student on the football team who'd never fried an egg or cashed a check. By the time they were buried, I was legally an adult. I was Jack's guardian, I had a mortgage, and I owned a business that was in the red."

Those first six months, Charlie had woken every night around three in the morning, gasping for breath, and had felt all over again the grief of remembrance slam into his chest. He'd lie there, in his childhood bed—because even though they were gone, there was no way he could sleep in his parents' room—no longer a child, but with no clue how to be an adult. A guardian. A business owner.

"It took me years to get everything together. A year before I could sleep without waking up from nightmares every single night. Five years until Jack left for college. Six until Matheson's Hardware was firmly in the black, but by then I was taking any extra work I could to help Jack pay for school on top of everything else.

"By then, all the friends I'd had in high school were long gone. Hell, they'd been gone within a month. I don't blame them. We were stupid kids. We played ball together. What did they owe me?"

For a while, he'd expected them to come. Expected Martin and Tom to stop by, or call, or…whatever. But within the month it had become clear how shallow those relationships were; what little capacity any of the guys on the team had to voluntarily march into Charlie's grief with him. He'd forgiven them. He couldn't say with certainty that he'd have behaved any different.

But it had still hurt. Charlie had never spent much time alone before that, always surrounded by the guys on the team and their classmates who hung around the edges. And suddenly he was more than alone. He was alone and full up with all these *feelings* he had no idea what to do with. Fear and anger and impatience and yeah, resentment.

He resented Jack because Jack had him. He resented his parents because they didn't have to do any of the work. He resented his father for not being better at business. And he resented every single friend he'd ever had for being able to walk away from him when he himself was firmly stuck in the bog that was his new life.

"Fuck," Rye said.

"After that I just kinda fell into a pattern. There wasn't really time to think about that kind of stuff. Romance stuff. Sex stuff. It wasn't…"

Charlie shook his head.

"Did you ever meet people you wanted to date?"

Charlie shrugged. Customers had tried to set him up with their daughters, sisters, cousins, and granddaughters often. He'd always demurred.

And the few times he had noticed someone he found attractive, it had made him think of Trevor, which had made him think of his parents dying, which...was a major anaphrodisiac.

Rye was worrying his lower lip and considering Charlie intently. Beautiful Rye. Full-of-life Rye who'd probably never been alone a night in his life if he didn't want to be. Rye who knew what he liked. Who asked for it. Who could pick up and move a thousand miles with nothing but his cat and the promise of a new adventure.

Charlie admired him. Charlie envied him. And Charlie was viciously, gut-churningly intimidated by him. At least when it came to sex.

Rye unfolded from the corner and came right next to Charlie. He took Charlie's hand in both of his and kissed it. His face showed so much pity Charlie wanted to run away from it.

"I'm sorry, Charlie. I'm so sorry you were all alone."

Charlie choked up. It hadn't happened in a long, long time.

Jane plastered herself to his chest, arms on his shoulder, and put her face right up to his face. She licked his cheek and he realized he was crying.

"Well, that's the cutest fucking thing I've ever seen," Rye muttered.

Then, very gently, he displaced Jane and put himself in her place. He put his arms around Charlie's neck and pulled him close, stroking his hair.

No one had done that since his mom when he was a little boy. His hair was white-blond then, and she called him her little dandelion. He hadn't understood why, because dandelions were yellow. So she'd taken him by the hand and searched the grass until she found one gone to seed. It was fluffy white. She stroked his halo of blond hair and held up the dandelion. Then, together, they blew, and watched the seeds cartwheel through the air.

"Baby," Rye murmured, and something pulsed through Charlie like lightning.

He folded Rye in his arms and squeezed him tight. They lay there for a while, Rye stroking his hair, him stroking Rye's back.

Then Rye said, "I think you're pretty amazing."

Charlie couldn't quite accept that.

"Why don't you think I'm a freak? Why are you so okay with this?"

Rye wrinkled his brow.

"You're not a freak. Well, I mean, you are, but not because you haven't had sex or dated people. That's ridiculous. Tons of people aren't interested in sex or dating. What's there not to be okay with?"

Charlie shook his head, feeling even worse now.

"I didn't mean it like that."

"I know. But it seems like *you* think there's something wrong with it?"

"Just for me," Charlie grumbled, and Rye snorted.

"Can I ask you something?"

Charlie nodded.

"The other night. When we... Why didn't you want to come? Whatever the reason was, I swear it's fine and I won't be upset or feel bad or any—"

"I get it, thanks."

Charlie smiled into Rye's hair. It was easier to talk like this, pressed together but not looking at each other.

"I was worried I might, um, do something weird."

"Weird how." Rye remained utterly relaxed on top of him.

"Don't know. Just, I wanted to concentrate on you and not worry about myself."

"Sounds like you do that a lot," Rye murmured against his neck.

Charlie blinked.

"Did you think of me later?" Rye's breath was hot against his ear and Charlie swallowed hard.

"Yeah."

"When?"

Charlie's heart beat faster and he knew Rye could feel it against his own chest. He couldn't get any words out.

"Did you touch yourself thinking about me?" Rye purred.

Charlie slid his hand up Rye's spine until his fingers rested at his nape, fingertips in his hair.

"Yeah."

"What did you think about?"

Charlie felt Rye's cock get hard against his hip.

"About, um. The way you looked when I pulled your hair."

"Mmm."

"And how you were so…free."

"Charlie." Rye stroked his cheek. "Can I touch you?"

"I— Yeah."

"Only if you want. Only what you want. I swear. Do you want me to?"

Charlie squeezed his eyes shut. He wanted it *so* much. He was scared of everything it could bring into his life—a flash-light beam exposing a hole that the darkness had concealed for years—but, goddamn, he wanted it anyway.

"Yeah, I want you to."

And once he'd said it, like magic, it wasn't quite so scary anymore.

Rye kissed his cheek, then the corner of his mouth. Then he nuzzled into the crook of Charlie's neck and just breathed there while he traced patterns over Charlie's chest.

"Just relax, okay? We can stop anytime you want."

Charlie nodded, but kept a tight hold on Rye.

Rye stroked down his ribs to the hem of his shirt, fingertips just resting on his skin.

"This okay?"

He nudged Charlie's shirt. Charlie nodded and he slid his hand underneath. He ran light fingertips over Charlie's stomach and Charlie gasped. Rye pressed a kiss to his neck. A finger dipped into his navel, then traced a path up to his nipple. His breath caught. Rye's fingers left a trail of fire and Charlie squirmed beneath his touch.

"You're so hot," Rye murmured, pressing another kiss under his ear. "Okay?"

Charlie nodded.

Rye touched him like there was nothing he'd rather do in the entire world than touch him. By the time he slid down Charlie's body a little and stroked Charlie's thigh, Charlie was aching.

"Want me to take these off?" Rye asked.

Charlie gulped, but he didn't feel scared; he felt...cared for.

"Okay."

Then Rye's face was in front of his, Rye's eyes gentle.

"You sure?"

Charlie tried to smile but he felt very serious. He nodded.

Rye kissed him, slow and sweet, then unbuttoned Charlie's jeans and pulled the zipper down over his erection. Charlie shimmied out of his pants. Rye kissed his collarbone, then settled against his side again. When he slid a hand to Charlie's inner thigh, Charlie gasped.

"Okay?" Rye murmured.

Charlie nodded.

No one had ever touched him there. He'd never really touched himself there. It was so sensitive he shivered.

Rye caressed the insides of his thighs, and Charlie squeezed his eyes shut to escape into the sensation.

"You're so gorgeous, Charlie," Rye murmured.

Charlie was so hard his erection threatened the bounds of

his underwear, and he was leaking into the thin fabric. Every stroke of Rye's fingers on his inner thighs crept closer to his aching flesh and each time Rye didn't touch him there his arousal ratcheted higher.

"Charlie, can I touch your cock?" Rye purred.

"Please," Charlie heard himself say brokenly.

Rye cupped Charlie between his legs and Charlie jolted, hips snapping forward, seeking contact. Rye moaned and fondled him through his underwear. Charlie threw an arm over his eyes because all he could bear to concentrate on was the way Rye was making him feel.

Rye stroked his cock through his underwear and squeezed his balls gently. Then he traced a finger along the line of Charlie's underwear in the crook of his thigh.

"You can, um…" Charlie tried.

"Want them off?" Rye asked, and Charlie nodded, arm still covering his eyes.

He expected to feel Rye's hand on his crotch, but instead he felt it on his cheek.

"Hey, look at me for a sec."

Charlie moved his arm. Rye's cheeks were flushed the way they had been in the woodshop, his eyes shining.

"Feeling okay?"

Charlie nodded. Rye studied his face for a moment, then leaned in and kissed him deeply. Then he moved his mouth to Charlie's ear and murmured, "I want to stroke your cock until you can't stand it anymore, and then I want to watch you lose it all over my hand. Then I wanna rub off on your hot-as-fuck thigh because these things are like tree trunks and it's sexy as hell."

A bolt of lust tore through Charlie and he made a choked sound.

"Do you want that?"

"Yes," Charlie said instantly.

"You sure?" Rye's voice was teasing now.

"Yes."

"What's the magic word?"

"Um." Charlie's brain was lust fogged. "Abracadabra?"

Rye snorted.

"The magic word is *please*, Charlie. Ask me. Say please."

White hot lust bubbled through Charlie's guts.

"Please, Rye. Please touch me."

"Touch you where?" Rye's voice was just breath.

"Touch me…touch my…my dick."

"Mmm," Rye said, and with a nip to his earlobe, he went back to Charlie's underwear, stripping them down and tossing them on the floor. Charlie groaned as his erection sprang free and kissed his stomach.

He kept his eyes open just long enough to see Rye's graceful fingers close around his length, then he let himself fall into darkness.

Rye stroked him soft and quick, hard and slow, and everything in between. Even Charlie had never spent as much time exploring his cock as Rye did. When he started running a finger around the tip, Charlie couldn't take it anymore. He was panting and sweating and his breath felt shallow.

"Please, Rye," he begged.

"Please what?" Rye murmured, all attention on Charlie's body.

"Please l-let me come."

Rye made a soft sound of satisfaction and went back to stroking Charlie's inner thighs. Charlie groaned and he didn't even have to open his eyes to see the wolfish expression that would no doubt be on Rye's face.

"There's so much to see if you like," Rye mused. Charlie truly hadn't expected this level of patience from him. "What would you think about me on my knees, sucking this gorgeous cock while you pulled my hair?"

The picture flashed through Charlie's mind like something out of a dream.

"Oh, god."

"I could spread you out on your bed and finger you until you're ready for me to fuck you."

Charlie heard a whimper. It was him.

"I could bend over in your huge shower and you could fuck me under the hot water."

Charlie groaned.

"Ooh, I could spread my legs and teach you exactly how I like to have my cock sucked. I wouldn't let you stop until you were an expert. Yeah, I like that idea."

"Rye," Charlie begged. "Rye, please."

"Good use of the magic word. Which? Which of those did you like the sound of?"

"I don't know," Charlie slurred.

"Yeah? Mmm."

Rye trailed a finger over Charlie's balls and up his aching erection to slide in the liquid there and Charlie gasped. Rye fisted his cock and began to stroke, hard and slow. It was like every touch Rye had scattered along his skin coalesced into a deep, throbbing ache, and now that Rye was touching him like this Charlie felt like he'd die if it stopped.

Rye shifted so he was pressed tighter to Charlie's side and started a slow grind against Charlie's hip. The denim felt rough against his bare skin, a flick of discomfort that stoked the fire between his legs.

"So fucking hot," Rye murmured.

His hand on Charlie was sweet torture and Charlie felt his orgasm building like a tidal wave. He tried to press harder into Rye's hand, and Rye moaned as Charlie's hip ground even harder against Rye's cock.

Finally, Charlie couldn't take any more. He was hot all over and his skin felt like it could hardly contain him.

"Please, please, please," he heard himself chant, and Rye moaned, his breathing getting heavier.

Charlie thought if he didn't come right the fuck now he

might die. He did the only thing he could think of. He slid a hand into Rye's hair and yanked.

"Oh, *fuck!*"

Rye's hand sped up on his cock and Charlie groaned. He gathered Rye's hair into his fist and pulled slowly, feeling Rye's rolling grind stutter and become more desperate.

There was a finger at the sensitive tip of his aching cock that sent sparks all through him, then Rye was jerking him hard and fast.

Charlie's orgasm barreled through him like a freight train, flattening every thought in his head to *Oh, god, Oh, god, Oh, holy fucking god*, as he came his brains out in Rye's hand.

The pleasure pulsed out of him, shattering the world behind his closed eyes to a supernova of light and bowing his body in ecstatic relief.

"Jesus Christ," he groaned, still shaking from the pleasure.

He'd let go of Rye's hair when he came, and now he grabbed it again, tugging sharply. Rye's hand tightened on his spent cock like he'd forgotten he still held it, and he thrust against Charlie's hip, moaning.

For the second time, Charlie saw Rye freeze for a moment and then go wild against him. He threw his head back as he came and Charlie gave his hair another long tug.

Rye was fully clothed while Charlie was naked except for his rucked-up shirt, but Rye still managed to look vulnerable in his pleasure. His cheeks and throat were red and he was writhing against Charlie, trying to wring one last moment of pleasure from his body.

With a final groan, Rye collapsed against him, still cupping Charlie's cock in his hand.

They lay together that way for a minute, as their breaths slowed. Then Rye kissed Charlie's shoulder and shifted so he could look at him.

"Are you okay?" It was probably the dozenth time he'd said it but this time he sounded tender, concerned.

Charlie cupped his face and drew him down for a kiss.

"I'm good," he said.

And he really, really was.

Chapter Sixteen

Rye

Marmot was laughing at Rye. She'd been laughing at him for the last week. He could tell.

"Stop laughing at me," he muttered.

Marmot cocked her head.

"Shut up."

But he couldn't muster much fire behind it because she was right—something was wrong with him.

He was all…*mushy.*

He scowled at himself in the mirror, but it was still there in his eyes. Mush.

Ever since the night Jack and Simon had come to dinner and Charlie had let Rye bring him to orgasm on the couch, Rye had felt this little place inside him soften.

When he saw Charlie doing something as mundane as pouring coffee, he remembered the way his breath had caught when Rye pinched his nipples. When he glanced over to see Charlie's muscles flexing as he lifted something down from a shelf, he remembered how those muscles had trembled when Rye stroked his inner thighs. When Charlie chuckled at something a customer said in the store, Rye thought of the wrenched sound he made when he came—like every inch of his body was experiencing this overwhelming pleasure.

Then there were the looks Charlie had been giving Rye.

Part shy, part dirty, and wholly distracting, he didn't think Charlie was even aware he was giving them, but every time Charlie hit him with one the soft place inside got a little gooier. And other parts of him got harder.

Rye had certainly lusted after people before. He'd even done the dance of the forbidden with people before, where the sexual tension between them became so charged that when it finally snapped it burned with intensity.

But none of it had anything on the soft, tender feeling he had whenever he saw Charlie.

And Rye wasn't sure he liked it.

He glared at himself in the mirror.

"Mush," he hissed.

Marmot hissed in sympathy.

On Saturday they made their way over to the Crow Lane house to continue construction. Jack and Simon were meeting them there, as were Vanessa and Rachel.

As they got out of the truck, Charlie handed him a thermos.

"Coffee," he said.

"Oh, thanks."

Charlie gave him one of those looks, paired with a shy smile, and Rye felt a treacherous mushiness threatening. He scowled at it, and Charlie's smile faltered. Oops.

He huffed and tugged Charlie's sleeve.

"C'mere."

Charlie blinked, eyes narrowed against the sun. He had wrinkles in the corners of his eyes when he squinted like that. Rye touched them with one finger. Then he pulled Charlie down so he could reach his mouth and kissed him.

He'd meant it to be a soft kiss of apology—balm to soothe the inadvertent hurt he'd caused—but when his lips touched Charlie's, Charlie's arms came around him and lifted him off the ground. Charlie kissed him with barely restrained passion and his arms were like iron, holding Rye tight.

Were they twirling around like some *Sound of Music* number or was Rye's head spinning?

When his feet hit the ground again he grabbed Charlie's arm to steady himself. That…wasn't supposed to happen from a kiss. Maybe he was just dizzy because he hadn't eaten breakfast yet? Yeah, he'd go with that.

But when Charlie slung an arm around his shoulder and pulled him tight to his body as they walked toward the house, the soft spot inside Rye grew larger still. Was he *rotting* like fruit? This was terrible. Terrible.

But Charlie's arm felt so damn good around him. Warm and strong and just so…present. Like Rye could lean into him and be held forever. And, really, how terrible could it be if Rye couldn't stop grinning. He pressed his face into Charlie's shoulder to hide the grin.

Jack's truck came around the curve of the road and Charlie's arm tightened around him like he thought Rye might try and shrug it off.

Jack and Simon were in the middle of a conversation and not paying much attention to their surroundings and for just a moment, Rye got to see a very different Simon than he'd seen before. Simon elbowed Jack and made a face at him, then smiled brightly, teasing him.

When Simon looked up and saw Rye and Charlie, he closed up like a crocus in the morning, shoulders hunching slightly and chin tipping down. Still, Simon greeted them warmly. It was only the contrast of a moment before that let Rye know this wasn't his always state.

Marie came next, sketching a good morning salute, then Bob with more tools and a boom box already playing honky-tonk. Vanessa and Rachel piled out of their car, looking sleepy and chugging coffees. Vanessa glared at the boom box and Bob tipped his hat to her.

Rye thanked everyone enthusiastically for showing up to help and promised them all the pizza they could eat. Charlie set them up with jobs.

They jacked up the house to replace the posts, then reframed the front door. Charlie set Jack and Rachel to work with Bob on the roof.

"Hey," Charlie said. "Let's talk layout."

"Huh?"

"Of the house. The next step will be framing in the interior walls, so we should walk around and talk about where you want the rooms to be."

"Oh."

Rye trailed after Charlie.

"Ordinarily we would've talked about it sooner, but given the limited budget we needed to keep the exterior walls since they were in okay shape." Charlie had already told Rye this. Rye nodded. "So, do you want to keep the bedroom upstairs?"

"Uh. Okay?"

"It's more private that way," Charlie said.

As if the fact that the house was in the middle of nowhere didn't make all of it private enough. As if he'd ever had privacy before in his life.

"Sure, sounds fine."

"Good. Since we're keeping costs down by not moving the plumbing or electric, that makes the most sense. Same with leaving the kitchen where it is."

"Why're you even asking me, then?" Rye grumbled.

"Well, it *is* your house," Charlie said, with a playful shoulder bump.

They stared at each other for a moment, and Rye felt suddenly awkward.

His house. Which meant his bedroom. Which meant him...living in this house. By himself. Waking up in a bed in that bedroom. Cooking dinner for himself in that kitchen. In Wyoming. Alone.

The treacherous soft spot in his stomach caved into a pit.

"I don't, uh... I'm gonna..."

Rye walked out the front door and toward the trees, sucking in fresh air. They were pine trees, but not the same pine trees he was used to from Seattle.

At the tree line, Charlie caught him by the shoulder.

"Hey! Are you all right? What's up?"

"I've never had my own place before," Rye said. "Not even a studio apartment. I'm used to living with a bunch of other people in a space we can't change. I don't... I don't even know what I'd *do* with a whole house."

"I think you'll find your life expands to fill the space you have."

"Is that what happened to you?" Rye asked.

"Sure," Charlie said. But somehow Rye didn't quite believe him.

The next day they left the construction to Bob and Marie and several of Marie's friends who'd volunteered to help, and Charlie drove them to an architectural salvage store two towns over.

"Seeing some options might give you a better idea of what you want the house to be," Charlie said. "I know it's hard to make it up out of nothing, especially if you never considered what you might want your house to look like."

Rye goggled at the enormous space broken into sections by type of merchandise. Kitchen cabinets in a Tetris against the left-hand wall, sinks and toilets of all shapes and sizes creating a maze to get to shelves packed with light fixtures. Bathtubs bloomed like upside-down mushrooms in the back right corner and steel girders held myriad pieces of wood, from molding to flooring. The entire middle of the space was long tables crammed with crates of doorknobs, drawer pulls, brackets, hinges, faucets, and every other decorative piece of hardware imaginable.

"Wow," Rye breathed.

Charlie, usually so practical and down-to-earth, was looking around them like he had stumbled upon a dragon's treasure trove.

"Heya, Charlie," a man called from the open barn doors in the back of the space.

"Hey, Lloyd."

"What can I find ya?"

"Just looking around for now. This is my friend Rye." Charlie put a hand on Rye's shoulder. "We're fixing up Granger Janssen's old place. Rye's his grandson."

Lloyd's bushy gray eyebrows rose over blueberry eyes and he nodded.

"Nice to meet you, son. Anything you boys need, just holler."

He tipped his hat.

"So, what do we do?"

"Thought we could just walk around first, see if anything jumps out at you."

Before Rye could say anything ridiculous, like, "boo," Charlie took his hand and led him over to the cabinets.

He was pointing at them saying words like *Shaker* and *modern* and Rye wasn't registering a single one because Charlie's hand was warm and rough in his. He squeezed Charlie's hand and Charlie squeezed his back, talking all the while.

"Sorry, what?" Rye said, when Charlie looked at him expectantly.

Charlie's brow furrowed and Rye cringed sheepishly.

"I got distracted by you holding my hand," Rye grumbled.

Charlie's eyes widened and a silly, delighted smile played at the corners of his mouth.

"Thought *I* was the one who'd never been in a relationship before?" he teased.

"Are we? In a relationship?"

"Well I…" Charlie began, then bit his lip. "I guess we never said that, no. I apologize."

He ran the hand not holding Rye's through his hair in a nervous gesture.

"Do you want to be?" Rye asked. And he realized that this was what all the mushiness had been leading up to. He didn't just want Charlie, he *wanted* Charlie for his own.

Charlie ran his hand over the lip of a cabinet, a casual assessment. Then he turned to Rye and ducked his head.

"Yes."

He said it like it was an admission, not a desire. Like it was a *finally*, not a *now*. And the soft, mushy place inside Rye grew softer and mushier still.

On Tuesday, Rye got off work at noon. Unsure what to do with himself, he picked up Marmot and drove over to the Crow Lane house with the intention of trying to figure out what the hell he wanted it to look like.

When he opened the door, the kids he'd met before were there and they had been joined by a fourth. Rye raised a hand in greeting.

"Hey," Greasy Hair Kid said.

They didn't seem surprised to see him. But when they caught sight of Marmot, they were all smiles.

They started playing with her, leading her on chases through the empty downstairs.

"So, uh, what are your actual names?" Rye stopped himself before he added *So I don't keep calling you Greasy Hair Kid, Bandana Kid, and Flannel Jacket Kid in my head.*

"Why, you gonna report us?" the new kid said, hands on her hips.

"Uh. No. Report you to who?"

"The cops."

"Well you're not doing anything illegal. I said you could hang out."

His actual words had been more like *Just don't burn the house down*, but whatever.

The kids exchanged looks.

"You don't have to tell me your real names. Just something so I can stop calling you Greasy Hair Kid and Bandana Kid and Flannel Jacket Kid in my head."

Oops. Slipped out.

Flannel Jacket Kid snickered. "Greasy Hair Kid," she repeated.

Greasy Hair Kid pouted. "I have above-average oil production," he protested.

"I don't *always* wear a bandana," Bandana Kid grumbled.

"This is what I was trying to avoid," Rye said.

"I'm Tracy," Flannel Jacket Kid said. "That's Nate." She pointed at Greasy Hair Kid. "That's River." She indicated Bandana Kid. "And she's Biscuit." The new kid.

Rye tried very hard not to laugh at Biscuit, who hadn't given any indication that she possessed a sense of humor about anything, much less herself.

"Nice to meet you," he choked out. "I'm Rye."

"I know," Biscuit sniffed.

Of course the others would've told her about him.

"That's Marmot," Rye added, as Marmot galloped back to him, holding something in her mouth, and dropped it at his feet.

Her offering turned out to be a bone. Before he could chide her for acting like a dog, River said, "That's a rabbit bone."

"How do you know that?" Rye asked.

"Oh, they know everything about animals and bones," Tracy said.

"My dad hunts," River said, like that explained it. And

maybe it did. Rye didn't know enough about hunting to evaluate.

River crouched on the ground and held out their knuckles to Marmot. Marmot sniffed regally, then bumped her little face against their fist.

"She's a sweetheart," River said, which made Rye conclude that they were either an optimist or delusional.

"She's got her moments," he allowed.

"Wish I could have a cat," Nate said. "Or a dog."

"Me too," said Tracy.

"Our dogs are evil," River bemoaned.

"If we had pets my mom would try and make them be in beauty pageants," Biscuit muttered bitterly.

"Biscuit and her sister have crushed their mom's dreams of them landing a pageant reality TV show," Tracy confided.

Rye wondered if Biscuit's sister's name was Butter or Honey.

"Well, we can stay for a bit if you wanna play with her," Rye told the kids. "But be chill about it. If she knows you wanna play she won't do it. Cuz, you know, cats."

For the next hour, Nate, Tracy, River, and Biscuit swung between fervently appealing to Marmot and pretending she didn't exist. If this was their idea of being chill about things, Rye was concerned for them.

In the down moments, they chatted, and Rye sat half turned away from them, scrolling on his phone and pretending he wasn't listening to every word.

What he took away from his eavesdropping was as follows:

Tracy had a girlfriend named Betsy whom her parents assumed was a friend because they lacked any creativity and which she allowed them to continue assuming because they would never let her leave the house again if they knew.

Nate wanted to do creature effects for the movies someday, and spent much of his spare time watching horror and fantasy films, trying to dissect how they did everything.

River's older brother, Adam, had gotten out of Garnet Run some years ago and River missed him horribly. They also worried about him because of something Rye couldn't divine from their conversation, but which the other kids clearly knew about. River hated their father and was scared of their mother and spent as little time as possible at home. They didn't say much, except about cats, so Rye learned this from things the others said about them.

Biscuit wanted to move to New York and be a Broadway star. Or maybe an astronaut. Possibly a famous chef. Clearly, she didn't know what she wanted, except to be far, far away from Garnet Run, and to do something extraordinary.

Rye felt a combination of amusement, sympathy, and tenderness for them all.

"We're gonna be working on the house this weekend, so you'll have to scram," he warned them.

"Sure."

"Where do you hang out if you can't hang out here?"

They shrugged and looked forlorn.

"We go to the diner a lot," Tracy said. "And usually the parking lot at school's empty on the weekends."

"There's the movie theater in Buckston," Nate added.

"Usually we just hang out in the woods if it's not too cold, though," said River.

"Sorry," Rye said.

He'd had a whole city to tramp around when he needed to escape his parents—which had been always. But it would've been nice to have a place like this. Free, safe, private.

They shrugged and Marmot jumped on River's shoulder.

They didn't startle but put up a hand to support her.

"Wow, she really likes you," Rye said. "She usually only does that to me."

And now to Charlie.

River smiled for the first time. A warm, pleased smile.

They all promised they wouldn't be here over the weekend and Rye was almost sorry when it was time for him to go.

Chapter Seventeen

Charlie

Marmot and Jane lay in a heap on Charlie's bed when he got out of the shower. Marmot was angry at Rye because Rye had insisted on thoroughly searching her for ticks the previous evening she'd run straight into the woods and come back covered in dust and bits of fern.

"He just did what's best for you," Charlie informed Marmot. Marmot yawned, unmoved.

Rye had been napping when Charlie got home from work. Rye was, it turned out, a joyous and dedicated napper, while Charlie only ever slept during the day when he was ill, disliking the groggy sensation that accompanied waking at any time other than morning.

Now Rye wandered into the room, bleary-eyed and rumpled and thoroughly adorable.

"Traitor," he muttered to Marmot and reached out to pet between her ears. She allowed it.

Seemingly unbalanced by sleep, he leaned a little into Charlie, and Charlie's heart soared. It happened every time Rye touched him. This affected him even more, though, because the casualness of it spoke of an assumption of intimacy which answered a call that came from Charlie's very depths.

Charlie ran his fingers through Rye's hair, combing out

the ever-present tangles and Rye dropped his head against Charlie's shoulder.

In moments like this, Charlie could almost imagine that he and Rye had been together for years; considered one another's bodies their own, to lean on as they wished.

When the pizza came, they settled in on the couch. The cats followed them one by one, wanting to sit on their laps at the exact moment they were trying to get pizza and seeming uninterested in them once they'd sat back, laps free.

Instead of *Secaucus Psychic*, Charlie turned on *Make it Home*, a new home renovation show he'd been wanting to check out.

Rye'd been so overwhelmed at his house the other day that Charlie thought maybe it would help him to see what happened during a home renovation.

The designer and the carpenter on the show were putting an addition on the house of a family with a teenage daughter who had recently been hospitalized long-term. They wanted to make her a space where she could enjoy privacy as well as be comfortable in bed for long stretches.

"This designer is pretty hot," Rye said. Charlie agreed, but he couldn't deny the pang of jealousy that shot through him too.

What, you think that once someone touches you they'll never find another human being attractive ever again?

"Jeez, the carpenter's even hotter," Rye said. "Is *everyone* on this show hot? No wonder you like it."

"I've never even seen it before."

"You could totally have your own show," Rye mused a few minutes later, when the designer and the carpenter were discussing the challenges of the space and bouncing ideas off each other about how to bring the girl's love of French architecture into play in the family's Rhode Island home. "Only you could be the designer and the carpenter."

"Nah," Charlie said. But he was flattered.

"Sure you could. You designed this place, didn't you?"

"Yeah. But this place was just for me."

Rye shot him a look from where he was splayed over the couch.

"Not all for you," he said.

Charlie froze.

No one knew. No one knew that Charlie had picked out things that were neutral enough that he hoped they would appeal to someone who might someday live here. Because what if he'd painted the living room green and they hated green? Sure, he could always repaint, but what if that paint color—or the drawer pulls, or the molding—was the thing that stood between that person seeing themselves at home here and not?

He'd made his bathroom exactly what he wanted and felt great about it for one week, until this had occurred to him. Tile wasn't so easy to change. But he decided he wouldn't make the same mistake with the rest of the house. He wouldn't give that person any reason not to stay with him.

It was cringeworthy, but once the thought had invaded his mind, no amount of visualizing windshield wipers had managed to clear it. This, he could control. This, he could manage. He couldn't know who they might be or what they might like—hell, he didn't even *really* believe they would ever come along—but he could make sure that nothing he chose was particular enough to push them away.

"What do you mean?" Charlie asked, keeping his voice completely neutral.

"You must've picked a lot of this stuff cuz you thought it'd help you sell the house," Rye said. "It's all so, what's the word? Neutral. It's not really like you. Except the bathroom. But that makes stuff easier to sell, right?"

Charlie swallowed his relief and cleared his throat.

"Right," he choked out.

★ ★ ★

"Bro. I know you're into him because I saw you together," Jack said, rolling his eyes.

He'd come into the store on the pretense of buying a new axe head, but obviously just wanted to grill Charlie about Rye. He'd tried texting Charlie about it but Charlie hadn't responded. He was too worried that he'd leave his phone lying out and Rye would see a text come through from Jack talking about it.

"Simon agrees with me," Jack continued. "He says Rye has that whole feral cat being slowly domesticated at the hands of a patient human thing going on."

Charlie couldn't help but smile at that description. Simon's powers of observation were nothing if not specific.

"Maybe. And much like a feral cat, when he decides it's time, he'll go back to the wild," Charlie said.

"I knew it."

"Jack. Do *not* say anything to Rye."

"I wouldn't do that," Jack said, looking affronted.

He fiddled with the stapler on the desk Charlie had set up in what was once their father's closet. It felt cramped with just Charlie in it. With both of them there was hardly room to move.

"I didn't… I didn't know you liked guys," Jack said.

Charlie shrugged.

"Why didn't you ever tell me?"

"Never told you I liked girls, but apparently you still thought I did."

Jack shook his head.

"Actually, I thought you were probably ace. Since you never mentioned being attracted to anyone."

Charlie was struck by an overwhelming wave of gratitude for his brother.

"So?" Jack prompted.

"So, what?"

"So, why didn't you tell me?"

"I don't know," Charlie told him. It seemed impossible to convey to Jack the cocktail of panic and desperation that had accompanied everything in those years after their parents died, and it wouldn't do any good to make him feel like part of what caused it.

"It's not something I was keeping from you," Charlie said. "I wasn't in that mode, in my head. I mean... I didn't...like anyone."

"Until now," Jack said.

Charlie slumped in his too-small chair and Jack clapped him on the shoulder.

"I'm really happy for you."

"Don't be. He's not gonna stick around."

"You don't think so?"

Charlie shook his head and forced himself to say his greatest fear out loud, because sometimes just saying it out loud took some of the sting out of it.

"I think he'll sell the house once we're done and get out of here. Probably go back to Seattle."

He stared at the wall but he could feel Jack's eyes on him. It didn't take any of the sting out of it after all.

"Hmm," Jack said. "I'm not so sure."

Jack stood, fiddling with the stapler on Charlie's desk.

"Listen," he said finally. "About what Rye said at dinner. The meatloaf thing. I'm really sorry."

Charlie waved it away but Jack caught his hand.

"Seriously. I've been thinking about it ever since dinner, and he was right. Why *didn't* I help cook? I was thirteen. That's plenty old enough. But I let you do all that shit for me. I let you...be a parent. It felt good, I guess. That even though Mom and Dad were gone, I still got to have that. I'm sorry I was so selfish."

Charlie's stomach lurched and he stood and put his hands on Jack's shoulders.

"No. You were a kid. And that's what I wanted—for you to still feel like you had someone taking care of you."

"I always knew you made sacrifices, Charlie. And I've appreciated them so much. I know how hard you worked to help me pay for school, and so many other things. But I didn't *think* about it. It's like… I don't know, like you did it so automatically and so instantly after they were gone that it never seemed like a choice. It was just the new way things were. We never talked about it. It…"

He bit his lip and Charlie was horrified to hear a catch in his voice that meant Jack was going to cry.

"It was so *unfair*, C. I didn't… Why… Why didn't I *help* you? Why didn't you *ask* for my help? You know I would have, right?"

Jack grabbed his arm and searched his face.

"I know."

"Then why? I don't understand. Did you think I couldn't help?"

"No. Course not, I just… I wanted you to be a kid. You shouldn't've had to do any of that shit."

He knew what Jack was going to say. That Charlie shouldn't've had to do it either. So he spoke before Jack could.

"Listen, even if I'd gone to UW, I was never gonna go pro. I would've wanted to come back here and work with Dad at the store. But you—"

"Are you saying you—you—you just *gave up* on having a future and decided I got to have one instead?"

Jack's eyes blazed with anger.

Charlie tried to figure out how to phrase it another way, but he must've stayed silent a beat too long because Jack's expression turned from anger to horror. Then his eyes filled with tears.

"You got the offer, didn't you? They asked you to play and you turned it down."

In an instant Charlie was back in Coach Tybee's office

at the end of March, six weeks after their parents died, the trifold papers lying on the desk between them. The poster yelling *THERE IS NO I IN TEAM* at him from above Coach's chair.

The assistant coach from UW had spoken with Charlie at the beginning of the season, had come to several games and a practice. He'd made a verbal offer, but Charlie had known that wasn't a guarantee.

He and his parents were invited down to Laramie in November to see a game, tour the campus, meet with coaches and players, but the snows had come early that year and after rescheduling twice Charlie accepted that a visit wasn't in the cards.

He'd been disappointed but he'd been to games there before and been on campus. So he just kept his head down, kept working hard, and waited.

When his parents died, the calendar he'd kept such a close eye on for months of recruiting came unstuck, fluttering into a jumble of days and weeks that fell unnoticed around him.

By the time he got into Coach Tybee's office in March he felt like a different person than the one who'd shaken Assistant Coach Brown's hand and smiled to himself as he pictured Saturday mornings in a Laramie autumn.

He'd pushed signing until the absolute last moment he could, hoping. But come the end of April he knew. Accepting the offer meant Jack either went to Florida with their grandmother or went into foster care. That he'd either have to sell the store or close it. Sell the house or rent it out.

If he played football for the University of Wyoming, his and Jack's life and their parents' legacy in Garnet Run were over.

He had told Jack the offer never came.

"I made a choice," Charlie said. "I chose to stay here instead of—"

"Charlie!" Jack's voice shook. "I can't believe you did that without telling me. Without *talking* to me, even!"

"And what would you have said? 'Sure, Charlie, go to college. I'll move to Florida with Grandma and not see you again for years'?"

Jack gaped. "I—"

"You would've hated Florida. You barely tolerated Grandma. I couldn't have helped you pay for school if I wasn't working. You would've ended up hundreds of thousands of dollars in debt at graduation with no place to live afterward, because I would've had to sell the cabin." He shook his head. "No. There was no way."

Tears were streaming unchecked down Jack's face. Jack was looking at him with a kind of helplessness Charlie hadn't seen in a long time. He slumped against the door frame and closed his eyes.

"I can't believe you." His voice was barely there. "I can't believe you never told me you could've had your dream. You fucking gave it up for me and you didn't even *ask* if I wanted you to."

Charlie pulled him into a hug and Jack squeezed him so tight it almost hurt.

"I didn't want that, Charlie," he said.

"I know," Charlie said. "That's why I never told you."

Then Charlie held him while he cried.

Saturday morning, Charlie came into the kitchen to find Rye sleepily stirring eggs in a pan on the stove, Marmot perched on his shoulder. He was a vision—all tangled hair and low-slung sweatpants and bare feet.

Charlie and Jane had had their morning nose bump in his room and she had curled back up on his pillow, her favorite place to sleep when he wasn't home.

"Morning," Charlie said, putting a hand out for Marmot to bump.

"Mmf," Rye said.

Charlie took advantage of his sleepiness and moved in behind him, snaking his arms around Rye's stomach while being careful not to dislodge Marmot. He kissed the top of Rye's messy head and pretended that he would get to do this every morning.

Pretended that Rye wasn't going to head back to Seattle after the house was done. That he wasn't going to be another memory Charlie took out and looked at like a faded photograph on sad days.

"Mmfmf," Rye said, and leaned back into Charlie with a little wiggle.

"Given any more thought to the layout of the downstairs?" Charlie asked. "Or do you want to leave it as it was?"

Rye didn't say anything for a while. He turned the heat off under the eggs and picked up two forks from the counter. He offered one fork to Charlie and held out the pan of eggs.

He seemed to intend for them to stand there and eat them out of the pan. Charlie reached over him and took two plates out of the cabinet. Much as he'd enjoy sharing a plate, he didn't trust sleepy Rye with a hot pan and a cat at the same time.

He dished up the eggs, put the pan in the sink, and drew Rye to the kitchen table. Marmot absconded for territories unknown and Rye stared at his eggs confusedly for a moment as if he couldn't quite track how they got from the pan to a plate.

Charlie had learned that it didn't pay to try and drag answers out of Rye. He liked to think things through in his own time and tended to be snappish when rushed. So Charlie ate his eggs and watched Rye poke and scowl at his own.

"Can we leave the downstairs open?" he said finally.

"Sure," Charlie said.

He wasn't sure what Rye was thinking about so hard, or

what his plans were, but he sketched plans on scrap paper while Rye ate his eggs in silence.

That night, after they'd showered off the day's work and were once again watching *Make it Home*, Rye slumped to Charlie's shoulder. He nuzzled into him and lifted Charlie's arm, draping it around himself. Charlie pulled him close, encouraging him to rest his head on Charlie's chest.

"One more?"

"Mmm-hmm."

Charlie pushed play on the next episode but hardly noticed what the renovation was, so distracted was he by the feel of Rye in his arms. He had molded himself to Charlie's side like a cat and his breathing was deep and even. He smelled warm and familiar.

Charlie rubbed the ends of Rye's hair between his fingers. It was usually messy, but Rye had combed it after his shower and though it would be mussed by tomorrow morning, now it was smooth and soft and Charlie could run his fingers through the silky strands easily.

Rye nestled closer when he did it and Charlie moved from the long strands to Rye's scalp, massaging gently with the pads of his fingers until Rye was liquid against him, practically purring.

Curious, Charlie moved from the pads of his fingers to the tips, lightly scratching Rye's scalp. Rye made a happy sound. He continued scratching for a while, letting Rye relax further, then slowly—so slowly—he gathered a handful of hair and pulled. Not a yank or a tug, but a gentle pressure.

At first Rye didn't seem to notice the change. He seemed as relaxed as before. Charlie pulled just the tiniest bit harder and Rye pressed his cheek into Charlie's chest.

Charlie gathered Rye's hair in his fist and tugged just a little harder and this time, Rye made a small whimpering sound, buried his face in Charlie's chest, and curled his arm around Charlie's leg.

"More," he said softly.

Charlie pulled his hair more. Still gentle, but definitive. Rye kissed his chest.

"Can we go to bed?" Rye asked, looking up at Charlie with big, liquid eyes.

"Tired?" Charlie said.

"Not anymore."

They walked hand in hand to Charlie's bedroom without discussion and when they got inside Rye wrapped his arms around Charlie's neck and pulled him into a kiss. Rye, who was often clumsy and awkward with tools or dishes, was grace personified when they kissed, when they touched, like it was his natural state and everything else was unfamiliar.

"Why does it turn you on?" Charlie asked. "When I..." He tugged on Rye's hair and Rye fisted his shirt.

"I don't know. Just does. Charlie."

Rye pushed him down on the bed. He climbed astride Charlie's hips, his eyes heavy lidded and his cheeks flushed.

"Charlie. I want you."

He said it like it was an invocation.

"What do you want from me?"

Charlie meant it like *I'll gladly give you anything* but Rye frowned and put a hand on his chest.

"Not *from* you. With you."

Charlie's heart pounded and he closed his eyes, but Rye already knew. Rye already knew he didn't know what he was doing. Rye already knew he couldn't expect him to take charge here, and it was okay.

Charlie opened his eyes.

"Tell me what you want?"

Rye licked his lips.

"I want... Would you want to maybe...be inside me?"

Desire rocked Charlie. He knew that wasn't the language

Rye would usually use. He *knew* it was for him. To make him comfortable. And it made him want Rye more.

"Okay."

"If you don't like it, we'll stop. Okay?"

"Or if you don't like it."

Rye almost rolled his eyes and Charlie saw the moment he stopped himself because he realized Charlie was serious.

"Okay."

Charlie's thoughts were all over the place. *I don't know what to do. I don't know how to be helpless in front of you. This isn't how I'm supposed to feel.* His heart was pounding so fast it felt like a fluttering creature escaping through his ribs. Rye put his hand over it.

"You're scared?"

Charlie nodded miserably.

Rye lay down on top of him.

"Of what?"

He hugged Rye to him tight.

"I guess because…"

He shook his head. He couldn't physically get the words out. It had only happened to him once before: when he'd had to tell Jack their parents were dead.

Because if I'm bad at it you won't stay with me. Because if I don't like it you won't stay with me. Then I'll be alone again, but even more alone because now I know what it feels like to be with you.

"Charlie? You know that not liking sex is okay, don't you?"

"I know that."

But it's not okay for me.

"And you know that penetrative sex is just one kind of sex, don't you? Lots of people aren't interested in it. And that's okay too."

Charlie nodded. He knew all this, intellectually. He had heard of the internet. But none of that knowledge made a bit of difference when the truth was that he was falling for

a man who liked sex—and clearly liked penetrative sex—
and wanted to have it with him and he just...didn't know.

"Do you want to try? See what you think? Or no?"

Charlie's head was spinning even though he was lying
down. What he wanted was to already know these things
about himself. To have spent years exploring and experiment-
ing the way Rye had so that these were givens; no big deal.

Rye's hand was still resting on his chest over his heart.

"Stay there, okay? Don't move. I'll be right back."

Charlie closed his eyes. He couldn't bear to watch Rye
leave.

Rye's warmth disappeared and Charlie was shivering. He
climbed under the covers and pulled his pillow over his head.

The bed dipped and he felt Rye's hand on his back. He
also felt the familiar feeling of Jane making biscuits. Rye had
brought Jane to him. He opened his eyes.

Rye's eyes were gentle. "Can I get in with you?"

Charlie nodded and Rye insinuated himself beneath the
covers while taking pains not to dislodge Jane. He was holding a pad of paper and a pen that he put on the bedside table.

Charlie turned onto his back and Jane curled up on his
chest.

"C'mere."

Rye snaked an arm around Charlie's stomach and arranged
them in a cuddle. Marmot yipped from down the hall and
Rye scratched the blanket in a sound that usually attracted
her. Within seconds she popped up onto the bed and curled
between Rye's legs.

Jane's rattling purrs and Marmot's tiny ones slowly relaxed Charlie.

"What's the paper for?"

"Can I sleep here with you tonight?" Rye asked. "Just
sleep."

"Yeah. Course."

"Then we'll talk about it in the morning. Okay?"

The morning. But… Everything was processing strangely slowly.

"So we're not going to…"

Rye shook his head and made an abortive gesture that looked like he was trying to turn the light switch across the room off with magic.

Charlie moved to get up but Rye stopped him.

"I got it."

"But I haven't brushed my teeth."

"I think you'll live just this once."

Charlie let his head fall back down on the pillow.

"I don't want to have bad breath." *If you kiss me*, he left unsaid.

Rye seemed utterly unconcerned.

"Everyone has bad breath in the morning, even if they brush their teeth. It's like a universal truth of bacteria. Go to sleep."

He crawled to the end of the bed, put one foot on the floor, and reached as far as he could, just nicking the edge of the light switch with his outstretched finger.

"Hot lava?"

"Huh?"

"Never mind."

He and Jack had played the game as children, jumping from bed to dresser to couch to TV console without touching the floor until, inevitably, one of them broke something and their parents yelled at them to stop.

"Charlie?"

"Hmm."

"Can I kiss you good-night?"

Charlie groaned and pulled Rye to him, dislodging both Jane and a disgruntled Marmot, who stood for a moment, waiting for the annoying humans beneath the covers to stop moving. Then, when Charlie and Rye were cuddled up holding each other, they settled into the empty space behind Rye.

Rye put his head on Charlie's shoulder and squeezed him tight and a lassitude like nothing he'd ever known spread through Charlie.

"Okay?" Rye murmured.

"It's perfect."

Chapter Eighteen

Charlie

In the thin light of dawn, Charlie Matheson woke up gasping.

For the first time in his life, arms tightened around him and a sleepy voice mumbled, "Ymkay?"

Rye.

Rye was warm and pliant and splayed half on top of him with his head tucked beneath Charlie's chin.

Charlie took a deep breath that smelled like Rye.

"Yeah."

Rye curled into him and fell right back asleep.

Charlie lay awake and thought.

He stroked Rye's back and felt the steady snuffle of his breath and thought about his life.

Usually he avoided thinking—especially about his life. Usually he acted. He filled his days with *doing*, and sometimes with worrying, but worrying was great because you could worry about *anything* and still not really think about it.

He had something with Rye. Something rough and new, but *something* nonetheless, and he didn't want to lose it. He didn't want to lose it because Rye left, but if that happened, it was Rye's choice. What was his choice was losing it because *he* was too scared to talk to Rye, too scared to be vulnerable.

He had to be braver. Try harder.

"I will be," he whispered.

"Hmm?"

Rye rearranged himself so he was completely on top of Charlie and buried his face in Charlie's neck, reminding Charlie so much of Marmot that he chuckled.

Rye grumbled a vague inquiry against Charlie's neck.

"I didn't know you were so cuddly," Charlie murmured, pressing down on Rye's back to keep him in place for the inevitable retraction of his cuddliness the second it was noted.

Sure enough, Rye went to move, muttering, "Mmnotcuddly."

"Stay." Charlie closed his arms around him. "I like it."

Rye grumbled, but stayed on top of Charlie.

"Mysquishingyou?"

"No."

Rye relaxed and Charlie went back to stroking his hair.

"There was one guy," he said so softly that no one whose ear wasn't an inch from his lips could have heard. "On the football team with me in high school. He was beautiful and we kissed, fooled around. Um, you know, jerked each other off."

Rye's breathing was deep and even, but he wasn't asleep.

"He moved the week before my parents died. He's the only person I've ever, you know. For a long time after they died, I didn't think about sex. I didn't think about anything. I don't know if it's normal or not, but I just... Everything that I didn't *have* to do to keep things going overwhelmed me."

"Fuck normal," Rye said. "It's not a real thing."

Charlie hadn't known it was possible to mutter aggressively into someone's shoulder, but Rye had certainly managed it.

"And when I would feel...that way, I just... I thought of him and that made me think of them dying and it got all... mixed up together."

Rye stroked the back of his neck.

"I feel like I missed it. The period of brave experimentation when people learn who they are."

And I'll never get it back.

Rye unburied his face.

"Baby, your parents died. You were totally traumatized. Of course you weren't playing spin the bottle in the college common room. Or whatever people do in college."

Charlie forced air into his lungs and made the words come out.

"I'm not quite sure why I'm so scared to have sex with you. I'm not sure why I can't tell whether I want to or not."

Rye squeezed him.

"It kinda sounds like you're cut off from your body. Like, you were turned on watching me come in the woodshop. You were turned on when I was touching you the way I wanted to on the couch. But both those times it wasn't—like, you weren't actively participating. You were kinda...being an instrument of my pleasure the first time. Then you were doing exactly what I told you the second time."

Charlie nodded.

"But that's all really different than us having sex where we're both physically connected at the same time, getting off at the same time. There's timing and expectation that we want compatible things at the same moment. It's a lot. Especially if you don't know what to expect."

Charlie's heart was pounding, but not from nerves. This... this made sense.

"Yeah, I...yeah."

"'S why I brought that notepad in," Rye said. "I was gonna kinda make a list of stuff that turned you on and stuff that didn't and see if you wanted to try some of it."

"And you're not...disappointed? I mean, you don't think I'm...?"

Charlie clamped his mouth shut on the torrent of remonstrances that accompanied these thoughts whenever they slipped in. Self-accusations that something was wrong with him; that he wasn't living up to an ideal he'd internalized.

Rye lifted his head up so he could look at Charlie.

"It seems like you've got some shame around what you think you're supposed to do and be, as a, like, strapping construction man, or whatever, and it's making you veer into pretty judgmental territory. Not wanting to have penetrative sex doesn't mean there's anything wrong with you."

His expression was serious, his tone severe.

"Masculinity isn't tied to, like, jackhammer cock drilling people or whatever."

The phrase startled a laugh out of Charlie.

"Jackhammer cock drilling?"

Rye huffed.

"You know what I mean. There are trans men and ace men and men who only like to get fucked and men who like it gentle, and people who are into pegging, and a million other things. I get that you've maybe only seen, like, porn where jacked cis dudes fuck each other, but that's only one way to have sex."

"I know that," Charlie muttered.

But he was embarrassed to realize that that *was* what he'd thought Rye might want from him. After all, he was big and muscular and generally powerful. So it stood to reason that Rye would look at him and…

He stopped himself again. No. Not *reason*. Stereotype.

"Maybe you think you know," Rye said. "But your fears clearly don't know."

"No," Charlie admitted. "You're right. I kinda did think that's what was…expected of me, I guess."

"Well, expectations are bullshit. Fuck expectations."

Charlie stroked Rye's hair. *Fuck expectations.* He could get behind that.

"So do you wanna make that list?"

Rye sat up.

"Yeah?"

Charlie nodded. It was harder when Rye was looking at him.

Fuck expectations.

"Can you, um, not look at me, though? While we…"

Rye grabbed the notebook and pen off the bedside table, then settled down on his side, facing away from Charlie.

"Okay," Rye said. "You can go with a Yes-No-Maybe, or a 1–10 interest level scale, or just general thoughts. Whatever."

"Are these all gonna be things you like?"

"No."

"Why?"

"Because!" Rye said. "The whole point is figuring out what *you* might like. Fuck expectations, remember?"

Charlie let himself pout just a little, since Rye couldn't see him.

"Fine."

Rye snorted and reached back to pat his leg.

"Okay. Me sucking your dick."

Charlie swallowed hard.

"I don't know."

"Don't answer so fast. Just think for a minute. Imagine me between your legs. Imagine me licking you, sucking you. Picture it. See how it makes you feel."

Charlie imagined Rye looking up at him, those extraordinary eyes locked on him. Seeing everything.

"I…maybe…maybe too much."

"Okay. What if you were blindfolded?"

Charlie gulped.

"What if I was blindfolded."

He could imagine it. Reaching down to stroke Rye's hair, touch the place where Rye's mouth opened around him, without being observed.

"I… Yeah, that's better."

"Okay. You fingering my ass."

That sent a pulse of interest to Charlie's cock.

"I think, yeah."

"You fucking my ass with your cock."

So close together, so intimate, so scary.

"I'm not sure."

"Be honest, baby."

"I'm... I... I don't think I want to."

"Okay. You fucking my ass with a dildo until I come."

Charlie was instantly hard.

"Yes," he said without hesitation, heart thudding.

"Okay. Me fucking your ass with my cock."

Scary scary scary scary.

"N-no I don't think so."

"Okay. Me, blindfolded, fingering your ass."

Charlie tried to picture it. He'd never touched himself there. Never really considered it. But it didn't scare him. Not if Rye couldn't see what it did to him.

"Maybe."

"Okay. Me, blindfolded, fucking your ass with a dildo."

"M-maybe."

"Okay. Kissing for an hour."

Charlie's heart fluttered.

"Yes. Definitely yes."

"Okay. Taking a shower together, naked."

"Yeah, okay."

"Okay. Kissing and touching each other in the shower."

"Yeah that's okay."

"Okay. Touching ourselves at the same time."

Charlie imagined Rye watching him jerk off and felt the same recoiling.

"C-can I just watch you?"

"Okay. Me, blindfolded, and us getting off sitting next to each other."

"Yeah, okay."

"Okay. Can I look at you now?"

Charlie started. "Is that...all?"

"It's not a comprehensive list of every sex act possible, no. But I think it's a good start. Is there something else you want me to ask about?"

Charlie blanked.

"No, I... No."

"Can I turn around?"

"Yeah."

Rye rolled over to face him. His cheeks were a little flushed but he looked serious.

"So," Rye said.

"So," Charlie answered, looking anywhere but at Rye.

But he couldn't escape hearing what he had to say.

"You don't like the idea of someone seeing you experience pleasure."

Charlie examined the blanket closely.

"I guess not."

"But you like to watch other people experience pleasure."

"You."

"What?"

"I like to watch *you*."

Rye paused, then nodded.

"Okay," he said softly.

He kissed Charlie's shoulder. Then he turned his back again.

"Okay, me spanking you."

Charlie choked.

"What?"

"Me, spanking you."

"I...why would you...how did you get to...what?"

"Picture it, Charlie. You, with your bare ass up, and me, spanking you."

The image fell into Charlie's head. His first instinct was to dismiss it. But something about it...

"I don't get it," was all he could make himself say.

"Okay," Rye said, and turned back around.

Charlie frowned.

"Why did you ask me about that?"

"Because I wondered about it."

"What'd you wonder?"

"Some people love being spanked. And more."

"I know that. I just…why did you think about it for *me*?"

"You don't want to be seen while you receive pleasure. I wondered how you'd feel about it while receiving pain."

"Oh. Do you…like that?"

Charlie's head was spinning.

"This isn't about me."

"Well, can it be? Or am I the only one who has to answer embarrassing questions?"

"I didn't mean for them to be embarrassing. I was trying to be neutral."

"You were," Charlie grudgingly admitted. "It's not you, I know."

"You can ask me all those same questions and more if you want. I'll tell you whatever you'd like to know."

Charlie wanted to take a shower. Alone.

"Maybe later."

"Okay," Rye said.

Charlie couldn't stop thinking about it.

Spanking.

And he didn't understand why. But over and over for the next two days, he kept coming back to it.

He went to the store, he worked on the Crow Lane house, he cooked dinner, he ate dinner that Rye cooked, they watched TV. And he couldn't stop picturing it.

Last night, he dreamt that Rye spanked him with a 2x4 they were using to frame in a wall. It was utterly unrealistic, Rye wielding it like a baseball bat, but still Charlie woke sweating with the feeling like he had a secret.

He was distracted all day, and when he saw Rye holding an actual 2x4 for a customer, he turned on his heel and shut himself in the office.

He couldn't even tell if it was that he *liked* the idea or he was just hung up on it.

What is wrong with me?

Rye's voice instantly answered, *Nothing's wrong with you. Normal doesn't exist. Fuck expectations.*

When Charlie got home from work, he didn't even greet the cats as he usually did, just tore through the house until he found Rye sweeping up wood shavings in the woodshop.

"What did you do to me?" Charlie accused.

"Um. Huh? When?"

Charlie's breathing was shallow and his heart pounded.

"When you…you said all those things! You said…"

He ran a hand through his hair, desperate not to say the word.

Rye narrowed his eyes and leaned the broom against the lathe. He approached Charlie slowly and put his hands on Charlie's shoulders. Charlie looked at the floor and Rye let him.

"Is this about spanking?"

Charlie's head jerked up.

"How did you know?"

Rye shrugged one shoulder.

"Just did." Charlie was vibrating with energy. Anger? Fear? He couldn't quite tell. "C'mere."

Rye towed him out of the woodshop and into his bedroom. He pushed Charlie to sit on the edge of the bed, then sat on the other side, facing away.

"Tell me what you're thinking."

Charlie dropped his face in his hands.

"I don't *know*."

"Okay. Tell me how you're feeling."

"Mad," Charlie snarled.

"How come?"

"Because you made me think about this shit that I don't understand, and I—I—don't know why I can't stop thinking about it."

Rye was quiet for a while, like he was waiting for more, but there *wasn't* any more. Charlie didn't know anything more.

"Sometimes we want stuff and we don't know why we want it," Rye said matter-of-factly. "Isn't it okay to just want something?"

"I *don't* want it."

"Okay. Isn't it okay to just be intrigued by something and not know why?"

"No," Charlie snapped. Instantly he was embarrassed, because obviously that wasn't true.

"Okay," Rye laughed. "Who knew you were such a grump when you're the slightest bit out of your element. I'll have to ask Simon if Jack is this way," he mused.

"What? Ask Simon?"

"Oh, we text now. Anyway. Charlie. You're thinking about something that struck some kind of chord with you. That's fine. What's your angst?"

Charlie slumped.

"I don't know."

But he did know.

"I shouldn't be interested in that. Why would I be? And I know what you're gonna say. There *is* no shouldn't be. But we can't all be from Seattle, okay?"

Rye snorted.

"Okay, sure, yes, you know, Seattle: den of universal spanking."

He giggled. Then arms came around Charlie's shoulders from behind.

"Your angst is adorable and totally unnecessary," he said. "You want to try spanking? I'll gladly spank the fuck out of you. Or ya know, just a little spank you. You wanna never talk about it again, no problem. You're the only one who has a problem. So maybe, like...deal with it. I'm gonna go make dinner."

He kissed Charlie's ear, squeezed his shoulder, and was gone.

The next day, Charlie woke up exhausted. He hadn't felt this way in a while—overwhelmed by the fact of his own life.

Rye found him in the living room after dinner, staring at the wall.

"Was I too harsh yesterday?" he asked softly. "I've been trying to be... I dunno. Like, casual about this because it's all fine. But I didn't mean to be like 'deal with it' and then leave."

Charlie sighed. "You weren't harsh."

In fact, it had been a surprise for him to find out how generally nonharsh Rye was, given some of their early encounters. Once Charlie had realized that Rye told the truth even when it would be more socially acceptable to offer empty niceties, he had no longer thought of him as harsh.

"What's up, then?"

Charlie let his head drop against the back of the couch and closed his eyes.

"If I can't stop thinking about it then it must mean something, right?"

"Probably."

"It must mean I want...that?"

"Not necessarily."

"Why would I want that?" he asked quietly.

This was the heart of things. Charlie didn't randomly fixate on things he cared nothing about. He wasn't someone who obsessively tracked down an etymology or historical oddity just because. Jack did that. Simon did that. Charlie didn't do that. If he was spending days ruminating on getting spanked, it was obviously because he wanted to get spanked. He just didn't understand why.

Rye sighed.

"It doesn't matter, baby."

"It matters to me."

"Okay," Rye said, curling up in the corner of the couch. "Well, it feels good. So there's that. For some people it kinda acts as a…what do you call it? Like a release valve? You're upset or sad or whatever and you can't quite tap into those feelings about that thing cuz it's hard, so then when someone spanks you, you can cry about that instead and it's a relief. Some people are into lots of different kinds of impact play, spanking included. Ummm…"

Rye stared up at the ceiling, like he was reading from a list.

"Oh, right, then there's people who were spanked as kids and linked it to sexual development. What else, uh? Some people like being forced to accept punishment or pain because it proves to themselves they're strong… There's lots of reasons."

Charlie blinked.

"What?" Rye said.

Charlie shook his head.

"I guess I wasn't expecting there to be a real answer."

Rye shrugged.

"Real? Whatever. People have all different reasons, including no reason at all. Whatever's useful to you."

"Fuck useful," Charlie muttered, because it seemed as useful a thing to say as any.

Rye snorted.

"That's the spirit."

The next thing Charlie knew, Rye was in his lap, hands on his face.

"I'm sorry," he said. "I didn't mean to weird you out.

You're doing all this shit to help me and I'm like 'Hey, never thought about sex, cool, wanna get spanked?'" He shook his head. "Maybe we should just hit pause on the sex stuff."

Charlie laughed.

"I like you so much," he heard himself say.

Rye's startled eyes shot to his.

"You do?"

"I really do."

He leaned their foreheads together.

"I...me too," Rye said, and Charlie could *feel* his forehead wrinkle as he scowled.

"Rye?"

"Hmm."

"Would you..."

Charlie cringed around words he couldn't speak and Rye's lips found his.

"You want me to spank you, baby?" Rye purred.

And impossibly, inexplicably, Charlie nodded.

Wordlessly, Rye stood and offered Charlie his hand, not looking at him. He led Charlie into the bedroom Rye had been occupying these last weeks. It was smaller and darker, shaded by a large blue spruce on the side of the house. With the sun setting, the room was cloaked in shadow and Rye didn't turn on the light.

He led Charlie to the bed and slowly, dreamily, helped him out of his clothes. He took off his own shirt but left his sweatpants—which were actually Charlie's sweatpants—on, and sat on the bed, back to the wall.

"Lie down on your stomach, here."

Charlie laid himself down.

"Close your eyes."

Charlie closed his eyes.

"I'll stop whenever you want," Rye said.

Charlie nodded, and tried to relax for the conversation that was about to come.

But what came wasn't words. It was a firm *thwack* to the meatiest part of his right ass cheek.

Charlie jumped in shock. Then Rye's hand rested on the small of his back.

"You okay?"

Charlie felt ridiculous. What the hell was he doing? What the hell was he asking Rye to do?

A sound came out of him that he'd thought would be embarrassed laughter but it wasn't. It was some kind of hybrid of a groan and a whimper and Charlie buried his face in his arms. He should tell Rye to stop. He should tell him this was absurd and mortifying and that he didn't have to do it. He should tell Rye that he was a grown-up and was perfectly capable of…of…

What?

The second hit was a quick stinging slap that sent prickles through his skin. It, too, was followed by a calming hand on his back.

"Nod if you're okay," Rye said softly, and Charlie found himself nodding.

He was in a dark cave and his flashlight couldn't illuminate far enough for him to know what he was entering into. He wanted to take one more step so he could see farther.

Rye spanked him.

Rye was *spanking* him.

What the fuck?

He hadn't done anything wrong! Spanking was a punishment. It was what happened when you messed up, when you broke a rule, when you didn't do what you were supposed to. But Charlie hadn't messed up. He never broke rules. He had always done what he was supposed to because he'd never had any other choice!

He'd never had the option to break rules or do things wrong because if he had, they would've lost the house, the business would've gone under, Jack would've starved or failed out of school or—or—or—just things! Terrible things!

So why? Why was he being spanked when he'd followed every single fucking rule for his whole damned life?

"Why?"

The word was ripped from him by the unfairness of Rye's hand.

"Why what, baby?"

But Charlie couldn't answer.

Why? Why? Whywhywhywhywhy?

"Charlie?"

Rye shifted and put an arm around his waist and it was only then that he realized he was saying the word out loud, over and over, and that Rye had turned on a lamp, was searching his face.

Charlie turned over, the burn on his ass barely registering, and threw his arm over his eyes.

"Charlie?"

"Why did I waste my life?"

Chapter Nineteen

Rye

Rye held Charlie as he cried. He was glad Charlie was finally crying. He was afraid Charlie might never stop crying. He was afraid that when Charlie did stop crying, he'd be embarrassed and push Rye away. People did that sometimes. Rye certainly had.

But although Charlie's weeping was raw and heaving, he was graceful in the aftermath.

"Jesus Christ," he said, and scrubbed hands over his face. "Guess that didn't turn out quite how you imagined?"

He pressed his face to Rye's neck. The opposite of pulling away.

In fact, it wasn't so far off from what Rye had imagined. Yeah, okay, he'd kinda imagined jerking him off afterward, but who cared what he imagined. Reality was so much better.

Because Charlie Matheson wasn't a Boy Scout. He wasn't Mr. Perfect. And he wasn't a goody-goody. Charlie Matheson was an adult who'd never gotten to be a child, and Charlie Matheson was finally mad about it.

Good.

"It turned out exactly how I wanted," Rye said.

Charlie snorted.

Rye'd never had much luck with offering people comfort.

He'd never felt he had much to offer, period. But here, now, holding Charlie in his arms as he fell apart, Rye had felt like he was exactly where he should be—where he *needed* to be.

Rye pressed them tightly together and tucked the blanket around them, cocooning them in the same atmosphere. He pressed kisses to Charlie's cheeks and the bridge of his nose. He pressed a kiss to the corner of his eye.

"I'm a bad boyfriend," he told Charlie in a rush. "Ask anyone. I've never been good. But I… I don't know. I could try. If you…if…if you wanted."

Rye scowled harder than he'd ever scowled at himself in the mostly dark. *Mush, mush, mush!*

Charlie cupped the back of his head.

"I cry like a baby and tell you I've wasted my life and *that's* what makes you wanna be my boyfriend? Your standards need work, Janssen."

But his voice was soft and rough, and his fingers on the back of Rye's head were so tender. He brought Rye's hand to his lips and kissed his fingertips.

"I disagree that you've wasted your life. And I can think of a couple of people who'd agree with me," Rye murmured. He pressed kisses to Charlie's cheekbones and his beard. "I thought maybe…we could start nonwasting them together. If you wanted. What's the opposite of waste? Conserve? That's not what I meant."

"Build." Charlie said it with such certainty that Rye felt the word like a lift in his stomach. "Build our lives together?"

His lips were a whisper against Rye's ear that made him shiver.

Rye reached for him and twined his arms around his neck. When they kissed it felt like sealing a deal.

A promise written in breath.

They kissed until the air between them was hot and they were pressed together everywhere. Rye ran a hand down

Charlie's muscular back and cupped his glorious ass, pulling him closer.

Charlie gasped at the touch. Rye had forgotten about his spanked-hot skin. But Charlie was hard against him, so Rye scratched lightly over the plump of his ass with his fingernails. Charlie groaned.

"Does it feel good?"

"I...yeah."

Rye squeezed again and Charlie shuddered.

Rye reached over and turned off the lamp, plunging them into darkness.

"You feel so good," he told Charlie softly, rolling his hips as he scratched across Charlie's other ass cheek. He felt rather than heard Charlie's gasp.

"So do you," Charlie murmured. "Kiss me?"

Rye kissed him and kissed him and kissed him. They moved without purpose, hands roaming for the sheer pleasure of learning one another.

Rye kissed along Charlie's neck to his ear and bit his earlobe. Charlie gasped and his cock throbbed against Rye's stomach. Without thinking, Rye gave Charlie's ass a swat from beneath the covers. There wasn't much power behind it, but when his palm connected, Charlie let out a sound Rye had never heard from him before. A desperate, needy sound that made Rye want to give him anything he wanted. Anything at all.

Charlie's breathing was heavy. Rye spanked him again. Again, that sound. And this time, Charlie slung his leg over Rye's hip, cocks grinding together. He tipped his head back like he couldn't get enough breath.

Rye pinched one of Charlie's nipples and Charlie writhed. Rye squeezed his nipple at the same time as he spanked Charlie again and Charlie started to shake.

"Rye," he gasped.

"Yeah," Rye whispered, but Charlie didn't say anything except Rye's name again and again.

Rye swallowed his own name on Charlie's tongue, kissing him deeply. He ground their hips together, and groaned at the feel of Charlie's erection against his own. Feeling him like this—needy and open and *there*—was intoxicating.

"This okay?" Rye asked.

"Mmf, yesss."

"Feel so good," Rye murmured again. "Just tell me if—"

Charlie shut him up with another kiss, deep and searching.

"Okay, but just tell me if there's anything you—"

"Don't make me think about it, just keep going."

Charlie kissed him fiercely and Rye obliged. He'd give Charlie whatever he needed.

Rye pushed the blanked down and hiked Charlie's thigh higher, exposing him. His palm landed hard on the meat of Charlie's ass, fingers catching his crack. Charlie let out a shuddering gasp and clutched Rye tighter to him. When Rye ran his fingernails over the tender skin he'd just spanked, Charlie hissed and bit at his jaw.

Rye ran a finger between Charlie's cheeks and over the tender skin of his hole. Charlie's breath caught and Rye went back to spanking him. He'd spank his ass two or three times, then run a gentle finger over his hole. After a few minutes of this, Charlie had his face buried in Rye's neck and was clutching Rye like a stuffed animal. It was fucking adorable. It was searingly hot.

Rye had first had sex at fourteen and he'd never been with someone who hadn't had a lot of sex. But seeing Charlie experience sex for the first time—even as fraught as it was for him—was something Rye would never forget.

He'd never thought of sex as anything but physical pleasure, or sometimes, with certain people, as an expression of intimacy. The depth of Charlie's feeling was moving. It was…humbling. It said: *I am letting you affect me. I am letting*

*you into the parts of me that I have never shared with anyone—
not even myself.*

"Charlie," Rye whispered, and kissed him, wanting to
give some of Charlie's beauty back to him.

They fed each other's breath and spit and heat and merged
closer and closer. With a cracking spank, Charlie whimpered
and thrust against Rye, and heat exploded between them.
Charlie's orgasm was a choked-off yell and a full body shudder as his hips stuttered.

He was breathing so hard that Rye wondered if he was
crying again, but when he cupped his face his cheeks were
dry. Charlie was looking at him in the darkness even though
they couldn't quite see each other.

When Charlie reached for him, Rye thought he'd once
more be held like a favored stuffed animal or a particularly
tolerant cat, so Charlie's tug on his hair shocked him. He'd
forgotten about himself or his own pleasure—forgotten he
even had a body in his concentration on Charlie's.

Now he blasted back into his own skin and felt how hard
he was, how heavy and aching. Charlie tugged his hair again
and Rye let himself feel all of it. In his head he chanted Charlie's name to the beat of his heart. *Char-lie, Char-lie, Char-lie.*

His heart pounded and his breath came faster and faster
as he lost himself. All it took was one more sharp tug on his
hair and grind of his hard cock against Charlie's muscular
thigh, and Rye tipped over the edge, his aching cock exploding as he dissolved into a starburst of pleasure.

They breathed in silence for what seemed like forever and
only a heartbeat and then Charlie breathed, "Wow."

It was heartfelt and worshipful and lovely, and Rye dissolved into giggles.

Charlie pulled back.

"No, no, sorry, I didn't mean to laugh," Rye laughed.

Charlie snorted and scritched Rye's scalp.

After a minute, Rye said, "Wanna take a shower?"

Charlie hesitated. Rye tried very hard not to feel hurt. He had seen firsthand how difficult all this was for Charlie.

"Doesn't have to be together."

Charlie pulled away.

"I'm sorry I didn't..."

He shook his head.

"Hmm?"

"I didn't... I didn't touch you."

"My dick? I don't care." He'd shot for casual but thought he might've hit dismissive when Charlie recoiled. *Fuck.* "I just mean—what I meant was that was great. It was perfect. You were hot as fuck and I loved every minute of it."

Rye wished so badly that he could see Charlie's face, but he didn't want to startle him by turning the light on.

"Do you promise?"

Charlie wasn't one for casual promises. When Charlie said *promise*, it was blood and bone and pain.

Rye fumbled for Charlie's hand and squeezed it.

"I swear."

"Okay. Good."

There were a hundred questions Rye wanted to ask about how it was for Charlie, but it obviously wasn't the moment. Meanwhile, he had Charlie's come all over his stomach and his own come in his underwear, and soon he was going to be pretty uncomfortable.

"I'm gonna take a shower," Rye said. He kissed Charlie softly on the mouth and left him in bed.

The hot water poured over Rye's shoulders and wet his hair, and he closed his eyes and breathed. The oozy, mushy place in his stomach had expanded to the size of a lake that threatened to swallow him. He was all mush now. Made of ooze, that was Rye Janssen. Ooze for Charlie Matheson.

He was in the middle of picturing himself as a bay when the bathroom door opened.

Charlie raised an eyebrow and Rye opened the glass door for him.

He wanted to search every inch of Charlie's face for the answers to questions he hadn't asked, but Charlie looked a little shy and was blinking against the light.

"Hi," he said.

"Hey."

Rye pulled him under the spray and they drifted together, warm and slick. It was the first time they'd both been naked at the same time and Rye reminded himself that Charlie had given this a thumbs-up on his list. He squeezed soap onto the shower puff and traced Charlie's muscular form in suds.

Charlie hauled him in, catching him in a tight hug.

"Thank you," he whispered, only just audible above the water.

"Thank *you*," Rye said, letting his arms come around Charlie.

"What are you saying thank you for?" Charlie asked, and Rye caught himself before he could laugh again.

Instead he shot Charlie a look that might be a glare when it grew up, but was now just a look that said, *You make me say all the dorky, smushy stuff that's supposed to go unsaid.*

But wasn't that Charlie, through and through? No assumptions with Charlie. No vagaries. No empty, scripted exchanges. Even his *Can I help you with anything today?* at the store was heartfelt.

"For making me feel good. And…for trusting me I guess," Rye said. "I know it was hard for you and I… It means a lot to me."

Charlie stroked down his spine and gave him a squeeze.

"Well what did *you* mean, then?" Rye asked, frowning at the suds running down the drain.

"I…you know," Charlie said.

Rye was going to let him off the hook. But Charlie tipped Rye's chin up and looked him right in the eyes. Charlie's eyes were shadowed and puffy from crying and there was a pillow crease in his right cheek. He was the most gorgeous person Rye had ever seen.

"Tell me," Rye whispered.

"Thank you for wanting to be with me," Charlie said, proving that previously Rye had *not* been entirely composed of mush, because he got mushier. "Even if you are a bad boyfriend," he said, with a wry little smile. "I guess I'll take what I can get."

Rye glared at him.

"Asshole," he said. Then, "Wait, what?"

"I want to try," Charlie said.

Rye felt the smile spread wide, wider. A grin. He was standing naked in the shower, grinning like a fool.

Chapter Twenty

Rye

Over the next two weeks, Rye fully immersed himself in his new life as Charlie's boyfriend. And not just Charlie's boyfriend; Charlie's Boyfriend Who Builds Houses and Sources Materials from Salvage Yards and Estate Sales and Says Hi to People in Town and Once Even Brought Charlie Flowers.

Charlie's eyes had gone wide and he'd snatched Rye up bodily and spun him around with joy. Then he'd carefully trimmed each stem, arranged them in a vase, and would have kept them even after they were a rotten mess if Rye hadn't convinced him to throw them away by promising he would bring him more. The next day, Charlie had brought *him* flowers. Now it was kind of a thing.

Every day when they got home from work, they greeted the cats—who had taken to curling up together just inside the front door before they arrived. They took a little while apart to shower and change and unwind.

Then they met in the kitchen to cook together. Slowly, Rye was teaching Charlie to use seasonings other than salt and pepper and Charlie was teaching Rye how to use Tupperware. They cooked and they listened to music—well, Rye put on music and teased Charlie that he didn't know any of it.

When Charlie liked something Rye played, Rye would ask him what he liked about it and try to spin those qualities into recommendations for other bands Charlie might like. He'd created a Charlie Matheson playlist that he added to, song by song.

At dinner, Charlie went into what he jokingly called "date mode," and what Rye unjokingly called interrogation mode. This consisted of questions like, *What were you for Halloween when you were ten?* (A cowboy; a zombie golfer who eats golf balls); *What did you want to be when you grew up?* (A football player; a rock star); and *Which is scarier, deep sea or outer space?* (Outer space because space is terrifying; outer space because space is *fucking terrifying!*)

But, while Rye teased Charlie for his questions, he enjoyed talking to Charlie so much that his grumbling was mostly for show. That Charlie wanted to know things about his childhood birthday cakes and the weirdest place he'd ever been made him feel seen and valued. Like Charlie was building his only kind of playlist—The Greatest (and Also Not Great at All) Hits of Rye Gregory Janssen. (See, Charlie also knew his middle name, and he knew Charlie's was Wallace, which was his mother's family name.)

"Wait, wait," Rye laughed. "You got a fishhook lodged in your own back? You...*caught* yourself?"

Charlie laughed with him.

"Fucking hurt."

This had been Charlie's answer to *What was a time you hurt yourself in an embarrassing way?*

"Your turn," Charlie said.

"Oh, god, mine's real bad." Rye pushed his chair back and pulled one knee up. "So I was dating this woman, Suzanne, and she took me to some ridiculous... I don't know, like, themed outdoor brunch. And there were living statues dressed like, uh, statues. You know, togas and shit. And there was a big buffet where all the food was, so people were milling around on the lawn, eating their food."

Charlie'd raised his eyes at *togas* and they'd stayed raised.

"So, we got our food and coffee and some mimosas and Suzanne saw her friends who had organized the thing, so she heads over to them. And I'm following her, just trying not to drop my plate or spill all my shit."

"You are very clumsy when you're holding dishes," Charlie confirmed. He was looking at Rye so fondly that Rye felt utterly possessed—like Charlie knowing this about him made Rye belong to him.

"Seriously. Um, so, I'm looking at where I'm walking so I don't trip over anything. And I'm concentrating so hard on the not spilling anything part that I walk directly into...?"

"You didn't."

"Yeah. Right into a fucking human statue—which, *why*?—and we both go down in this cacophony of plates and cups and toga and elbows, and, jeez, this poor lady. My hot coffee spilled all over her and her hand landed on my spleen, I swear, and I had her gray body paint smeared all over me."

Charlie was laughing into his hand.

"So, but Suzanne didn't notice I wasn't still behind her, so she's talking to her friends, all 'Hey, guys, great event, I'd love you to meet my date,' and her friends are watching this happen behind her, like, 'Who's this utter train wreck of a person who full-body tackled a statue?' and Suzanne turns around to present me and..."

Charlie was laughing deep belly laughs.

"There I was, in a heap. But when I tried to get up and to help the statue get up I kind of, um, knelt on my plate and it shattered and cut me, so then I stagger to my feet and there's blood and mimosa and eggs all over everything."

"Stop," Charlie wheezed. "Stop." He collected himself. "You made that up, right?"

"No! Hand to god, I have a scar!"

"Show me."

Rye narrowed his eyes but Charlie sat, arms crossed, waiting. "Fine."

He pulled down his sweats and put his foot on Charlie's thick thigh.

"See?" He pointed to a fine web of scars on the outside of his right kneecap. "Wounded by brunch-time human statue."

"Wow. Did you get a second date, though?"

"That was the second date," Rye said. "But we didn't have a third."

"I'm terribly sorry about that," Charlie said, clearly not in the least bit sorry.

But when Rye went to pull his leg back, Charlie caught his calf in a warm hand and leaned down to place a soft kiss on Rye's knee.

Rye's cheeks warmed. With any other partner, Rye would've assumed it was the prelude to sex. Hell, he already had his pants down. But that wasn't Charlie.

Rye just waited. After a moment, Charlie pulled Rye onto his lap.

"I didn't know you had dated women as well," he said.

"I'm pan," Rye said.

Charlie nodded.

Was this going to be something that made Charlie feel his lack of experience even more acutely? But, no. Charlie said, "I guess technically I did too."

"You did?" Rye felt a flash of hurt that Charlie had lied to him about never dating anyone. Then he saw the humorous curve to Charlie's mouth. "Oh my god. Don't say it. I know what you're gonna say and you can't say it. Don't tell me you dated cheerleaders while you were on the football team because I simply can't deal with that level of *Friday Night Lights*-ness. Or whatever the Wyoming version of *Friday Night Lights* is."

"I don't know," Charlie said. "I never—"

"Yeah, yeah, you never saw *Friday Night Lights*, I know."

Charlie shrugged.

"Wow. I can't believe I didn't know about this," Rye said.

"I guess that decides our Halloween costumes. Also I have to text Simon immediately because, sheesh."

It was only because he was grinning directly into Charlie's face that he saw the flicker in his expression.

"What?"

"Oh. Well. Nothing," Charlie said, making it absolutely clear that the one thing it wasn't was nothing.

"Charlie."

Charlie ran a finger over the bridge of Rye's nose.

"Will you be here. For Halloween?"

Rye blinked. They hadn't talked about this since they'd become...what they were. Boyfriends or whatever. But every time he had a question about something in the Crow Lane house, Charlie talked about it like he assumed Rye would be there. Like it was Rye's house. So why was he questioning Rye's presence now?

"I... Yeah?"

Charlie bit his lip and nodded.

"Okay."

"Do you think I won't?"

Charlie shook his head.

"No, no. I... I just wanted to check."

But later, when Charlie pulled him close in bed as they fell asleep, his arms were tight around him like he feared Rye might disappear in the night.

Chapter Twenty-One

Charlie

Build a life together. That's what Rye had told Charlie he wanted to do. And that's what they were doing. On days when Rye was scheduled to work at the store, they drove in together. They cooked dinner together. They slept together, curled up under the covers of Charlie's big bed, Jane and Marmot staking out territory around their feet once they'd settled.

The more they talked, the more they had to say. The more they touched, the more they wanted to touch. The more time they spent together the more time they wanted to spend together.

And the plans. They couldn't stop talking about them. Rye would mention a book he liked, and Charlie would instantly want to read it to understand what Rye liked. Charlie would say he wanted to go to the Grand Canyon, and Rye would describe the road trip they could take there. One of them would see a food that appealed to them while watching a movie and they would plan to cook it together.

It was giddy, this planning of the things that made up a life.

But a life wasn't the only thing they were engaged in building. Crow Lane was progressing each weekend. It was no longer a house of horrors. It almost looked like a place someone could live.

And that was a huge problem.

Because it meant that soon Rye would leave. Charlie was no longer so concerned about him going back to Seattle—Garnet Run seemed to endear itself to him with every local restaurant and friendly shopkeeper. But he would leave. He would take his bag full of black band T-shirts and his cat and he would move into the Crow Lane house.

That was the plan, anyway. That had always been the plan.

The thought of not falling asleep next to Rye every night, not waking up beside him every morning, not stirring in the wee hours and reaching for him…it filled Charlie with a different kind of sadness than he'd ever felt. A delicate, maudlin sadness built of yearning for something that wasn't even gone yet.

"Hey, bro," Jack said with a goofy wink from under a pile of dogs. "Come here often?"

Here was Jack and Simon's house, where Charlie had come on his lunch break.

Simon waved from the couch and made a gesture toward Jack that indicated he was in silly, roll-around-with-the-dogs mode.

Jack and Charlie had had lunch together several times since their conversation at the store, and it had been good. They'd talked more. About their past, their present. About everything. Everything except Rye. Rye and Charlie's future.

Jack and Simon's cat, Mayonnaise, yawned hugely and stretched out a paw to Charlie as he settled on the couch beside Rye. Charlie scooped Mayonnaise up and lifted her onto his lap.

"Hey, kitten," Charlie said. He stroked between her ears.

"We still working on the house tomorrow?" Jack asked.

"Yeah, thanks. And Rye says thanks too."

"Sooooo," Jack drawled, eyebrow cocked expectantly.

"So?" Charlie said, looking between Jack and Simon.

"So what *about* Rye?" Jack asked impatiently.

"Rye's good."

Jack and Simon wore matching expressions of exasperation.

"Fine." He ran a hand through his hair. "Rye's..." *Amazing, perfect, dazzling, adorable, sexy, hilarious, beautiful.* "Rye's pretty great."

Simon leaned in, chin on his knees, as intent as a child at story time.

"Soooo, are you together, then?" Jack asked.

"Um. Yeah."

Jack let out a celebratory *whoop*, which scared several dogs and Mayonnaise, who tried to bound off Charlie's lap but failed when her claws stuck in his jeans.

"Shit, sorry, babies," Jack said.

"I'm really happy for you, Charlie," Simon said.

"We knew weeks ago," Jack said. "But still."

"Yeah, yeah."

Jack, having lost his companions on the floor, went into the kitchen and brought out sandwiches for lunch.

Charlie thanked him and smiled when he saw Jack had made him peanut butter and honey just the way Charlie used to make it: a thin layer of peanut butter on both slices of bread to seal them, then honey in the middle.

While Jack and Simon were distracted with their food, Charlie said, "I was thinking that maybe Rye should stay with me."

"Rye's already staying with you," Jack said through a mouth of peanut butter.

"Yeah, but. I was thinking maybe he should keep staying with me."

Simon raised an eyebrow.

"Is this a Penelope and the shroud situation?" he asked.

Charlie had no idea what that meant.

"Huh?"

"She said she'd remarry when she was done weaving a burial shroud, but every night she undid the work she'd done that day to put off ever having to choose a suitor."

Charlie blinked.

"He's saying do you want us to go dismantle the house bit by bit so Rye can't move in and has to keep staying with you until he falls in love with you and you both live happily ever after," Jack said, as if this were a totally reasonable request that they'd both be happy to execute under cover of night.

"Well, uh, I was more thinking I'd see if he wanted to rent the house out for a year. But I guess your idea has merit too."

He looked at Simon, searching his memory of tenth grade English class.

"Is that the one with the giant horse that had people living inside it?"

Simon smiled kindly. Simon was unfailingly kind.

"Yep, same story. Different plot line."

"Oh. Okay. Um, so, do you think I should ask Rye?"

Simon and Jack exchanged another look.

"That's a pretty intense way to start a relationship," Jack said. "But I guess you already started out that way, so..."

Jack shrugged and turned to Simon. Charlie forced his face to be neutral.

Simon smiled at them both. "Well, the Mathesons do seem to have kind of a thing about asking people to move in fast. Maybe it's genetic."

Charlie was going to do it. Who cared if it was faster than usual? *Fuck expectations*, as Rye would say. He knew what he wanted. He knew it because he finally felt like he was awake after years of sleepwalking.

He didn't want to keep making choices that were neutral,

preparing his life like a surgical field. He wanted to make choices *with* Rye. *For* both of them. He wanted all of it.

He felt reckless, impulsive.

After leaving Jack and Simon's, he stopped at the Crow Lane house to see what materials he'd need to bring the next day. He drove with the window down, and the midday chirps of swallows and the fluffy scuffles in the trees made him smile.

The smile faded when he emerged into the clearing from the trees and saw the people *in* the Crow Lane house.

These must be the squatters that Rye had seen evidence of when he first arrived. Dammit, he *knew* he should've put a front door on last weekend. There wasn't anything inside to steal yet, so he'd let it slide.

"Hey, folks," he said, raising a hand to say he came in peace. "This house is owned so I'm afraid you can't stay here."

When they stood, Charlie realized they were just kids. Maybe sixteen or seventeen.

"Shouldn't you all be in school?"

They exchanged eye rolls, and one of them gave him a withering look.

"We have permission," she said.

"Permission from who, miss?"

The girl snorted.

"From the owner."

"How do you know I'm not the owner?" Charlie said.

"Cuz we know him," another kid said. He had angry acne and drawn features. "Rye said we were cool to hang as long as we were careful and didn't die or burn the house down."

Charlie's heart started to pound, anger skittering through his veins. He wanted to dismiss the kids, but that sounded awfully like something Rye would say.

"You know Rye."

They nodded as one stubborn body.

"And *Rye* said you could hang out here."

Another collective nod.

Charlie pictured one of the kids tripping down the stairs, breaking a leg, or their neck. Their parents suing Rye. He pictured one of their candles falling over and setting the house aflame by accident, burning to the ground long before the fire department could do anything to save it. He imagined the bank loan defaulting to him when Rye was unable to pay it back, his father's store being claimed as collateral.

He tried to windshield wiper it away. But with each pass of his mental blades, a new potential disaster bloomed, and all of it added up to the same thing.

Everything he'd worked for, everything he'd built, everything he'd sacrificed for, gone in the capricious kiss of flame and wood. And all because the man he wanted to build a life with let it happen, with a shrug and a careless quip.

Fury struck like a snakebite.

Charlie stormed into his own house. He was shaking. "Rye! Rye, are you here?"

There was a thump, then the sound of Rye swearing, then he padded out of his bedroom, hair wet and wearing only Charlie's sweatpants, which he now considered his own.

"Hey, what's u—"

"How could you let those kids stay at the house?" Charlie thundered.

"How do you know about that?" Rye grumbled, crossing his arms defensively.

Charlie's heart was racing and he was vibrating with the effort it took not to scream.

"I know about that because I was just there. What is wrong with you? Do you have any idea what could happen? They could get hurt, they could burn the house down, they could...*anything* could happen!"

Rye glared.

"Nothing's gonna go wrong. They just need a place to hang for a little bit. Once it's finished they can't come in anymore, probably."

"*Probably*? They can't come in anymore, *period*. No more. Done. Do you not understand the stakes if something were to go wrong?"

"As you've said a zillion times, it's my house. Which means I get to decide what I do with it."

Rage and fear mixed like epoxy and spilled over.

"Yeah, it's *your* house so you're the one who will get sued. But *I* cosigned the loan! How could you be so careless? Do you even *get* what the potential disasters are? If one of those kids gets hurt on the property—your property—you're liable! One of them trips and breaks an ankle on a board outside and their parents could sue you. One of them smokes a cigarette and flicks it, the house goes up like a tinderbox and you have no recourse because you told the kids they could be there," Charlie roared.

"Their parents are not gonna sue me," Rye snapped. "Why do you think those kids need a place to escape to? Their parents don't give a shit about them."

Rye's naivete was unbelievable.

"You think just because those kids don't get along with their parents that your ass won't get sued if it means their parents can get someone else to pay thousands of dollars in medical costs? Grow up, Rye. You're leaving yourself wide open! And what happens to me if you lose the house, huh? I'm on the hook with the bank!"

Rye's eyes burned and his mouth trembled.

"I never asked you to help me! You're the one who rode in on your white fucking steed and told me I was doing everything wrong and you couldn't stand it. Which, come to think of it, is exactly what you're doing now."

"Well and if I hadn't, you still be sleeping in a rotting, falling down shack with your cat, eating nothing but granola

bars and getting tetanus from rolling over onto a rusty nail
in your sleep! Hey, the kids could live there with you, since
you've all got about the same amount of sense."

Rye's quicksilver eyes narrowed.

"Sense. Interesting. You think when people don't have any
other choices it means they've got no sense? That's good to
know. What's also good to know is that you'll move heaven
and earth and give up everything in your life to take care of
your own family, but you're not at all interested in taking
care of anyone else's."

Rye's eyes were so piercing that Charlie had to look away
from them.

Rye turned on his heel without another word and Charlie followed him to his room to see Rye pulling a shirt over
his head. He couldn't coax a single word out of his mouth.

Charlie looked around the room that had been Rye's for
the last two months. His few clothes were still in his duffel
bag next to the bed. There was nothing hanging in his closet.
Except for toothpaste, he hadn't bought a single thing since
he'd moved here as far as Charlie could tell. He'd borrowed
Charlie's sweats and shirts for pajamas, and he'd washed his
own same few garments over and over. He hadn't bought so
much as a pack of T-shirts.

Had he ever felt like this was his home? Had there ever
been a chance he might stay?

Charlie's guts were coiled in his throat, his tongue so dry
he couldn't have spoken even if he'd known what to say.

Rye stepped into his boots and walked past Charlie silently, careful not to touch him.

He shut the door behind him quietly, but it echoed
through the house as if he'd slammed it.

Chapter Twenty-Two

Rye

Rye drove and drove and drove. With every mile that he put between himself and Charlie the storm clouds in his stomach grew. So did the likelihood that his car would crap out and leave him stranded somewhere in rural Wyoming.

But it wasn't anger he felt; it was a snakier, sneakier, more uncomfortable feeling.

Disappointment. He was disappointed in Charlie.

Yeah, he'd known that Charlie wouldn't like him letting River, Tracy, Nate, and Biscuit use the Crow Lane house. That was why he hadn't told Charlie in the first place.

But over the last month, Charlie'd learned so much about himself. He'd faced demons that had been long buried, delved into his relationship with Jack, laid himself bare to Rye when it came to sex.

When he'd told Charlie about his own parents, Charlie had raged against them, and agreed with Rye about how lucky he'd been that he had friends who could give him the affection his parents never had.

Rye had thought he understood. How cruel people could be. How powerless it was possible to feel. What a relief it was to find ways to rebuild that power.

But was Charlie only sympathetic when it cost him nothing to be so? When there was no risk involved? Did he only care about the people he loved, and everyone else in need could go to hell? Rye didn't want to think it of him, but the pit in his stomach wouldn't let him dismiss the idea.

Rye pulled off the main road and turned off the car. It was mostly dark now and drizzling, a fine mist that delicately beaded his already damp hair like dew on a spider's web. It smelled clean and green out. How could rain through trees in Wyoming smell so different than rain through trees in Seattle? It was just one more reminder of how far Rye had moved from everything he once knew.

Rye sat in the car, in the dark, in the middle of a road no one drove down. The night critters were emerging and the day critters were bedding down; a brief, noisy overlap.

Rye had begun to think of Charlie as the person he might be able to have a life with. A life with joy and comfort, silliness and fun. Care. A life that was also about something bigger than themselves. But if he and Charlie didn't even agree that it was good for kids in need of a safe place to have one… what hope was there?

Rye sighed from the depths of his being, turned the car on, and started back toward Garnet Run; to the Crow Lane house. *His* house.

He shoved his book in his back pocket and used his phone's flashlight to guide him, and he went inside out of the rain.

Out of habit, he settled on the spot where he'd laid his sleeping bag when he first arrived, in the corner, facing the door. He wished Marmot were with him. If she were, she'd be sticking her nose out the front doorway and into the rain right now. She'd let the rain dampen her whiskers and cheeks and then she'd retreat back indoors, shaking her head like a dog to dry off before curling next to Rye.

He leaned against the wall—which, he noted with a combination of grudging satisfaction and grim resentment, didn't squish the way it had before Charlie reframed it.

Ugh, damned Charlie with his way of making everything better and stronger.

Everything.

Rye slumped. Everything about his life—except, fine, maybe his takeout options—was better now than it had ever been. He had a job. He had a place to live that he didn't constantly worry about losing, whether for monetary reasons or interpersonal ones.

He had a relationship that he loved with someone who truly saw him for who he was and cared about all of him. He had the space to contemplate a future—futures, really. All the possible futures.

And it was all because of meeting Charlie.

Without Charlie this house would currently be falling down around him, unnavigable by all but Marmot, who could flit through the most intimidating of rubble like it was a kitty amusement park.

The image reminded him of a video he'd seen: of a woman who had turned her small, suburban house into a maze of cat ramps with archways and tunnels between the rooms. He thumbed through his phone to find the video again.

God, Marmot would love that. He could just imagine her appearing in the kitchen while he was making breakfast, sticking her little head in at the smell of bacon cooking. Or seeing her pop into the living room and jump onto his shoulder from the ramp near the ceiling.

If Jane were there too, they'd probably chase each other. Jane would take up residence on a platform and snooze there peacefully until Marmot pounced on her and got her to play, exhausting them both until they curled up in a fluffy pile on the floor.

Fuck, that was an adorable picture.

He wished he was with Marmot and Jane. Wished they were curled up with him on the couch, purring, Marmot's a light rumble and Jane's the sound of tearing metal.

Which means you wish you were back at Charlie's.

"Shut up," Rye grumbled at his treacherous brain.

He let his eyelids fall half-shut to better see the cat playground he was envisioning. Tracy and Nate, and especially River, would get a kick out of a cat playground in the house.

He pulled up the hood of his sweatshirt and let his eyes drift the rest of the way shut as his mind wandered in the dark.

Ramps a little below the ceiling, yeah. Cat-sized holes between the rooms so Marmot could sneak attack. Maybe some textured places for her to rub her cheeks or scratch her back on. Steps leading to a platform with a cat bed, or a scratching post, or her litterbox.

Rye smiled. Yeah, the kids would definitely get a kick out of it. And River *loved* animals; they'd said so several times. Maybe they'd like to help build the ramps and things. Or probably they'd just really like to play with Marmot. And Jane. Any cat, probably. They should try and get a job at an animal shelter—that would be ideal for them.

Rye googled animal shelters in Garnet Run only to see that there weren't any. He widened his search and found no shelters or pet adoption locations anywhere nearby. Shit. So much for that idea for River.

Rye shoved the phone back in his pocket and drew his knees up. He closed his eyes again and let a vision begin to form in his mind. It started off hazy, but as more and more pieces fell into place Rye wondered if maybe he was onto something.

The sound of tires crunching on dirt yanked him back to attention. A moment later a human-shaped bulk slightly darker than the darkness outside was silhouetted in the doorway.

Charlie.

Something leapt in Rye's stomach, dolphin bright and joyous. Then he cringed farther into the corner as the beam from Charlie's flashlight shone directly in his eyes. Rye threw his hand up.

"Dammit, Charlie."

The flashlight beam dropped and Charlie walked over to him. He loomed, then he sighed, then he lowered himself to the floor beside Rye.

"I thought you'd go to Jack and Simon's."

"Didn't want to make Jack feel bad for turning me away."

"Jack wouldn't have turned you away."

"You're his brother—he should have. You've got dibs on him in a fight."

"Doesn't work that way," Charlie said softly. "Not anymore."

Rye's joyous dolphin, dormant since Charlie had sat down, gave a little quiver and popped its nose out of the water.

"So how does it work, then?"

"Jack's your friend. He'll be there for you," Charlie said simply.

"Oh." Rye couldn't tell if Charlie was happy about that or not.

Charlie sighed audibly, his large shoulders rising and falling in a motion that seemed like surrender.

"Jack wants me to be happy. I want you to be part of my life. So Jack would be there for you."

"Oh."

Want. Want, present tense. That was something.

Even though it was warm during the days now it still got chilly at night and Rye wished he'd brought his coat. Or that they weren't fighting so Charlie could wrap his arms around him. Charlie was always so warm.

After an awkward silence, Rye said, "They won't burn down the house."

Charlie tensed, but Rye wasn't trying to fight.

"Just listen. Charlie, I know those kids. I was those kids. They're gonna treat the place with care because it's the only place they have that's just theirs. If they just wanted to smoke weed or hang out they could go anywhere. There's, like, *nothing* here. They could sit in any field or clearing. But they wanted someplace that felt like home, that felt safe. Private. So they'll be careful. I know they will."

Rye could feel Charlie's eyes on him even in the dark.

"You wanted a place to escape to."

"Hell yeah. I wish I'd had a place like the Crow Lane house."

"Where'd you go instead?"

"Oh, uh. Bad places."

"That's ominous."

"Just places I shouldn't've been been. When you're thirteen, fourteen, fifteen, and you don't have any money, the only places you can hang out are places where, like, anyone can hang out, you know? And lots of the people I met were great. But some of them weren't."

Charlie didn't need to hear these stories right now, though.

"When I was a kid I thought I was so tough," Rye said. "I did stupid shit to seem grown up and invincible. It's just better if you have someplace to go that's safe, where you don't have to do those things."

Charlie frowned.

"Charlie. Jack isn't the only teenager who deserved someone to step in and take care of him. You cared for him because he was your brother. But what about everyone who isn't lucky enough to have someone like you?"

Charlie's frown deepened, but he turned toward Rye in the dark and reached for his hand.

"I...haven't thought about it before," he said slowly. "I never thought about a connection between taking care of Jack and taking care of other teenagers. It's... I don't know why I didn't make the connection."

"I get it. You were totally focused on just making sure you and Jack made it day by day."

Charlie cleared his throat.

"Back then, I tried to do what I thought my parents would do. Be the kind of parent they were. They were generous." His voice sounded tight. "And I thought that I was too, I guess. But... I guess there are ways that I'm really not."

Rye hated to hear the defeat in Charlie's voice, but his heart sang at the acknowledgement. He hadn't been wrong about Charlie.

"Charlie, you *are* generous. You've been nothing but generous to me. You help all these people who come into the store. You protected Jack when you were kids. Made sure he had everything he needed. But you're not a kid anymore. You don't have to just think about what your parents might've done. You can make your own choices now."

"You really know what you think is right. In here," Charlie said, touching Rye's chest with two fingers. "It's not about following rules or being polite or doing what other people expect. You just *know* your values for yourself. I really admire it."

Rye leaned his head against Charlie's shoulder.

"Thanks. With a shitbird father you kinda have to make sure you know your own mind or there's a chance you could end up believing his. Anyway, you have time now," he said. "To figure out what your values are, you know?"

"They might not be the same as yours," Charlie warned.

"That's okay. As long as they're compatible."

"Yeah?"

"There are definitely things that wouldn't be okay. But then those wouldn't be compatible. Like, if you thought about it and decided you *didn't* think people should be equal or that money was more important than lives or that you wanted to destroy the planet, then yeah, we're not compatible. But I'm pretty sure we're okay on all those fronts. Right?"

"Yes."

"We can talk about stuff," Rye said. "Whenever you want.

That's...that's what couples do, right?" he ventured, gritting his teeth in case Charlie wasn't sure he wanted to be a couple anymore.

But Charlie leaned in and gathered Rye in his arms.

"Right," he said.

They sat that way for a while, then Charlie said very softly, "I've never had a fight before."

Rye knew what he meant: a fight with a lover, a partner. He meant: *Is it over now? Are we okay?*

"We're okay," Rye said. "As long as we keep talking, we're okay."

Chapter Twenty-Three

Charlie

When he'd gotten to Jack and Simon's and found Rye not there, something had happened inside Charlie's heart. Something primal and screaming and afraid. He'd thought Rye had left. Even though he *knew* Rye would never leave without Marmot, his silly, simple heart had thought Rye was gone.

And his silly, simple heart had broken.

Now he texted Jack to tell him he'd found Rye and tried to get his body to catch up with his brain.

He watched Rye in the rearview mirror the whole drive home, like if he took his eyes off him for a second, Rye would vanish. Rye drove with his window down despite the chill, hair whipping around his face.

When they got home, Charlie drew Rye down on the couch in front of him and started the task of untangling his hair.

"I've been thinking more and more about why I came here," Rye said. "I mean, I left Seattle in *minutes*. I never met my grandfather. I didn't even know he lived in Wyoming, but that lawyer said I had a house here and I was gone. And so I've just been thinking about how I fucking *want* that, man. I want a *home*."

Rye turned to look at Charlie and squeezed his hand hard. He looked lost and beautiful.

"Well, you'll have one soon," Charlie said.

Rye nodded but he was scowling and looked confused. Charlie remembered what Rye had said in the dark of the Crow Lane house. *As long as we keep talking, we're okay.* He swallowed hard and forced himself to speak.

"Rye, I— Earlier, before we fought... I was going to ask you to stay here with me. To not move into the Crow Lane house. To live here."

Charlie's heart beat a furious tattoo and Rye's eyes went wider than Charlie had ever seen them.

"This... I'm in this," Charlie said. "I want it. A home, like you said. I mean I know I have a house, but I've wanted...to share it. I—" Mortification flowed from an unknown source outside him. "I built this house for you."

Rye's eyes opened even wider.

"Not for *you*, I don't mean, but for *a* you." He shook his head. "This is so embarrassing. You know how you said I picked neutral things for this house because of the resale benefit?"

Rye nodded slowly.

"I didn't. That wasn't why. It was... I had this dream. This...fantasy." Charlie's voice broke. "It wasn't even something I ever admitted to myself. Not consciously. But I chose things that could appeal to anyone so that maybe someday my *someone* would feel at home here. God, that sounds so stupid when I say it out loud."

Charlie cringed. He stared at his hands and the rug and Jack's illustration on the wall. Anything to avoid seeing whatever might be in Rye's eyes.

Rye tipped his chin up and Charlie met eyes of mercury. A tear spilled down Rye's cheek and he made no move to brush it away.

"Baby," he said. "I can't believe you."

It was the tenderest chiding, the most loving headshake.

"Actually, I can," Rye corrected himself. "I can absolutely

imagine you choosing the desires of an imaginary future partner over your own."

It stung, the accuracy of that statement, delivered so gently, and with Rye's hand on his cheek. As if Rye saw the truth of his home's yearning—its nearly silent, beige-and-white cry into the darkness: *Love me. I won't assert myself. I am made of space for you. I have emptied myself of any identifiable desires so that yours may flourish.*

Charlie had made himself a ghost house, and he wanted the most colorful, alive person he'd ever met to make a home with him there.

He would have laughed, but he thought it might come out as a sob.

Instead, he looked at Rye's hand, slim fingers newly roughened by work, and he kissed his knuckles.

"I know I haven't done this before," Charlie continued. "But I also know that having you here feels right to me. That has to count for something?"

Rye's grip on his hands was so tight it was almost painful. He looked deep into Rye's eyes and he saw there the same desire as his own. The desire to fall into their future like a child into a pile of autumn leaves—cushioned, enveloped, with just a little bit of chaos flying around the edges.

"It counts. It counts so fucking much, Charlie. I just... I'm scared, I guess. I don't wanna mess this up."

"Well, then we talk about it, right? Isn't that what you said?"

Rye nodded. Then he glared, the glare Charlie had learned was his thinking glare—not to be confused with his pissed-off glare, his annoyed glare, his why-are-people glare, or his exasperated-but-amused glare.

"If you're serious..." Rye began, then shook his head and cut himself off.

"I'm serious."

Charlie pulled him into his lap and Rye snorted, but settled there, regal as a cat.

"I had this idea," he said slowly. "It's probably not possible.
And it wouldn't make any money. I don't know, it's not—"

"Tell me," Charlie said, kissing his cheek.

"If you're serious about me staying here, I was thinking...
Maybe I could turn the Crow Lane house into a cat shelter.
And we could hire River to work there because they love
animals. And we could build cat ramps and little passages
between the different rooms so the cats could play, and also
it would help spread them out so they didn't fight over territory."

"Sounds like you've thought about it a lot."

"Nah," Rye said with a faraway look. Then he continued
excitedly, "And then people could bring in cats they found
outside or kittens they couldn't keep. A vet could come in if
there were any injured cats. And then anyone who wanted
to adopt would be able to, but also maybe people could foster the kittens?"

Rye was bouncing more and more with every idea, his
words coming faster as he laid out his dream.

"I'd have social media for the shelter so people could see
how cute the cats were and want to adopt them. Oh! And
we could have little activities for the cats, like little themed
things around the holidays or about movies or whatever,
and dress them up or have them play with thematic toys and
then those pictures would hopefully get people who were
into those things to like that particular cat and adopt them."

Rye's eyes burned with excitement and intensity. He
looked like he was thinking about fifty things at once.

Charlie had known he was in love with Rye Janssen for
a while now. He might not ever have been in love, but he
knew it when he felt it. But now he found that love opening
up to encompass not only Rye but this big, beautiful dream
that Rye had.

Rye, who hadn't been able to think about how he'd want a house for himself to be designed, but had designed this entire space for cats he'd never met to live the best lives they could until they found other homes.

Charlie hadn't thought it was possible for love to double, but he felt it, in his gut. And lo and behold, he had space for it. He had all the space in the world for loving Rye.

He swallowed the tears he could taste in the back of his throat and nodded.

"And you'd... What do you think about living here, with me, then?"

"Yeah, isn't that what I've just been *saying*?"

Rye glared, and this was a new glare. A variation of the exasperated–but–amused glare, yes, but it was clearly a why-are-you-making-me-be-mushy glare. Charlie liked it a lot.

He couldn't keep the smile off his face for another second.

Rye isn't leaving. Rye is putting down roots, building something, creating something. Rye isn't leaving you. Rye wants to build this with you. He is saying we. We, we we!

"Then I think it's a fantastic idea. There isn't a shelter around here. Nearest one's in Casper, I think."

"I know!" Rye said, brightly. Then he said, "I have no clue how to start a shelter," even though it sounded like he had a pretty good idea of how to start.

"I'm sure you can figure it out. I'll help you if you want. Probably funding is the biggest thing."

Rye wrinkled his brow.

"Yeah. Maybe there's grants and stuff? Or state funding? We could do a GoFundMe. Or like... I don't know."

"You'll figure it out," Charlie said. "You've got this. And I've got you."

Rye's eyes burned.

"You do?"

Charlie nodded somberly.

"Me too. I mean, I've got you too." Rye rolled his eyes at himself. "I was trying to make that shit sound romantic."

Charlie laughed and drew Rye close.

"It was, honey. It really was."

Chapter Twenty-Four

Rye

Once Rye had resolved to turn the Crow Lane house into a cat shelter, the pieces began to fall into place almost faster than he could keep up with them. Now when he and Charlie walked through the house, he could see his vision perfectly. Though he hadn't been able to picture himself living there, he could imagine in great detail everything the building should have to best care for the cats he imagined helping there.

The cabinets they'd originally sourced for the kitchen were recommissioned into storage in what could now be turned into a sterile place for the cats to be spayed, neutered, and chipped.

The area inside the front door where Rye had once stomped through his own floor would be converted into a front desk area and where Rye had slept curled up in his sleeping bag would be walled off and turned into a space for the cats to stay, as would the room that opened onto the back porch.

The only room left was the upstairs bedroom.

"Do you want to turn that into an office so you can work on business related to the shelter there?" Charlie asked.

"Actually, I have another idea," Rye said. He anticipated resistance, but they'd promised they'd always keep talking. "Just hear me out, okay?"

* * *

It took about a week (and some awkwardly Big Brother-ish watching) for Rye to track down River. They arrived at the Crow Lane house by themself the next Monday after-noon and were reading when Rye startled them by bursting through the front door in his excitement.

"Hey, River!"

River clutched their chest and swore.

"Jesus, you just took ten years off my life."

"So sorry." Rye grimaced. "You okay?"

"Yeah," they muttered.

Rye couldn't resist any longer.

"You still looking for a job?"

"Always."

"I've got one for you." Rye was vibrating with excitement. "I'm gonna turn this place into a cat shelter and I want you to help me."

River's eyes went wide but they didn't say anything.

"You know, if you want?" Rye added, realizing he'd phrased it rather bossily.

River swallowed hard and finally nodded.

"I… Are you serious?"

Rye let his energy spill over and told River all about it. He told them about how he wanted to encourage people to get to know the cats before adopting them to minimize the chances of returns. How he planned to provide spaying and neutering on the premises so that if people found cats they wanted to keep they could bring them in for services.

"Of course that requires a vet and we don't have a bud-get for one, so we'll have to see if we can find someone to volunteer their time."

"Maybe a retired large-animal vet in the area would be willing to help out," River suggested.

"Large-animal vet, yes. Wyoming. Of course. See, this is why I need you!"

River made an aw-shucks face and waved Rye away.

"Okay the other thing is. You know the bedroom upstairs?"

"Course."

"You want it?"

River's eyes narrowed.

"What?"

"It's already got a bathroom since I was gonna sleep up there. Now…" Rye shrugged. "I'm, uh. I'm gonna be staying with Charlie, so. It's there. You hate staying with your parents, so I thought…" He shrugged again.

River blinked blankly for a moment.

"We'll put a lock on the door so no one can get in there and you'll have your privacy. And really it'd be you doing me a favor because if you're here at night and anything goes wrong with the cats, then—"

River hugged him with a desperate relief Rye recognized down to his bones. It was the relief he'd felt when his friends let him stay on their couches; the relief he'd felt when Charlie pulled him out of his sleeping bag and gave him a home. The relief he felt now, knowing that he could provide a safe place for someone else who didn't have one where they should have.

"Thank you. Fuck, thank you so much," River said.

Once River was on board everything seemed more real. Rye finally let Charlie do what he'd been wanting to: tell what seemed like every person living in Garnet Run (and a few who lived outside it) about the new business that would be coming to town.

"That's what it is," Charlie insisted. "You're a part of the community so the shelter is a community business. People want to know what's going on in the community."

Rye had his doubts, but Charlie's big mouth began paying dividends almost immediately. Marie, it turned out, had once

worked for a nonprofit arts organization in Cheyenne and offered to help Rye apply for grant money to fund the shelter.

Simon's grandmother, Jean, volunteered to do some land-
scaping in the front of the shelter—"To give it that established, been-here-forever look!" she explained. She also
offered to experiment with recipes for gourmet cat biscuits
that Rye could sell when the shelter opened. Simon had encouraged him to take her up on it since she wanted to help
in some way but was extremely allergic to animals.

Mike at the bank turned out to be invaluable in helping
them do whatever legal zoning blah blah boring was required to have the space be both residential and a nonprofit,
and pointed them toward his accountant uncle who helped
them set up their nonprofit status and do something that Rye
didn't understand or care about but which Charlie assured
him would help come tax season.

The next step was to raise the money they'd need to buy
equipment, food, toys, litter, and everything else for the cats.

When Jack and Simon came for dinner that weekend, they
all sat sprawled around the living room, brainstorming. Marmot took advantage of the preponderance of laps suddenly
available to her and prowled from person to person, seeing
whom she preferred.

The expression on Simon's face when she finally plopped
down on his lap and curled up was tender satisfaction, and
the look on Jack's face watching Simon was as mushy as Rye
felt watching Charlie.

They batted ideas back and forth. A GoFundMe seemed
like the most basic first step. Jack had done them before and
offered to take point on it. Simon offered to design a website
for the shelter so that any donor could click over to the site
from the fundraiser and see what they were supporting. He
also put the creation of social media accounts and graphics,
and a logo for the shelter on his own list.

"The only thing I still need to make the logo and sites is the name of the shelter," Simon said.

Jack had thus far insisted on referring to it as The Cat House when discussing it, even though Simon had pointed out to him that *cathouse* had another meaning.

"Uh, Paw's Place," Jack threw out. "Wagging Way."

"Wagging is more dogs," Simon said. "And Paw's Place sounds like an apostrophe nightmare. Is it one single paw's place? A place for all the paws?"

"The Hopping Home," Jack said, rolling onto his back and addressing the ceiling.

"Sounds like somewhere dying bunnies go to cross into the next dimension," Rye said.

Charlie snickered. "Aren't you supposed to be good at naming things, bro?"

"Hey, books are different," Jack said with a faux pout.

They batted names back and forth for a while, each one worse than the last, until Simon got bored and suggested that they do a fundraising auction. They could ask local individuals and businesses to donate something to auction off with all funds to go to the shelter.

"We can tell business owners that we'll list them on the website if they donate something to the auction—or if they just want to make a direct donation," Simon explained. "And it will help them gain visibility to new clients and goodwill with the community. I can donate a website redesign."

"I'll donate some copies of my books, if you want?"

"Thank you both. Seriously," Rye said. "Um, this asking people for donations thing sounds like a Charlie job?" Rye said, looking at Charlie hopefully.

"Sure," Charlie said, and squeezed his hand.

"Soooo," Jack said, eyes on their hands. "How's it going? You two, I mean."

Rye scowled at Jack but Charlie just smiled.

"Going real good," he said. "Real good."

★ ★ ★

And it was. At least, it felt good to Rye. The last few weeks had been the happiest of his life. Being with Charlie had already felt good. Having something to work on together, though—something that Rye felt could actually make a difference—had made it so much better.

Now he was here because he was Charlie's partner. They shared chores and expenses and dreams for the future. They shared a bed and showers and a plate sometimes, if Rye was too sleepy to get up and get his own.

They collaborated like a dream, Rye good at coming up with ideas of what they could do, and Charlie good at the practical steps of achieving them.

It was all going so well that sometimes Rye caught himself staring at his new life like his brain was trying to figure out how they had gotten here.

Rye was cooking dinner when the text from Simon came through.

GUESS WHAT???

Uh, what?

PetShare is going to link to the shelter gofundme!

The fuck is PetShare?

It's the app that matched me with Jack when he needed a dog walker. Dog and cat walker. I emailed them and told them the whole story of how I met Jack and what you wanted to do with the shelter and they said no at first but then I guess someone higher up in the company is a huge rescue cat lover and heard about it, so we're in!

Dude that's amazing.

There was an ellipsis that showed Simon searching for a gif, then one of a circus ringleader bowing low.

You're a fucking star at this shit! What do I have to do? Rye asked.

I got it, Simon replied. But I need a name SOON!

Rye wasn't sure why the name for the shelter was proving such a challenge. Nearly every shelter he looked up online was either named after the place it was located or had a cutesy, animal-punny name.

Just pick something, he told himself for the hundredth time. But nothing felt right. He'd thought of naming it after his grandfather, since it had been his house, but Granger sounded like *grungy* and The Granger Cat Shelter didn't sound good. He didn't want to use the Janssen part of his grandfather's name because then it would seem like he was naming it after himself. Besides, he knew from a lifetime's experience that everyone would leave out the second *s*.

He was still agonizing over the name when he walked into Peach's Diner to meet Clive for breakfast. He was excited to tell his grandfather's best friend that he was honoring Granger's legacy. At least, he hoped Clive would see it that way.

Clive was in the booth he'd shared with Granger—the booth Rye had gravitated toward when he first met Clive—and he raised a hand in greeting.

"Hey, Clive, thanks for meeting me."

"Morning, son. I'm glad you called."

In fact, Rye hadn't called. He'd texted and Clive had called him, saying he didn't mess around with buttons.

Melba poured them coffee and Rye said hello without insulting her name, so he thought things were off to a pretty good start. Rye ordered biscuits and gravy and Clive got a fond expression in his eyes. He didn't order, just nodded to Melba who clearly knew what he wanted.

While they waited for the food, they chatted about the bird feeders Clive had built out back of his house. Clive, it turned out, was an avid birder, and regaled Rye with the many species he'd seen from his porch. Rye knew nothing at all about birds, but when Clive invited him on a bird walk he accepted immediately.

One of the things Rye had been thinking about a lot the last couple of weeks was how little he knew himself in this new context.

It was Charlie who'd inspired the thought. After their disagreement about the risks and rewards posed by letting River and the other kids hang out at the Crow Lane house, Charlie had thought about it a lot. Charlie'd said that trying a lot of different interests felt like one more thing he had missed out on in the wild crush of responsibility foisted upon him. The more he'd thought about it, the more Charlie had discovered opinions and curiosities he hadn't known he had.

And Rye had realized that although there were parts of himself that felt constant—his values, his ethics, his politics— there were other parts that had been formed in Seattle and weren't relevant anymore. Things he'd hewn to because of necessity, habit, and lack of imagination, but that he didn't have to. He'd begun to wonder what this new Rye—this Garnet Run Rye—would be like. And he was taking every opportunity to find out.

Their food came and Rye savored the first bite.

"So, um, I wanted to tell you about what I'm gonna do with my grandfather's house. Granger's house."

"You aren't going to live there?"

"Well I was, but, um."

Rye had no idea if the well-oiled rumor mill of Garnet Run extended to Clive. Rye had watched with twinned delight and horror when a customer at Matheson's Hardware had tried to set Charlie up with her daughter and Charlie had pulled Rye close to him and said politely. "Thank you so much for thinking of me, but I already have a boyfriend."

The woman had goggled for a moment, then nodded, given Rye a rather thorough perusal, and raised an eyebrow at Charlie.

"Good for you," she'd said, and although Charlie insisted she had included both of them in that "you," Rye disagreed. But he hadn't minded, because although the encounter had resulted in a sudden after-lunch epidemic of sudden-onset DIY fever that required a mob of people who'd never patronized Matheson's before to purchase one nail each, it had also put a smile on Charlie's face and made him walk around like he was even taller for the next several days.

"I'm living with Charlie now." At Clive's head tilt, he added, "Charlie Matheson? Who I was with when you—"

"I know who he is, son. He's your fella, then?"

"Er. Yes?"

"You asking me?"

"No," Rye said. Then, because he hated the idea that Clive might think he was ashamed, he clarified. "Just running *fella* through my dustbowl-to-contemporary-speech translator."

Clive let out a full-bellied guffaw that turned heads in the diner. After the tension was broken Rye felt a lot more comfortable.

"So tell me about this thing you're doing with Granger's house."

"I'm turning it into a cat shelter."

Rye excitedly told Clive all about it, and about his plans for the shelter and about the catch-and-release program he wanted to start, to spay and neuter local cats who clearly enjoyed being outside cats, so they didn't have more kittens. Clive let Rye lay out the whole plan, listening attentively and eating his bacon and spinach omelet.

When Rye ran out of steam, Clive nodded once, a soft expression on his face.

"Your granddaddy woulda liked that just fine. He had a cat. Years ago. Thing just showed up on his porch in the middle of the night, yowlin'."

"What was its name?"

Clive snorted.

"Dirt Road. Granger called her DeeDee for short. She was a dusty little thing with a gray belly and brown paws and face and a lighter brown back. Granger said she looked like ten miles of dirt road, all crying and starving. He took her in and washed her off, fed her. Kept saying she would just stay for one more night, but she never left. Granger was a softy, really."

An image fell into Rye's head of his grandfather's cat running around the house just as Marmot had. Leaping and scratching and getting into trouble. Curling up in his grandfather's lap the way Marmot curled up in his. Granger's shaking fingers stroking the cat's soft back as a fire crackled merrily before them. What comfort his grandfather must have taken from her, when he had little interest in communing with others.

The ghost of a whole life suddenly unfurled itself for Rye in a way that he'd never been able to picture before. And with it came a pang of sadness that he would never know the man who lived there. The man who had given him the gift that had changed his life forever.

For a guy who'd renovated his own house into the design equivalent of khakis, Charlie was shockingly creative when it came to ideas for the kitty castle, as he'd been calling it. The cat ramps had been Rye and Charlie's design project for the last two weeks, and they must've drawn them a hundred different ways—googling plans, watching videos, and dreaming wildly. to Rye's great surprise, the biggest problem turned out to be reining Charlie in.

That was something Rye had learned since they began planning: Charlie might've been ruthlessly practical by default, but when Rye gave him an opportunity to do something impractical, he leapt in with both feet and gloried in doing it.

He'd proposed an elevator that sank when a cat stepped into it, depositing them on the floor and then rising again when empty. He'd proposed steps that swung out from one platform and reconnected to another when a cat pushed a lever. He'd proposed a machine that projected holographic cats for the real cats to chase.

Tonight, after Rye told Charlie about his breakfast with Clive, Charlie pulled out yet another iteration of the kitty castle. He pushed the notebook toward Rye proudly.

"It's a windmill, like at a mini golf place, and the blades cover the tunnel entrance until the cat spins it out of the way! Also they can just spin it to play."

It was honestly one of the more adorable things Rye had ever witnessed—the design and Charlie's enthusiasm for the project. But he had to get it back under control.

He put his hands on Charlie's shoulders and moved his face in front of Charlie's. Charlie, thinking he was going in for a kiss, closed his eyes in happy satisfaction.

"Why," Rye said, touching the tip of his nose to Charlie's, "are you trying to kill me?"

Charlie's eyes opened.

"Huh?"

"Baby, these plans are amazing. They've all been amazing. But I'm not letting you spend a ton of your own money on this build. Everything you're drawing is way out of budget."

Rye took a moment to marvel at how responsible and business savvy he sounded, talking about budgets.

"But, but," Charlie spluttered. "But it's my money."

And that was a full-on whine.

Already, the ramps had become a labor of love for Charlie, beginning as a seed that Rye had planted and growing into a project that found him in his woodshop at all hours of the day and night, testing things, trying things.

Rye kissed Charlie. He'd intended it to be a quelling kiss, but he found himself hauled onto Charlie's lap and kissed quite thoroughly.

"It's so sweet that you wanna do that," Rye said between kisses. "But I know you can find a way to do it without spending a lot of—mmf. Okay, you've distracted me and I'm dropping it but don't think I'm gonna forget!"

Satisfied that he'd made his point, Rye pressed closer to Charlie so they could grind together. Slowly, Charlie had begun to relax when they tried to get off at the same time. Rye didn't need it—he was happy with Charlie every way he could get him—but one night Charlie had confessed that whenever he fantasized about being with Rye what he saw was them locked together in passion. He wanted it, he'd said. He just wasn't sure how to shut his mind off enough to get it.

Rye had been ever so happy to help him practice.

Rye felt the bulge of Charlie's erection and rubbed against it, drinking in Charlie's rumbling groan.

They moved together, hips grinding, breaths shared, until liquid heat coursed through Rye's veins.

"Charlie," he gasped, latching onto Charlie's neck to suck hard at the hot skin of his throat. His teeth scraped gently and Charlie gasped. Then Charlie's fingers found his hair and pulled.

Rye let his head fall back and lust shot through him.

"That good?" Charlie murmured.

"Yeah, fuck, so good."

Their mouths met again and this was mutually assured destruction. Charlie pulled his hair and Rye fed on Charlie's mouth and their hips fucked and strained. Rye's cock ached with the need for relief and he could feel Charlie's erection throbbing against him.

With his mouth on Charlie's, Rye snaked a hand between them and freed their cocks. Charlie's moan was almost pained as their hot flesh came into contact, and Rye could feel his shiver of pleasure.

"Okay, baby?" Rye asked.

Charlie's answer was to growl and pull him even closer, fist tightening around his hair. Rye whimpered and went to work.

He jerked them together, their flesh burning with the heat between them. Charlie's hand came down over his own to help, and he squeezed them tighter, jerked them harder.

Rye opened his eyes to find Charlie's on him as well. They burned green in his passion and Rye drank in every flutter of his eyelashes and every tremble of his lips as they pleasured each other. Charlie's beautiful mouth fell open and Rye rested their lips together—not kissing, just breathing in each other's every breath.

Rye felt the moment that Charlie's pleasure crested in the tightening of his lips before he felt it in his hand. His flesh shook and his mouth drew into a grimace of pleasure too extreme to be contained. He threw his head back and roared as he came, his come a scalding brand across Rye's hand.

Rye loved it when Charlie came first because of what always happened next.

For the space of two breaths, or maybe three, Charlie was lost in his own pleasure. But then, his eyes fluttered open and with a groan he claimed Rye's mouth in a brutal, loving kiss. He used his hands on Rye like he was playing a delicate but necessary instrument and he intended to pull out every note.

Rye let himself be played by Charlie, because the music was always shattering and sublime.

Tonight was no different. Charlie's kiss was pure passion and he used his come to ease the slide of his hand on Rye's aching flesh. Rye's hips strained and his ass clenched with the need for release.

Charlie wrapped his other arm around Rye's back, locking them together, and slid his hand back in Rye's hair.

He tugged in counterpoint—Rye's aching cock and Rye's hair—until Rye was a moaning, trembling, begging mess.

"I love you," Rye said. "Please. Please, Charlie, I love you so much."

The words left his mouth without thought or regret. Because although it was the first time he'd said them, he'd thought them a hundred times.

"Rye." Charlie groaned the word like his heart was being ripped from his chest. "Oh, my Rye. I love you. I love you."

He kept saying it, over and over, and Rye said it over and over. They layered *I love you*s, sharing the taste and the feel of the words until they were as familiar as one another's breath.

Then Charlie leaned his forehead against Rye's and took Rye apart. The pressure and friction were unbearable and so Rye didn't bear them. He leaned back and let go and orgasm tore through him like a ribbon unspooling. Pleasure clawed up from his balls to his guts and left him shaking.

Shock after shock rolled through him until he was trembling with overwhelm.

He didn't realize he was crying until Charlie wiped his tears away.

"My Rye," Charlie said, and carried him to bed.

Chapter Twenty-Five

Charlie

It was the last weekend in August and the sun shone hot and bright through the trees outside the Crow Lane house. Only it wasn't called the Crow Lane house any longer—The Dirt Road Cat Shelter was opening its doors in two hours and Rye was rocketing around the place like a feral cat himself.

Somehow, everything had come together in the last week. Molly Simmons, a large animal vet who had been a friend of Charlie's father's, had agreed to volunteer at the shelter one day a week to do medical procedures and checkups. The fundraising auction had been a huge success—due in part to Charlie calling in every favor he'd accrued over the years—and that final push had given them the funds they needed to kit the shelter out right.

Last night, they had done a final walk-through and everything had been fine. Now Rye was standing in the corner of the cat room where once he'd slept, and declaring that the entire thing was a disaster and they should probably call off the launch.

You're on, Charlie texted Jack.

Ten minutes later, Jack knocked on the door, then pushed it open, a disgruntled Marmot in his arms.

"Little fucker didn't wanna come without Jane," he muttered. Then he whistled. "Looks great in here. I hadn't seen it with everything all orderly yet."

Charlie pointed above the front desk to where hung a framed drawing that Jack had done of the shelter, complete with cats hanging out of every window and roosting in the eaves. Jack had given away and auctioned off multiple artworks of animals to raise money for and spread the word about the shelter.

He smiled at the drawing.

"Thanks, man."

Marmot let out a crow that meant she wanted to be put down. Rye came thundering into the front room, looking confused.

"Marmie?" When he saw the cat and Jack, he said, "You brought her?"

Jack nodded.

"Charlie thought she might like to do the honors of testing the ramps."

As the word *ramps* left Jack's mouth, Marmot seemed to see them and was off like a shot.

She pranced up the stairs that led to the ramp over the front desk, sniffing as she went. It sloped up to near ceiling height and when Marmot got high above their heads, she looked down on them like she should be waving a scepter.

"Oh my god," Rye said. "It's like I'm seeing her from the perspective she always felt she was at on my shoulder."

Rye spotted the hole that led through the wall and into what had been the living room and was now a room outfitted with large cat cages and pens, toys and pillows and perches. She darted through the hole and the humans opened the door to follow. They watched her rocket around the ramps for a few circuits of the room, then slow down enough to see the toys. She sniffed some, batted at others, and danced over the different pillows and perches as if to say, *I'll be back later but you are mine and don't you forget it.*

From there, she disappeared into the wall again and Jack raised an eyebrow.

"It goes to the room upstairs," Charlie explained.

"River's room," Rye added.

Charlie said nothing. This was a topic about which Charlie was still anxious, but Rye had been immovable: even though River wouldn't be eighteen for six months, Rye had insisted that they be allowed to sign a lease and have the room.

Rye had said very calmly and very quietly that he was not going to change his mind. That River didn't feel safe at their house and that Rye didn't care what negative consequences he had to shoulder—he was giving River a safe place to stay.

Then he'd put his arms around Charlie and told him not to worry. That following rules and laws wasn't always the way to stay safe. That sometimes breaking rules and laws was the way to keep everyone okay. Charlie knew that he was right, and he was working on not worrying so much about the consequences. Charlie liked River a lot and he dearly wanted them to feel safe. But it wasn't easy letting go of years of believing that rules were a protection.

"We told them that putting an entrance there would mean they were sure to get cat bombed in the middle of the night," Rye said. "And they said they didn't care. Well, actually they said they couldn't wait to get cat bombed."

Rye grinned.

As they started up the stairs to follow Marmot, there was a scratching sound from the porch on the back of the house that they'd closed in. They went through the smaller room where a cat could have some alone time, or where potential adopters could take a cat to spend some time together. It didn't have any entrances to the cat ramps.

On the other side of it was cat heaven.

Charlie had respected Rye's wishes that he stay within the budget of their fundraising efforts in constructing the ramps even though Charlie would have happily used his own money to fund it. But Rye hadn't been able to put any limits on his time, and Charlie had poured it into the project. Where the budget didn't allow for something, Charlie found a way to build it or scavenge it himself. He'd regularly called around to locals for scrap wood and metal, bits and bobs that he knew they might have leftover from projects—and he *knew* the projects people did because he routinely sold them the supplies to do them.

But this—the cat heaven they were about to see—this, Charlie had done as a surprise for Rye. Under the cover of lunch breaks, lumber deliveries, and with some sneaky assistance from Jack, Marie, and Bob, he had made something he thought any cat would be happy to have.

He just hoped his favorite cat, Rye, would like it too.

"How did she get through there?" Rye asked, confused. "Charlie, what…"

Rye turned to look at him, expression half suspicion and half confusion.

"Go through," Charlie said.

Rye put his hand on the doorknob and turned around again to look at Charlie.

"What did you do?"

"Go through," Charlie said again, and put his hand at the small of Rye's back as he opened to door.

Out the back door was a porch screened in with metal strong enough that cat claws couldn't tear it. The floor was carpeted with a layer of cheap Berber carpet, perfect for cats to scratch and easy to replace when destroyed. The cat ramps ran over the wall of the porch attached to the house, and that was where Marmot had scampered to. She was frozen in awe of the vista before her, though: the entire back was open to the land outside the shelter. The grasses waving in the breeze and all the animals that jumped around them. The trees past that, and the animals that played through them. A vast expanse of sky and all the birds and bugs that flew across it. The smells and sounds and tastes of nature, all there to be enjoyed. Charlie had a plan for winterizing it, but now didn't seem the time to burden Rye with details.

Rye looked around the huge space with his mouth open. He clapped a hand over his mouth and turned to Charlie, so that all Charlie saw were his extraordinary eyes, ringed in kohl and sparkling with tears.

"What did you *do!*" Rye accused.

"I just—"

But Rye wasn't looking for an explanation. He flung himself into Charlie's arms and buried his face in Charlie's chest. Charlie could feel him shaking with sobs.

"I love you so much," Rye sobbed. At least, that's what Charlie heard. Rye was pretty incomprehensible, but Charlie didn't mind. He wrapped Rye in his arms and rubbed his back and stroked his hair, just as Rye had done for him more than once over the past few months.

Emotional growing pains, it turned out, were as painful as physical ones.

"Moment of truth," Charlie murmured, watching Marmot over Rye's head.

Rye made a snuffling sound of query and Charlie turned him so his front was to Rye's back but he could still have his arms around Rye.

"I did a lot of research on what metal mesh would stand up to claws," Charlie explained. "But you never know with cats." He didn't add that he'd chosen something that would withstand any potential claws possessed by animals *outside* the shelter as well. The last thing Rye needed on opening day was the image of a coyote attacking the cats.

Marmot's shoulder blades bunched and she launched herself to the floor from her perch high on the inside wall. Slowly she approached the screen, sniffing delicately at the air. She rubbed her cheek against it, then out came the claws.

In an instant, she'd climbed it and was hanging off it, tail twitching.

The screen held, and Marmot made her clinging way to a perch hooked into the screen.

"Yesss!" Charlie said.

Jack, whom Charlie had forgotten was still there while he'd held Rye, said, "Damn, what is that, plutonium?"

"Adamantium," said a soft voice. Simon had arrived.

Jack's face lit as he pulled Simon to him.

"Hey," he said, like every time he got to see Simon was special to him.

Simon kissed him, then said, "You mean adamantium. The metal that Wolverine's skeleton is made of? Plutonium is a radioactive element."

"Oh, yeah, adamantium, right. Thanks."

Not content to stay on the perch, Marmot was attempting to traverse the screen one paw at a time. When she lost patience she leapt back to the floor. Then she ran around smelling and rubbing her cheeks on everything.

"Welp, I'd call that a success," Jack said.

Charlie winked his thanks to Jack, let out a sigh of relief, and pressed a kiss to Rye's cheek.

"You okay?" he said softly.

Rye nodded. When he turned back around to Charlie, his eyes were glowing with joy.

"Thank you," he whispered. "Charlie, thank you so much. For everything."

He looked like he had more to say, but it wasn't the time. Besides, Charlie knew what *everything* meant. He knew, because Rye had given him everything too.

"What's the plan here, guys?" Jack asked.

"Doors open at eleven," Charlie said. "People can wander around, see the place, we'll give them information about how things work."

"Who knows," Rye added, "maybe people will even want

to get on the waiting list for cats right away. We've got the pamphlets you made, Simon, so if you all can make sure those get passed out. And your grandma's bringing, like, one million kinds of cookies."

Simon grinned.

"Snickerdoodles?" Jack asked, hopeful as a puppy.

"Course," said Simon.

"Molly will pop in for a while, answer any questions people have from a vet's perspective," Charlie went on. "And we'll have that newsletter whatsit..."

"Newsletter sign-up," Rye said, all business now. "Which will also link them to the website. So make sure you get them to sign up. There's an iPad on the desk so they can do it here. Do *not* believe anyone who says they'll do it later."

Rye was bouncing on the balls of his toes as he listed things off.

Weeks before, after hours of swearing, googling, and some glares and fisted hands that Charlie feared would lead to the actual throwing of his laptop across the room, Simon had come over and showed Rye how to interlink the website he'd designed, the newsletter Rye had set up, the social media accounts, and the GoFundMe. After that initial tutorial, Rye had navigated it all effortlessly.

He'd put out a call for people to send him pictures of their shelter-adopted cats and had flooded the shelter's Instagram with their stories of love. He'd linked to every other shelter he could find, getting on their radar, and then contacting them for any insights they could offer about the process. He'd also reposted those shelters' pictures of cats to spread their reach and linked back to the GoFundMe donation page until that, too, provided them with enough funds to get started.

Charlie hadn't been at all surprised to find out that despite Rye's bluntness and lack of interest in small talk in person, he was stellar at drawing people into his orbit.

After all, that was what had happened to Charlie.

At first, Rye had been genuinely shocked by the way the citizens of Garnet Run had shown up for him. How many of them had donated their goods and services for the fund-raising auction, donated to the GoFundMe, included links to the shelter on their business' websites, donated old towels, sheets, and unused pet supplies.

He'd insisted, at the beginning, that it was because of Charlie. But little by little, as people stopped him in the grocery store, at the gas station, at the library, and wanted to talk to him about what he was doing—wanted to *help*—he began to believe that it was him. That people were invested in him and his vision. That they cared about him. Accepted him.

And with that newfound sense of belonging, Rye had begun to meet Clive Wayne for breakfast at Peach's Diner on Tuesday mornings, just as his grandfather had done.

Last week, Rye had been quiet all day at work after his breakfast with Clive. He was quiet all through dinner. After dinner, he took a shower and went to bed. Charlie had followed him, crawling into bed with him and lying silently beside him, confident that Rye would tell him whenever he was ready.

"I can't believe I had someone this whole time," Rye said after a long quiet spell. "Family. A...connection. Maybe he'd've hated me as much as the rest of my family if he met me. But maybe...maybe we would've gotten along."

It had broken Charlie's heart to watch him swallow hard around the grief of losing someone he'd never known. There was nothing Charlie could say. All he could do was hold Rye close, stroke his back, and rock him as he cried.

Jean's voice called, "Helloo?" from the front door and they trooped back inside, leaving Marmot to her own devices.

Simon's grandmother was a force of nature—and a damn good baker to boot. Simon rushed to take the teetering pile of Tupperware from her arms. She patted him on the arm and told him there was more in the car.

"There's a cat here," Simon told her. "But just one, and she just got here."

"Don't worry about me, dear. I took an allergy pill. I won't stay too long, but I wouldn't miss this for the world."

They arranged the cookies on platters around the front room. Jean had made up little signs that listed the ingredients in everything.

"You're a gem," Jack told her. She handed him the snickerdoodle he had clearly been about to help himself to, along with a napkin that he clearly hadn't.

At eleven, people began to arrive. Rye looked horrified as the trucks pulled in.

"What's wrong?"

"There's no parking lot," he said. "I didn't even think of that?"

Charlie squeezed his arm.

"Any place you can park is a parking lot in Wyoming." He winked.

"Is that a joke?"

"Nope."

"Oh. Okay. So it's fine?"

"It's fine. Now go greet people. And be—"

"Polite, I know." Rye grinned.

Charlie had actually been about to say *Be proud of yourself*, but Rye was already padding toward the front door.

Garnet Run came, with Clive Wayne leading the way.

Charlie had known they would. Even people he knew very well thought of cats as nuisances wanted to see what Rye had done with The Dirt Road Cat Shelter.

Watching Rye talk about his vision for the shelter made Charlie so proud he could burst. When excited, Rye had an energy that couldn't be denied. He spoke passionately about finding cats homes, about gentling them, and about releasing them back into nature after spaying and neutering them, if they didn't seem to want to stay indoors. He introduced

River as the manager of the shelter to people, an arm around their shoulder the whole time, sending the clear message: *You mess with this kid, you mess with me.*

And no one wanted to mess with Rye.

Part of the town now or no, Rye still cut an intimidating figure. With his wild hair, his habitual scowl, his tattoos, the kohl smeared around his intense eyes, his willingness to stare you down, and his unwillingness to accept an ounce of bullshit...yeah, Rye was a force to be reckoned with.

Around one, Van and Rachel arrived. Jack and Van had been friends since high school, so Charlie'd known her forever. Van was grinning and she made a beeline for Rye.

"It's a sign!"

"Uh, what?"

Van tugged on Rachel's arm to reveal a very tiny, very asleep black kitten.

"Oh my god." Rye stroked the kitten's back worshipfully.

"She was curled up against the wheel of my car," Van said. "No other kittens around, no mom cat. And I watched for a while. That's why we're late. Just this little angel. I almost didn't see her. But here she is, just here and obviously wanting to be your first customer. Patron. Adoptee. Whatever."

"Jeez. That's wild. Hang on."

Rye pulled out his battered phone and snapped a picture of the tiny kitten in the crook of Rachel's arm. Charlie could almost imagine the Instagram caption Rye was writing. *A cat visitation on opening day!* or *Look who wandered in?* or *Our first customer!*

Charlie waved at Molly Simmons, who'd just arrived, and pointed at the kitten. She took it from Rachel and held it gently. A crowd was starting to form around the tiny fur ball. Charlie took a couple of pictures of the crowd, in case Rye wanted to use them later, then ushered Rye and Molly into the medical room, closing the door behind them.

"It was out by Van's car," Rye was telling Molly. "It's so tiny. Is it okay?"

Molly turned the kitten onto its back, gently exploring its tiny body. As she did, it fell asleep, head lolling, mouth open, tiny paws flung above its head.

Rye was making choked noises like he was working very hard not to ooh and ah over its adorableness.

"She seems fine," Molly said. "But she's very young. We'll need to dropper feed her. Do you have a box we can let her sleep in?"

Rye fetched one of the many donated shoeboxes and put a fluffy washcloth inside. He handed it to Molly and she gently lowered the sleeping kitten into it.

"Let's let her sleep for now and we'll feed her in an hour," Molly said, all business.

But Rye was staring at the kitten and there might as well have been hearts coming out of his eyes. He stroked her head with one fingertip and cradled the box for the rest of the opening.

"That went okay, huh?" Rye said.

They were home, and Rye was lying on the living room floor with one hand on Jane and the other on an exhausted Marmot.

"Are you kidding? It went great."

Charlie sat beside him on the rug and slowly reached out a hand to rest on Rye's stomach. Now Charlie was touching Rye who was touching both cats. They were all connected. Rye's smile was sweet and Charlie stored it away. A beautiful moment. He was trying to notice more of those.

Charlie loved Rye. Adored him. Wanted to bask in his company like a cat in a patch of warm sun. But sometimes he still got scared—so fucking scared that because he loved Rye, he would lose him.

"Since you gave River the room above the shelter, you

should have a real office," Charlie said. "We could move the bed out of your old room, and I could build a desk and shelves and stuff. Or you can find your own. Whatever you want."

"I can't believe we just opened the shelter in a house you basically built and you're ready to start another construction project," Rye said fondly.

He shook his head but sat up and put an arm around Charlie's neck. He kissed Charlie slowly.

"Your office at the store is crap," he mused. "Your shoulders don't even fit. You should turn that room into an office for yourself."

The picture of John Matheson doing the books at the kitchen table while Charlie, Jack, and their mom circled around him flashed in Charlie's mind. It was a nice memory—if disadvantageous for the books.

"What if we share it," he offered. "I could build us a double desk and shelves so we each have room."

Rye's cheek was pressed against his so he could feel Rye's smile.

"Can you make the desk so we're not looking at each other?"

Charlie felt a brief pang of hurt and tried to will it away. "Sure."

"Cuz if I'm looking at you while I'm trying to work," Rye said, trailing fingers down Charlie's neck, "I won't get shit done."

Charlie shivered.

"And we probably shouldn't build cat ramps in there," Rye murmured against Charlie's ear. "Too distracting."

He sucked a mark behind Charlie's ear and Charlie shuddered.

"Yeah," Charlie agreed. He pulled Rye on top of him and the movement disrupted the cats, who glared at them and then slunk off, no doubt to curl up together somewhere they wouldn't be disturbed by pesky things like unpredictable limbs.

Rye's eyes were heated.

Charlie said, "We can draw up some designs. See what would work best."

"Mmm-hmm." Rye kissed Charlie's throat and pinched his nipple, making Charlie jump. "Later." Arousal flushed through him and he gave himself to it.

They were good at this now, letting the moment unfold and carry them away. Charlie didn't think so much anymore. He gave himself to it. Gave himself to Rye. Trusted that Rye wanted him. That Rye wanted to be wanted. Trusted that his pleasure wasn't unfair. That he could have things for himself.

For both of them.

"Want you," Charlie breathed.

It was all he had to say. Rye's mouth was soft and hot and devoured him so sweetly.

"Take your clothes off and turn over," Rye said.

Arousal ripped through Charlie. The second he was naked, Rye was on him. He kissed the nape of Charlie's neck, making him shiver, then kissed down his spine. Each touch of his lips was electric.

"Close your eyes," Rye murmured. He always said it and Charlie always did it. "You're so fucking hot." He kept talking to Charlie, praising him. His body, his skin, his ass. His heart.

He grabbed heated handfuls of Charlie's ass.

"I wanna spank you till this is hot and pink and then I wanna rub my cock all over it," he said, squeezing. Rye's words always took Charlie apart.

"Ah! Fuck, yes, fuck, please."

The first *thwack* of Rye's hand shorted out Charlie's brain. He couldn't think anymore—didn't have to think that he didn't deserve this, that he shouldn't have it, that it wasn't allowed. By the third, there were starbursts exploding behind his tightly shut eyes and his shoulders relaxed.

"You're amazing," Rye said. *Spank*. Then Rye's hand, soothing the skin in gentle circles. "I couldn't have done any of this without you." *Spank. Soothe.* "I can't believe we live here together." *Spank. Spank. Soothe.* "You're the best thing that ever happened to me."

Spank. Soothe. Soothe. Soothe.

Charlie could hear the words this way. He heard them with his body instead of his mind. They were branded on his body with every impact of Rye's hand and set with every soothing caress, the proof of them there when the words had long faded into the air.

There was a pause and when Rye pressed himself against Charlie's back, it was skin on skin. Rye's erection, hot and silky, rubbed his ass. Charlie's cock was hard and hot, trapped between his stomach and the rug.

Rye bit the back of his neck and thrust, grinding his hips against Charlie's ass. He squeezed a cheek, groaning as he felt the heat of Charlie's flesh.

"More?" he asked.

Charlie moaned, helpless to form words.

"Mmm, 'kay," Rye purred. "Touch yourself while I do it."

Charlie reached a hand to his erection and jumped at the brush of his hand.

"That's good," Rye said. "Just like that."

Rye spanked him and he touched himself because Rye wanted him to. Rye wanted him to because Rye *wanted* him to feel good. Rye wanted him to feel good, Rye wanted him to feel—

"Fuck, so good." Charlie's voice was strangled.

"Good, baby. I love seeing you like this. You look so fucking gorgeous."

Rye patted his ass, then kissed each cheek. Then he parted Rye's ass and slid his erection in the cleft. They moved together, Rye rubbing himself off and Charlie tightening his muscles and flexing his own cock into his hand.

Rye thrust harder and faster and then Charlie felt a rainbow of heat fall across his back and ass.

Rye cried out as he came over Charlie, then pressed hot kisses all over his neck.

Rye's hand slid underneath him, encouraged his hand away. Rye stroked him hard and fast and pinched his sensitive ass for good measure. Electricity zinged up and down Charlie's spine and the heat in his gut became an inferno.

"So fucking sexy," Rye said. Then he pushed Charlie onto his back and swallowed his aching cock.

They'd only done this a few times and every time Charlie felt overwhelmed by the intimacy of it. Now was no different. Rye reached for his hand, lacing their fingers together, and Charlie squeezed. The other hand he put on Rye's head, just resting there, on his hair.

Rye moaned around his cock, and Charlie lost himself to Rye's exquisite mouth. As his pleasure grew, Charlie clenched his ass and pressed his hips up. The carpet scraped his ass, his muscles tensed, Rye swallowed around him, and Charlie exploded like a supernova, body arching and muscles going rigid as he shook apart.

He felt raw and trembly when Rye had licked the last traces of pleasure from him, and he pulled Rye back into his arms.

"I love you," he said. Simple and extraordinary.

He said it to Rye every day. He made sure of it. But still sometimes Rye seemed unsure.

When Rye's face appeared above him, his eyes were bright and wide.

"You do?" he said. Then, before Charlie could even open his mouth to reassure him, "Do you really?"

"Yup."

A smile started at the corners of Rye's lips. He swallowed

hard, then he caught Charlie in the tightest hug. For a moment, Charlie thought he was crying and stroked his shaking back.

Then he realized Rye was laughing.

"I...what's so funny?"

"I just can't believe this," Rye said. "I can't believe I'm in *Wyoming* and that I *live* here and there are, like, *bison* here, and that you *love me* and I *love you*."

He buried his face in the crook of Charlie's neck and squeezed him even tighter.

"I love you so fucking much, Charlie," he said. Rye was just lying on the floor, naked, giggling about Charlie's love. Loving him back. Giggling and loving him.

In all the visions Charlie Matheson had over the years—all the visions of partnership and love and romance, because okay, *yes,* he'd had them—never once had they included this: the kind of love that made you giddy, that made you laugh with the sheer overwhelming joy and surprise of everything that love could be.

They hadn't included it because he had never been in love so he couldn't have known. He couldn't have known that *this* was the truest thing: he was happier to be in the world when he got to share it with Rye. And Rye felt the same.

Charlie smiled. His smile became a chuckle of pure happiness. He caught Rye's hand in his and kissed his palm.

"I'm so proud of you." He said it softly, like a bubble blown from a wand into the breeze of Rye's laughter.

Tears leaked from Rye's eyes and he pulled Charlie down on top of him. It reminded Charlie so much of the way Marmot would pounce Jane that he couldn't help but smile even bigger.

"Are those laughing tears?"

Rye's arms were around his neck and his legs were around Charlie's legs.

"Yeah," Rye said. "No. Both."

Charlie kissed *I love you* and *I'm proud of you* into Rye's hair and to Rye's cheeks and to every other part of Rye that his lips could reach while he was caught in Rye's surprisingly strong grip.

Eventually, Rye loosed his arms and they lay on their sides, facing each other.

"We love each other," Rye said, voice a whisper.

"We love each other," Charlie confirmed.

Looking into Rye's eyes, Charlie grinned. Rye grinned. They grinned and kissed each other and grinned some more.

Eventually, when they could bear to part, they cleaned up a bit, and the cats ventured back into the living room. Rye and Charlie lay on the rug, still facing each other, and Jane and Marmot insinuated themselves into the circle. Marmot spread herself out fully so that no humans in the vicinity could fail to notice that her belly was *right there* for the petting. Jane sat in a dignified floof. She would accept pets if they were offered but it was beneath her to beg or pander.

Charlie stroked Marmot's sleek stomach and Rye pet Jane's magnificent coat.

Both cats had begun purring loudly when Charlie spoke.

"You want that kitten that Van and Rachel brought in today don't you?"

Rye looked up, kittenish himself.

"So fucking much," he said sheepishly.

Charlie looked at Rye. His best friend. His love. The person he wanted to do everything with—even housebreak a kitten.

"Anything for you."

Epilogue

Rye

Eight months later

"River, Godzilla sat in my lap!" Rye called from the foot of the stairs, uselessly brushing white cat fur off his black jeans.

River skipped down the stairs, eyes wide.

"She did?"

"Hand to god."

"Aw," River said. "What a good baby. She'll get adopted, don't you think?"

River said this like they knew it was a good outcome, but Rye was pretty sure River would be happy just caring for an ever-growing household of cats. They'd been devastated when Milquetoast, a little orange and white cat with a silent meow, had gotten adopted and left the shelter.

"There'll always be more."

River nodded. They'd been living in the bedroom above the shelter since it opened, and the difference in them from August to April was palpable. They'd stopped slouching so much, they didn't muffle their laughter, and they were quicker to speak up and offer their opinion. Just having a space of their own and a purpose had shown them what life could be.

Not only had River turned out to be a great help around

the shelter, they were much savvier at social media than Rye was. They'd had the idea to set up a cat cam in the playroom so that people could watch the livestream online, and did amazing photo shoots with the cats to encourage adoption. The shoot they'd done with the fluffy white cat with two different colored eyes named Jasper had been incomparable. It had included a deck of tarot cards, a piece of black velvet, and a disco ball, and had resulted in a couple driving four hours to adopt Jasper, as well as donate a trunk full of supplies.

"Okay, I'm gonna take off," Rye said.

"Oh, hey, I have something for you. Hang on a sec."

They ran upstairs and emerged with a flat square wrapped in a paper towel. They handed it to Rye shyly.

"I wouldn't be here if not for you. I just … thank you."

"Aw come on, hey, no," Rye said.

He didn't want River to waste their money on him. He'd told River it was his and Charlie's anniversary by accident the week before, too lovestruck to keep it to himself. Not the anniversary of their first kiss, or their first *I love you*. Rather, at Charlie's insistence, the anniversary of the day they'd met. Because, Charlie said, that was the day his life changed forever. Rye hadn't argued the point. He felt the same way. But it had never occurred to him that someone might get him a present for it.

"Rye, uh. Thanks, man. Seriously. You don't know what you've done for me…"

Their voice got thick and Rye nodded. He did know. He knew what providing someone with a safe home felt like because it was exactly what Charlie had done for him.

"I'm glad," Rye said. "Thanks for being the best employee ever. I think. I mean I've never had employees before, but you know. Employee of the month every month."

River smiled and Rye tore off the paper towel.

It was Theo Decker's new album. Rye hadn't even known he'd put out a new album.

"It's the dude who used to be the lead singer of Riven. You're always playing them, so. And I know today's your anniversary and I don't mean it as a present for that, cuz that's… weird. Is it weird? I don't know. I don't anything about anniversaries, but—"

Rye dragged them into a one-armed hug.

"Thanks, Riv. It's awesome. I really love it. And I have no idea," he added. "I've never had an anniversary before."

River beamed.

"Okay, get outta here," they said.

"I'm gone. Call me if you need anything."

Rye said it every time he left, and every time, River waved him away, heading into the cat playroom, where Rye had no doubt they'd spend many happy hours covered in cats.

It was only 4:00 p.m., but the sky was darkening with the promise of a spring storm. Charlie'd be at Matheson's for a few more hours, which should give Rye time to finish his anniversary present.

He'd started working on it the week before, and quickly realized he was in over his head. Though he'd spent many an evening over the last few months with Charlie in his woodshop, watching, helping, learning, all it took was trying to make one thing by himself to show him how much he still had to learn.

The gift was a laptop desk. Charlie didn't like to admit it, but being on his feet all day, combined with lifting heavy things and working on the lathe, often left him with an aching back.

"I'm old," Charlie muttered whenever his back twinged.

"Pssh, you're not old, you're just bad at taking care of yourself," Rye would reply.

"Pretty good at taking care of you," Charlie would say, leering or burying his face in Rye's neck.

After which excellent and inarguable point, Rye would drop the conversation in favor of other things.

In any case, since they shared an office, Rye got to see firsthand how bad Charlie was at taking care of his back. He was a large man and he used a small laptop to do all the store's records. Though Charlie had built their desk a bit taller than a standard desk, it wasn't enough. If he put the laptop up on books, his shoulders ached from not resting his arms on the desk.

Rye had seen a laptop desk on someone's Instagram one day and thought such a thing would be perfect for Charlie. Adjustable, angled for maximum comfort, and with a place to store a Bluetooth mouse and keyboard, which Charlie could use at home.

He'd gone to order one, then decided that it would be far more personal (and, fine, romantic) if he made one for Charlie. After all, Charlie *loved* woodworking, he loved handmade things, he respected craft.

How often had he run his fingers along the silken curve of a wooden bowl after he'd finished it? When he thought no one was watching, he'd sometimes stand back and admire the double desk and built-in shelves he'd created for their office. He would test the continued structural integrity of the cat ramps every so often, making sure they were still sturdy and plumb.

So, yeah, Rye would make it for him. What could possibly go wrong?

Answer: everything.

When he'd begun the week before, he'd thought it would be the work of four or five hours. Six hours in and he had a hunk of wood that jutted at an obscene and useless angle and was liable to stab Charlie as soon as hold his laptop.

So much for winging it.

But no problem, he'd just look up some plans online. A tutorial. You could learn anything online.

And he had found plans. And tutorials. But the problem with YouTube woodworking tutorials was that although they only ran twelve minutes, they never really told you the full working time of the project. He'd barred Charlie from the woodshop all of Sunday while he worked on the desk, pausing and rewinding the video on his phone so many times that he ended up with a drained battery and a damning film of wood glue on the screen.

But today was the day. Tomorrow was their anniversary, so this was his last chance. If he could just figure out how to calculate the angle for the miter saw, he'd be fine. Right? Well and he had to figure out the whole adjustable part. And sand it. Oil it. Shit.

The rain was coming down hard now, spattering his windshield, gusting from tree branches when the wind blew.

He rolled the window down just a bit, just enough to smell the rain on the air. When Charlie's house—their house—came into view, Rye knew he was smiling. It still happened every time. He saw the big pine tree, then the corner of the house, then there it was.

Home.

He parked off to the side, leaving room for Charlie's truck when he got home. He wouldn't listen to Theo Decker's new album while he worked in the woodshop. Too much noise; the album deserved his full attention.

He wiped off his shoes outside, then opened the front door slowly because—*Blam!*

The second he could see inside he was hit with a fuzzy black projectile. She was still a kitten, really. Not even nine months old. Charlie had let him adopt her from the shelter after he'd fallen in love with her at the launch.

Once she was big enough to explore on her own, she'd revealed herself to be a bit of a hell-raiser, accelerating Charlie's construction of the cat ramps and tunnels in their own house to keep her from tearing things apart.

Murder cat, Charlie had started to call her, since he'd stopped calling Marmot that long ago.

"What's with you and the murder cats?" he'd asked.

"Guess I'm just attracted to trouble," Rye'd said, winked, and kissed him.

Rye had begun to call her Redrum instead, and Charlie had been confused. Which was how Rye realized Charlie had never seen *The Shining*, which led them down a week-end-long Stephen King movie marathon that reminded Rye that Stephen King was awesome and reminded Charlie that he didn't care for horror movies.

Still, she was Redrum. Red, or Rum, or Rummie, or Drumbot, or Asshole for short.

Redrum liked to perch atop tall things and drop down on unsuspecting passersby. She also liked to perch atop tall things and remain as still as a statue until you panicked because you couldn't find her and thought she'd somehow gotten outside and been hit by a car or been eaten by a bear. *Then* she'd drop down on you unawares, when you were so grateful she hadn't died that you couldn't be mad at her for scaring the shit out of you.

Murder cat for real.

But she also slept curled up in between Rye and Charlie's pillows, purring sweetly, licked Charlie's beard like it was a kitten of her own, and had been thoroughly adopted by Marmot and Jane so that Charlie and Rye were now outnumbered. They stalked the house in a phalanx of paws and tails and eyes that saw everything and Rye was pretty sure that he and Charlie were living at their pleasure.

"Hi, Murderbaby," Rye said, stroking her ears. "Where are your comrades?"

Jane sauntered down the hallway, then gave Rye a quick *mrow* and went into the living room when she saw he wasn't Charlie. Marmot was no doubt off running the ramps and would emerge in time.

"You wanna come play in the woodshop?"

Charlie had originally wanted Redrum kept out of the

woodshop at all costs. He'd had visions of her getting so amped up she tried to jump into a saw or something. But it turned out the one thing Redrum feared was loud noises, so if a tool was running she wouldn't get anywhere near it.

She yipped and Rye took that as assent. He dropped his stuff on the table inside the door, hung up his coat without dislodging her, and walked into the woodshop.

He hung the *Stay the Fuck Out* sign (handmade by him) on the door in case Charlie came home before he was done, and got down to work.

Several hours, a great deal of swearing, and one near accident later, Rye was at his wits' end. Tired, hungry, and doubting that wood was a suitable medium for *anything*, he kicked at the floor and swore.

There was a soft knock on the door.

"You need some help, love?"

Charlie.

"Um, you can't."

"Why?"

"Because, Charlie, it's *your* present! But I fucked it all up."

The door opened.

"I have my eyes closed," Charlie said.

Rye threw a drop cloth over the abomination on the table before him.

"Okay you're good," he told Charlie.

Charlie crossed to Rye and scooped him into a warm hug. He'd clearly gotten home from work, showered, and cooked without Rye noticing.

"Time is it?" Rye murmured, burying his face in Charlie's neck. He smelled so good. He smelled like home.

"Almost eight. Come on and eat."

"Can't," Rye said. "Gotta finish."

Charlie's hand went to his hair like it always did, untangling the long strands. It always soothed Rye. He pressed even closer to Charlie. He didn't want to work on this thing anymore. But he didn't have anything else for Charlie and no way was he showing up empty-handed for their first anniversary together.

Maybe he could still order one online? No, it would never get here on time.

"I haven't seen you all day," Charlie said. "I want to spend time with you. I don't care if it's in here working on my present or in there hanging out. But we're not spending another evening apart."

The flush of warmth that always suffused Rye when Charlie said things like that rushed through him. He squeezed Charlie around the waist.

Rye was a fighter, but one thing Charlie had taught him was the honor in knowing you were beaten. And this damn computer desk had absolutely beaten him.

"I fucked it up," he murmured. "I'm sorry. I wanted it to be perfect for you because you've made me so many things. You built me a whole…" He shook his head. "But I messed it all up."

Charlie's rough hands were so gentle on his cheeks.

He looked up into Charlie's gorgeous hazel eyes and saw no disappointment, only love.

"I bet we can fix it. Or if we can't fix it, we can make a new one."

"Shouldn't have to make your own present," Rye muttered.

"I like making things. And I love making things with you. So it's still a present."

Rye snorted. "Cheesy," he said.

But he liked it.

"Okay, fine. So, you know how your back hurts a lot and you're always hunched over your computer. This is—was supposed to be—an adjustable laptop desk thing. It sits on your desk and it's angled and you put the laptop in it, then you have the keyboard on the desk and type there so your shoulders don't hunch forward and it doesn't strain your back."

Charlie blinked. A slow smile spread across his face and he stroked Rye's hair back.

"Wow. That's a great idea. Thank you."

He said it like he'd opened a gift that was the ideal of what Rye just described.

"Well, uh, don't get too excited cuz I messed it all up."

Charlie dismissed this and reached for the drop cloth. Rye bit his lip. Maybe it wasn't as bad as he thought. Maybe Charlie would unveil it and it would be like a magician pulling a rabbit out of a hat.

Charlie tossed the drop cloth aside and made a choked sound.

It hadn't been miraculously fixed. In fact, if anything, covering it up and revealing it again showed its flaws to full—and horrifying—effect.

"Um," Charlie said.

Then he started laughing.

For a moment, Rye's pride was hurt, then he started laughing too.

The laptop desk looked more like an emboldened wooden grasshopper, reaching its claws out to consume a laptop. It was crooked, both vertically and horizontally. And somehow Rye hadn't noticed before that the screws he'd used were too long and now posed a bloodletting hazard for anyone who tried to adjust the desk.

Charlie was whooping with laughter. He grabbed Rye in a tight hug.

"You're so damn cute I can't stand it sometimes," he said.

Rye scowled and mumbled, "Mnot cute."

But do you want to know a secret about Rye Janssen?

He liked that Charlie found him cute.

Don't tell.

Rye gestured helplessly at the hunk of misshapen wood,

about to tell Charlie what he'd been trying to do. But Charlie spun him around so they were facing each other, put his hands on Rye's shoulders, and said, very seriously, and very gently, "That is beyond saving, my love. But the idea is great and we should absolutely make one."

And somehow, even though Charlie had told him all his hours of effort had amounted to garbage, Rye was grinning. Because he loved that Charlie was honest. It meant he never had to guess what he was thinking. Charlie always told him.

"Okay," Rye said.

He rested his head against Charlie's chest and pulled Charlie's arms back around him. They fit together perfectly. Rye never felt safer or happier than when he could feel the steady thump of Charlie's beautiful heart.

"Remember our first bowl?" Rye murmured.

Rye thought about that night all the time. The feeling of Charlie's warm bulk behind him and Charlie's sturdy arms around him, guiding him. How Charlie's mouth had been hot and sweet and welcomed him so perfectly.

"How could I forget." Charlie kissed his hair. "Everything's been different for me since then."

He sounded so sure. So sure that Rye was what he wanted. That *this*—this life together was what he wanted. For someone who'd been so uncertain about his own desires in the beginning, once Charlie knew what he wanted he *knew what he wanted*.

Rye'd had more doubts. He'd worried he would fuck it all up, this amazing thing between them. Worried he'd drive Charlie away or annoy him or disgust him. That something essential about Rye would prove to be the pin in the grenade that destroyed them.

But each day that they spent together eased his heart. Each disagreement they had that didn't break them; each time he got annoyed and Charlie didn't punish him for it; each time Charlie asked a question and he found himself answering it not just truthfully but honestly. Each time they held each other in the night and Rye could *feel* Charlie's love in the way he touched him. Each one had been a brick in the home of their relationship, shoring up this thing they shared.

"Me too," Rye said. And he smiled against Charlie's chest. He smiled at Charlie and at this woodshop, in this house, in this strange town of Garnet Run. He smiled at himself.

Charlie

Charlie used to think that the opposite of *alone* was *together*. Now he knew that the opposite of *alone* was being yourself with another person while they were also being themselves. It was more than *together*. It was *in partnership*.

He'd never known partnership before Rye. He had needed people and he had been needed. He had worked alongside people. He'd had friends and he'd been a friend. But until Rye Janssen stormed into his life Charlie had never known what it felt like to coexist with someone and share dreams, goals, plans.

Cats.

"Yeah, I see you there, you little monster," Charlie said, flicking a gaze to the cat Rye had named Redrum and Charlie still thought of as Murder Cat the Second (Marmot's initial incarnation in his life having been Murder Cat the First). Even Rye nearly always called her Murder Cat. The kitten was sitting on top of the refrigerator, no doubt preparing to set upon any food a fool human prepared. She yawned and stretched out a paw lazily toward him as if to say, *Okay, you got me.*

It was their anniversary. Last night he and Rye had made popcorn and sat in front of the fire, talking as flames consumed wood. Rye had suggested they should burn his benighted laptop desk in effigy as an offering to the gods of woodworking and a blessing for their union, but Charlie had nixed it on account of the truly staggering amount of wood glue that Rye had used on the project.

"We'd die of asphyxiation. Not a good way to start our next year together."

Rye had snorted and not seemed too upset that his supremely sweet idea for a gift wasn't even suitable for kindling.

"Need help?"

Rye sidled into the kitchen, hair damp from his shower, wearing his worn skinny jeans and a gray and orange sweater of Charlie's that he'd claimed as his own though it was far too big for him. Charlie loved seeing Rye in his clothes, as if the sweater was hugging Rye all day long in Charlie's stead.

"Nah, I'm just making meatloaf," Charlie said. "Made it a million times."

Rye froze, eyes comically wide.

"Kidding."

Rye grinned.

Charlie still liked meatloaf just fine. He still made it sometimes. But he didn't make it every Thursday. In fact, he didn't follow a set schedule for when he made certain dishes at all anymore. He made what he was in the mood for, or Rye did. He made whatever he wanted.

"I'm making pizza with your dough."

"Yum."

Rye moved fluidly around the kitchen, getting things from the cabinets and the refrigerator.

He was closing the refrigerator when he jerked back, cried, "Jesus!" and the cheese went flying across the floor.

A small black face peered from above them, and a relaxed *merow* followed.

"Fucking *murder* cat!"

Rye clutched his chest and gathered the cheese off the floor.

Charlie laughed. Murder Cat purred and curled back up on the refrigerator.

"You're not gonna get me again," Rye muttered to her. It was the twentieth or thirtieth time he'd said it.

The doorbell rang just as they were sliding the pizzas into the oven and they herded Simon, Jack, and an allergy-medicated Jean into the living room. It was still storming outside and the whole world looked gray and wet and chilly.

When Charlie had asked Rye what he wanted to do for their anniversary, he'd expected him to suggest going out to dinner or driving to Laramie to see live music. But Rye had said they should invite Jack, Simon, and Jean over. He'd walked it back, grumbling, "Wait, is that weird? I don't know what the hell you do on an anniversary."

But it had been his first instinct to invite Charlie's family into their love, and Charlie, who'd never been celebrated for anything, had been more moved than he could say.

Rye told them the story of the misbegotten laptop desk and Jack raised an eyebrow.

"I should get you one of those," he told Simon.

"I'll make one for you after I make mine," Charlie told him.

Rye bit his lip, no doubt keeping himself from informing Charlie how wrong it was that he was going to make his own anniversary gift.

After pizza, Jean unveiled the most beautiful cookies Charlie had ever seen. They were individually decorated flowers, frosted in delicate swirls of pastel icing with silver streaks, glittering with sugar.

"The first anniversary is traditionally paper," Jean said. "But who wants cookies that look like paper?"

They crunched the cookies delicately, all remarking that it seemed a pity to eat something so beautiful, until they tasted them, after which no one seemed to have a problem eating more.

After they'd eaten their fill and Rye had put on the new Theo Dekker album, Jack got up and went to the front door.

He returned with a plain manila folder that he handed between Charlie and Jack.

"Happy anniversary, guys," he said, sitting back beside Simon.

Charlie opened the folder and rested the contents on his knee between them.

Inside was a sheaf of papers that had been sewn into a little book. The cover sported hand lettering in Jack's signature font that read: *The Adventures of Marmot and Jane.* A caret had been added at the end of the title, under which was lettered, *And Murder Cat!*

The cover image showed the three cats, Marmot and Jane curled up together in a ball, eyes looking up at the title and Redrum perched atop the letters looking like she was about to pounce.

"Oh my god," Rye said worshipfully.

They read through the little comic together. The illustrations were more cartoony than the style Jack used in his children's books; they were more like the style of the graphic novel he was nearly done with. He managed, as always, to portray real depth in the expressions of the animals.

The story was charming too. In it, Redrum had recruited Marmot and Jane to her nefarious attempt on the refrigerator. It loomed, gleaming, like the monolith in *2001: A Space Odyssey*, just waiting for the cats to conquer it.

Working together, they toppled the refrigerator and feasted on its contents. The final page showed them all curled up together in a heap of furry paws and tails and ears, crumbs and bits of food surrounding them as they slept, dream bubbles above their heads as they dreamt of even more food.

Rye cracked up at how Jack had drawn each of the cats eating their favorite foods—Marmot with a chicken leg in her mouth, Jane with her face in a tub of yogurt, and Redrum chowing down absurdly on a wheel of brie.

"It's wonderful," Charlie told Jack, as Rye said, "Fucking awesome, thank you."

Jack just smiled but Charlie could see how pleased his brother was. He'd always loved seeing people appreciate his work.

Jack, Simon, and Jean didn't stay late, though. Jean's allergy medicine only protected her from the animals for so long, and Jack and Simon clearly wanted to get home to their own animals, their own fireside, their own evening.

Once they'd seen everyone out into the rainy night with promises to get home safe and get together soon, Charlie and Rye were alone.

"It's nice they all came over," Rye said. "Was it weird for them to celebrate our anniversary?"

"Who cares, you loved it. You love anniversaries."

Rye's eyes widened and he looked like maybe he was going to deny it, but then he slumped and peeked up at Charlie.

"Yeah, I kinda do."

"Nothing to be embarrassed about."

Rye shot him a look like, *Isn't it, though?*

"Nah," Charlie said. "It's sweet. You love our anniversary, just own it."

Rye huffed, but relaxed.

"Just own it," was what Rye had repeatedly told Charlie to do. "You like to be spanked, hot stuff, just own it," he'd said with a wink. "You're a neat freak, just own it," he'd said when they started sharing an office. "You hate hummus, just own it," when Charlie had tried Rye's over and over to no avail. And, more recently, "You love sucking my cock, just own it." Charlie had flushed deeply at that one, but he'd had to admit that it was true.

Charlie had thought long and hard about an anniversary gift for Rye. He knew Rye would bristle at anything expensive or extravagant. He already felt that Charlie had given him too much for a lifetime.

He'd thought about grand romantic gestures involving rose petals and baths, but he was pretty sure they would just make Rye very uncomfortable. He had learned that while Rye loved small romantic gestures, anything too dramatic, anything that announced itself too loudly, made him cringe.

He had considered unveiling a grand new addition to their ever-expanding cat amusement park, but they'd been working on that together and it was for both of them, so it didn't seem like a good gift just for Rye.

Finally, though he wasn't quite confident in his instinct, Charlie had used a number he found in Rye's phone, and gone the sentimental route.

"Want your present?" he asked Rye softly, not wanting to interrupt his snoozy meditation of the fire or the cats that were splayed out around him.

Rye turned dreamy eyes to him.

"Present?"

He sounded like an excited kid.

"Stay there, I'll bring it."

He got the wrapped package from the coat closet where he'd stashed it, confident it wouldn't be found because Rye never hung his coat in the closet, always draping it over a banister or a doorknob or simply laying it on top of the vent. ("It dries it off faster!" Rye insisted. "It blocks the vent," Charlie said.)

He handed the gift to Rye and sat next to him in front of the fire, a hand on Jane so he didn't startle her. Murder Cat jumped into his lap the second he created one.

"Can't believe I'm making you make your *own* anniversary present *and* you got me one," he muttered.

"Hush," Charlie told him.

Rye tore the paper off and Charlie watched his face intently.

"That's the shelter," he said softly, tracing it on the large framed photograph. "The house I mean."

Charlie nodded.

"Is that him?"

"Yeah."

He put his face up close to the picture.

"Clive said we look alike but I don't see it."

He sounded disappointed.

"I do. The way he's scowling at the camera, like he wants Clive to fuck off. That's pure you."

Rye snorted. "Okay."

"And look at his chin. Pointy just like yours. Same high cheekbones."

Rye scrutinized the man in the photograph, searching for traces of himself in the family he'd never known. When he looked up at Charlie his eyes were wet.

"I can see it now." Charlie brushed a tear away with his thumb and Rye scrubbed at his face with his sleeve. "Wow, look at the house. It was nice before it...fell apart."

It was a classic winterized Wyoming cabin but when the picture had been taken some twenty years ago (or so Clive had told him) its porch was still level and its roof didn't sag. It had a neat woodpile next to the house and there was smoke streaming out the chimney.

Based on the trees it looked to be the end of autumn. Granger Janssen stood before the house, scowling, hands in his pockets, and a scarred brown cattleman hat over his wild gray hair. Hair the color of his eyes and Rye's.

"Where did you get this?"

Rye stood the frame up against the wall and leaned into Charlie.

"From Mr. Wayne."

"Whenever you call him that I picture Batman," he said absently. Then after a while, "I hope he was okay. He was all by himself. I hope he was happy."

"Are you happy?" Charlie asked.

Rye paused long enough that it might have made Charlie nervous had Rye not been holding on to him so tight.

"I'm so happy," he said finally, voice choked with feeling. "Sometimes I feel this, this feeling and I don't know what it is at first and then I'm like, oh, shit, that's happiness. But like *actual* happiness. It's like being a balloon."

Charlie eased Rye around so he could see his face. Charlie's heart was so full he felt at any moment that it could leap from his chest and spring like a buck out into the falling rain.

Last year at this time, Charlie had driven home from work alone after Rye's initial visit to Matheson's Hardware. He had put on sweats and built a fire and stared at it, just as he was staring at one now. He'd gotten out a thick wool blanket and slept in front of the fire. Jane, confused, had curled up next to him, giving him little flicks with her tail, as if to say, *Just checking: You do know we're not in bed, correct?*

He'd slept in front of the fire because that day he'd met someone new, and meeting someone new had reminded him that he was alone, and because he didn't want to be alone. He'd woken in the middle of the night. The fire had burned out and Jane was gone. Cold and dejected, Charlie had gone to his bed.

Now the fire crackled merrily, Rye's eyes on him were luminous, and the cats lounged languorously around them.

"Actual happiness," Charlie echoed.

Rye kissed him and Charlie tasted his tears and his love and his perfect Rye-ness.

"Can we sleep out here in front of the fire?" Rye asked, as if he'd plucked the memory from Charlie's very head. Charlie was startled, but it felt right somehow.

"You…yeah, sure. Okay."

Charlie went to their bedroom and got an armful of blankets. He turned out all the lights as he returned, and they made a bed in front of the fire. He piled on more logs and they watched tongues of fire consume them, wrapped to-gether in blankets, bracketed by cats.

This year, Charlie had a life that he was building with himself at its heart, not one that he checked off like a to-do list, like an obligation, like a Tuesday-night meatloaf.

This year, Rye had a life that he was building with an eye toward the future, not simply eking out each day as it came.

This year, Charlie and Rye were dreaming a dream for both of them.

★ ★ ★ ★ ★

Acknowledgments

Many thanks to Jenny and Anni, whose thoughts on this book, as on all the others, were invaluable.

Thank you to Wyoming, which made me fall in love with it, and the chipmunks, moose, dogs, fish, and other beasties that graced me with their presence.

Thanks to my agent, Courtney Miller-Callihan, who makes magic behind the scenes, and to my editor, Kerri Buckley, for shepherding this project so generously.

Thank you to my sister, as ever, for listening to me ramble as we amble.

Thank you to Timmi, for your excitement, your support, and your presence.

This book was written entirely during quarantine, with only my cat for company. Our animals are quiet (or sometimes not so quiet) witnesses, cuddlers, and often reminders that we are needed in this world—even if only to feed them and scratch their ears. So my tenderest thanks of all to Dorian Gray, my little furry heart.

Moving to eclectic New Hope, Pennsylvania, and running The Beautiful Things Shoppe is a dream come true for elegant and reserved fine arts dealer Prescott J. Henderson. He never agreed to share the space with Danny Roman, an easygoing extrovert who collects retro toys and colorful knickknacks.

And yet here they are, trapped together in the quaint shop as they scramble to open in time for New Hope's charming Winter Festival...

Keep reading for an excerpt from
The Beautiful Things Shoppe
by Philip William Stover

Chapter One

Prescott

"What is that hideous object doing in the window of *my* store?" I turn my head away from the large section of plate glass to avoid looking at the horrible tchotchke. The tiny mounds of dirty snow on the sidewalk offer more visual appeal than whatever that thing is. Bravely I push through the cerulean blue-trimmed door and enter the shop. A man is standing behind the counter wearing a hoodie the color of a traffic cone and a T-shirt with some sort of bear in a polka-dot tie and tiny hat.

I need my move-in to go smoothly today so I can be ready to reopen the shop for business at the Winter Festival next week. This is my opportunity to become a serious antiques dealer and I don't need a detour through the Island of Misfit Toys. "Who are you and why are you putting such vile merchandise in the window of *my* store?"

"Excuse me. Did you say *vile merchandise*?" the man asks, walking over to the window and grabbing the offensive object. He holds it in his hands like a newborn infant. "I'll have you know this is a genuine *Muppet Show* lunchbox with the Kermit the Frog thermos in mint condition." He inspects the object for a moment. "Somebody will fall in love with this and cherish it as much as I do."

I'm about to move in some of the finest antiques from the

nineteenth century and this confused man is putting a *lunch box* in the window of my new retail space. There must be some mistake. I take out my phone.

"Who are you calling?"

"I should be calling the police to let them know a deranged criminal with horrible taste has broken into my shop but I'm calling the man who leased it, Arthur." This was his shop for years but he invited me to take over so he could finally retire.

The confused man goes back to unpacking a parade of items from a grade-school show-and-tell in hell. Somewhere in this quaint town on the river there must be an empty store waiting for his horrible toys. Does he have the wrong address or wrong town? A quick glance at the things he's unpacking makes me think he might be on the wrong planet. I begin to dial when the vintage brass bell above the door rings and Arthur, the man himself, walks in carrying his cane.

"Uncle Arthur, I'm so glad you're here," the man with bad taste says.

"Uncle?" A sinking feeling descends. "Arthur, you know this man? You're related?" I ask.

"Oh, it's an honorific. Many young people in the queer community call me Uncle Arthur. Frankly, it makes me feel old." He smooths his white beard.

That man walks over to Arthur and kisses him on the forehead. "You aren't old. You're cherished."

I've known Arthur only a few years. We'd seen each other at estate sales and auctions and he'd always been very kind to me as a fellow lover of antiques. Eventually he noticed I keep to myself at these events and made gentle, repeated attempts to coax me out of my shell. I eventually felt comfortable enough with him that I looked forward to our exchanges. Knowing he was going to be at big events made tackling the social aspects of them much easier. When he asked me to take over the shop I was thrilled. I had always wanted a shop of my own so I could establish myself as a serious collector. I left the entry-level position at Fisher Fine Arts Library that I'd had since finishing graduate school, gathered my growing collection of antiques and moved to this charming town on the banks of the Delaware River—not far from the spot depicted in the Emanuel Leutze painting of Washington's crossing.

I was more than ready to leave Philadelphia after half a dozen years as a student and almost as many at the library. The Georgian stone farmhouses with painted wooden shutters and stunning view of the river made moving to New Hope an easy decision, but clearly I should have pressed for more details about how the lease would work.

"Arthur, would you mind helping me understand what's going on here?" I try to smile and remain as pleasant as possible. This can't be Arthur's fault. But then he gives me a look that says I'm not going to like what comes next.

He takes off his vintage bowler and puts it over the silver Labrador head that tops his cane. "Prescott, I would like to introduce you to Danny Roman. He has been running an online shop for a few years, selling all sorts of fun collectibles from midcentury to kitsch."

"I have a large inventory of Beanie Babies if you have any holes in your private collection," this Danny says. If the situation is making him nervous he isn't showing it.

"What on earth is a Beanie Baby?" I ask.

"Sure, play it coy like you don't have a Dinky the Dodo you sleep with every night," he says, that confident grin returning.

"Dinky the…" I start but Arthur cuts me off.

"Gentlemen, please," Arthur says. His warm voice is kind yet firm. "Now I apologize that I didn't have the opportunity to explain the arrangement in greater detail but I was quite busy moving my things out and getting the shop ready so the two of you could move your collections in. I want nothing more than for you to put your own marks on this place." Arthur looks around the mostly empty store. The freshly painted white walls and barren space must be difficult for him to take in, considering the decades he spent operating one of the finest shops in the region.

"Arthur, I don't understand," I say. How could comic-book-in-a hoodie fit into his plan?

"The Beautiful Things Shoppe has enough space to accommodate you both. You each signed a lease that allows you half."

"You're telling me that I have to share the shop with *him*?" I say, scanning Danny from head to toe.

Danny looks back at me, unfazed by my dig. He looks at Arthur. "Where did you find this one? He's wound more tightly than the corset on Lady Footlocker at gay bingo." He then turns to me and says, "Look, you uptight snob, I'll have you know that my collectibles are some of the hardest to find items anywhere."

"Maybe your things need to stay hidden." I've raised my voice just enough to make my point but this guy takes it as an attack. He raises his finger and is about to jab back when Arthur interrupts.

"Gentleman, please. Both of you. I just came by to make sure you were settling in nicely and make a formal introduction but I see that isn't needed. I realize this is a bit unconventional, but Prescott, you are one of the sharpest antique appraisers I've ever met and Danny, no one understands how objects can bring people joy more than you. How you two divide the shop is entirely your decision. I do suggest you be ready for Winter Festival next week. The streets will be filled with winter shoppers." Arthur puts on his hat and grabs his cane. "After decades in this business I can tell you both one thing. People come in this shop thinking they're looking for one thing and walk out loving something different entirely."

He leaves and I am alone with Danny.

We stare at each other in silence, each of us sizing up the other. This guy barely looks like he has the maturity to run a paper route let alone half of an established antique store. He's my age or maybe a few years older than me. I'd guess at least thirty-five but he's dressed like he's late for homeroom and forgot his homework. In addition to the weird T-shirt and hoodie, his jeans are too big in the waist and too short in length. He has a thick brown scruff and even thicker hair sticks out from the collar of his T-shirt above his chest.

My eyes linger there a moment longer than they should before I realize this person is going to destroy my chances of being taken seriously in the fine art world. I will not let that happen. I stare him down and smile with a sense of determination.

Danny

Just keep smiling, I tell myself. Ignore his blue eyes and the flecks of gray-green sparks that circle his pupils. Just pretend they don't exist. I move my gaze up to the severe side part in his perfectly combed blond hair. He looks like he's about to start his first day of prep school in his blue blazer and khaki pants. I begin to wonder what his body is like under his crisp white button-down when I gather my senses. This man had the audacity to insult my Muppets lunch box. Is Miss Piggy not a sacred diva? Still, Uncle Arthur seems to have given him his stamp of approval. How bad can he be? Maybe we got off on the wrong foot.

"Let's start over," I say and extend my hand. He looks like he expects my palm to have a gag buzzer lurking. Slowly he extends his arm and we shake.

Big mistake.

His hand is thinner and more delicate than mine but just as strong. I look down and see my hairy knuckles against his golden smooth fingers and suddenly I'm wondering what mysteries might be lurking under those perfectly ironed kha-kis. You know what they say, the firmer the crease...

I pull my hand away as quickly as possible so I can refocus.

"I'm Danny Roman," I say gathering as much formality as I can—which for me is not very much.

"I'm Prescott J. Henderson," he says. His voice reminds me of Fred Astaire dancing lightly across the silver screen—smooth elegance and refined precision.

I chuckle, glad that he has made a small joke to lighten the mood. "No, what's your real name?"

"That *is* my real name," he says so firmly the words almost come out as a growl.

"Oh, I'm sorry. It's just... I mean... Prescott J. Henderson? It sounds like a hoity-toity character in a comic book. Like Scrooge McDuck or something."

"You think I sound like a duck?" He's clearly annoyed.

"Well, I didn't say you sound like a duck, but to be fair I haven't heard you quack yet." This guy is so uptight that any physical charm he may or may not have is completely pointless. Arthur knows how much I hate these pretentious poseurs who think taste is reserved for the privileged. How could he do this to me?

I've known Arthur for years and when he told me he wanted to lease out the shop I jumped at the chance. I needed a change. A big change. After getting dumped on my birthday by a guy I thought was serious about me, I realized I needed something to help me take my focus off romance. I've learned I have great instincts when it comes to vintage collectibles and lousy instincts when it comes to men. I'd love to turn my collectibles into a thriving business, but having something to ground me is just as important. The whole reason I took on this lease was so that I could stand on my own two feet.

"Listen, you're going to have to move these boxes. I have a van arriving with some of my things in just a few minutes." Prescott is talking to me as if I work for him. I ignore the tone.

"What time?" I ask.

"Noon," he says like I just challenged him to a duel.

"Well, I hope your van can find a place to park," I say nonchalantly and move back to unpacking, knowing it will eat him up.

"There's a loading zone right in front of the shop. Obviously the van will park there," Prescott says, falling into my trap.

"I don't think so. That's where my truck will be." I take a short yet dramatic pause. "At 11:45."

Prescott blinks, slowly and steadily, then breathes in. "I have some very fragile and valuable pieces. I'll need a clear path and don't want the movers spoken to or otherwise distracted in any way."

"Spoken to? You don't want the movers *spoken to*? Who do you think you are, the Queen of England? Cher?"

"I just mean don't distract them. They are serious about their work." Prescott opens the door and a rush of cold air sweeps around the store. Arthur usually had the potbelly stove keeping the place toasty warm and without it the shop is chilly.

Prescott starts measuring the doorway. "I don't have time to argue with you. I need to make sure the Chippendale can fit through the door."

"Chippendale? Here I am, thinking you're a stuffy prude. I stand corrected. I hadn't thought of bringing in male strippers but it's not a bad idea—and if you're worried his piece might not fit through the door then it's beginning to sound like a great idea," I say in my best impersonation of Fozzi Bear, who just so happens to be on the shirt I'm wearing.

"I suppose you're trying to make some type of vulgar joke. I'm assuming you know full well *Chippendale* refers to a neoclassical style of furniture from Yorkshire, England."

He rattles off the description without hesitation. He certainly knows his stuff. "Excuse me for not laughing but I am unaccustomed to such crass humor in a place of business." His tone is all serious, but I can tell there is a chip in his polished exterior from the way the corners of his mouth have to fight moving upward. This is the kind of guy that wants to belly laugh but thinks it wouldn't be proper. Just because he looks like he should be playing the lead in a Merchant Ivory film doesn't mean he needs to act like the Dowager Countess of New Hope.

I hear a series of screeches from the street so loud they can most likely be heard on the other side of the river. They're followed by hissing, a jangle of chains and the grinding of gears. I look out the window and see a truck that looks like it has just competed in Thunderdome and in the driver's seat is my old pal and current roommate, Lizard.

★★★

Don't miss The Beautiful Things Shoppe
*Available now from Philip William Stover
and Carina Adores
www.CarinaPress.com*

Discover another great contemporary romance from Carina Adores.

Their collections may clash, but their hearts are a perfect match.

Moving to eclectic New Hope, Pennsylvania, and running The Beautiful Things Shoppe is a dream come true for elegant and reserved fine arts dealer Prescott J. Henderson. He never agreed to share the space with Danny Roman, an easygoing extrovert who collects retro toys and colorful knickknacks.

Danny has spent years leading with his heart instead of his head. The Beautiful Things Shoppe is his chance to ground himself and build something permanent and joyful. The last thing he needs is an uptight snob who doesn't appreciate his whimsy occupying half his shop.

And yet here they are, trapped together in the quaint shop as they scramble to open in time for New Hope's charming Winter Festival…

Available now!

CarinaPress.com

CARPWSTBTS0321TR

IF YOU ENJOYED THIS BOOK
WE THINK YOU WILL ALSO LOVE

Carina Adores is home to highly romantic contemporary love stories where LGBTQ+ characters find their happily-ever-afters.

ONE NEW BOOK AVAILABLE EVERY MONTH!